THEN COMES THE CHILL OF N

D0447059

PICK-UP ON SUNSET

"So what do you do, Mr. No Names Please?"

"Just drive around."

There was something sweet about her . . . something that made him want to take her along with him for a few hours and try to beat back the night.

But before they made it to the All American Burger they came up on a tricked-out pickup on the other side of the street.

"Stop!" she said. "I know those guys."

She jumped out.

"You're sweet," she said in a way that doesn't mean anything.

Then she kissed him on the cheek.

She pulled back, *spooked*. She stepped away from the car. She touched her lips.

Jimmy drove away, up Sunset.

When he looked in the mirror, she still stood on the side of the street where he left her, watching him go, holding herself as if from a sudden chill.

THE QUICK

DAN VINING

JOVE BOOKS, NEW YORK

THE QUICK

A Jove Book / published by arrangement with the author

PRINTING HISTORY
Jove edition / June 2004

Copyright © 2004 by Dan Vining
Cover art and design by Larry Rostant
Book design by Kristin del Rosario

For information, address: The Berkley Publishing Group,
a division of Penguin Group (USA) Inc.,
375 Hudson Street, New York, New York 10014.

ISBN: 0-515-13719-7

A JOVE BOOK®
Jove Books are published by The Berkley Publishing Group,
a division of Penguin Group (USA) Inc.,
375 Hudson Street, New York, New York 10014.
JOVE and the "J" design
are trademarks belonging to Penguin Group (USA) Inc.

PRINTED IN THE UNITED STATES OF AMERICA

10 9 8 7 6 5 4 3 2 1

CHAPTER 1

A RUGGED MALIBU CANYON, A CLEAR NIGHT. THE smooth black road ahead, unstriped, wound through slow turns, the headlights igniting the underbrush. There was a song on the radio over the low rumble of the engine. The windows were down, the air sweet with something that picked that night to bloom. For now, Jimmy Miles was just eyes in the mirror. The half-moon came into the corner of the frame, dancing with the vibration of the motor, full of intent, hung up there like a spotlight over the scene. Jimmy watched it until it slid away again.

A few more turns and there was an iron gate flanked by a pair of fifty-foot-tall jacarandas, like purple fireworks against the night sky. On up the canyon there was a dome of glow and noise, but the house wasn't even visible from here.

A guard stood next to a fat white plain-wrap Chevy.

Jimmy was ready for him. "What's the square root of eighty-eight?" he said.

The guard didn't have an answer, just waited, keeping whatever he thought off his face.

Jimmy held up his engraved invitation.

"Thank you, sir," the rented cop said and stepped back, and the Porsche—it was a '64 Cabriolet, a ragtop, black—passed through the gates, nice and slow, behaving itself, and up the drive. The guard watched until it went around the next bend then leaned back against the door of the Chevy. The moon flushed, the shadows changed. The guard looked up at the half-round light high out over the water, but didn't think a thing about it. After a minute, a raggedy coyote crept out of the manzanita. There was a plate of chicken *sate,* or what was left of it, on the dash of the Chevy. The dog lifted his nose at it from twenty yards out. The guard squatted, picked through the gravel until he found just the right-sized rock and sent it back into the night.

The big house was all glass and steel and hard edges, like a cruise ship rammed into the back of the canyon, the bridge facing the Pacific, all the lights burning as if there was some enormous emergency. Tall black doors stood open. Music and laughter. Jimmy got out of the car, said something in Spanish to one of the valet car parkers that got an honest laugh and went aboard.

In the foyer, he tossed the invitation onto a side table and walked toward the noise. The card read:

MENSA: A NIGHT OF MYSTERY
Joel Kinser's
June 13th   8 p.m.
12122 Corpo Grosso Road, Malibu

The party was two hours in. Here was a crowd of fairly ordinary people wearing the best clothes they owned, except maybe for the guy in Bermuda shorts, flip-flops and a Cuban guayabera. They all had drinks in their hands, trying to hold them the right way, and they were a little loud, as if they felt out of place in the big rich house, which inside looked more like a Beverly Hills bank than a ship. Money trumped smarts, at least when you were in the middle of it, even smart people knew that.

Everyone turned as Jimmy stepped down into the main room. There was an Oscar on the piano so there was always the chance a movie star would show. Jimmy was a bit of a clotheshorse. Tonight it was a charcoal suit, a white shirt, a black tie—and pastel suede shoes he somehow made work. There was something about him that was pre-acid sixties, a little Peter Gunn, smoky jazz, cool. He was nice to look at but he wasn't a movie star so the party people went back to their smart conversations.

The host, Joel Kinser, who produced movies, sat on the arm of a white couch, his finger to his chin as he listened to a woman a foot taller than he was.

Jimmy caught his eye. Kinser winked at him.

A waiter came past with a silver tray of martinis, an actor *playing* a waiter actually, in black and white, more waiter than any real waiter. It was the way with movie people, they rewrote their lives to look like movies, cast them like movies, spoke dialogue, saw their houses as sets, their clothes wardrobe, their bodies things to be reworked perpetually by backstage craftsmen. Jimmy went along with the gag, took a martini, let the waiter bow at the waist, didn't giggle. He waded into the crowd. He walked past the guayabera guy just as he was delivering the punch line to his story.

"And it had already been calibrated!"

It got a big laugh.

A woman stood at the bar along the far wall under a Ruscha, her face turned away, quarter profile, talking with someone, maybe watching herself in the plateglass window beyond the man. There was something Old School about her look too, black hair over the eyes, a silk dress that caught the light, shoes taller than they needed to be. In another time, or at least another *movie,* she would have had a cigarette smoldering and a little chrome .25 automatic in her clutch bag. And a hurt in her heart.

Jimmy was watching her when Joel Kinser came up.

"Maybe I could see some I.D.," the host said.

Kinser was just over five feet. He wore a suit the color of raw clay, a black silken V-neck tee underneath, thin-soled slip-ons, no socks, a belt that picked up the hardware on the tops of the shoes. He had his hands in his pants pockets, pockets which were always empty. He hated bulges.

"Look who's talking," Jimmy said. "It takes an I.Q. of one-twenty to get into Mensa. What'd you do, have one of your story editors take the test for you?"

Joel Kinser loved talking about how very intelligent he was. It was almost his favorite subject. He smiled in an oddly feminine way.

"Don't hate me because I'm perspicacious," he said.

Jimmy couldn't look away from the beauty.

"Who's she?"

"Jean Kantke. Go talk to her. We don't bite."

"Oh, I could never *talk* to one of you."

"Funny."

"What would I *say?*"

"Right."

A television star, a comic, came in from the foyer, even later to the do than Jimmy. He stopped on the steps, looking for Kinser, or making an entrance, letting them all get a good look at him. He had a face that made you smile or at least think of smiling. He had a can of beer in his hand and wore a black Hugo Boss suit over a Day-Glo Dale Earnhardt Jr. T-shirt.

"*He's* not Mensa is he?" Jimmy said.

"Just a friend. Like you, Jimmy." Kinser turned up the wattage in his smile and started toward the comic.

"Have fun," he looked back and said. "And, by the way, it's one thirty-two."

Jimmy went over to the bar, stepped behind it, poured out the martini and started making a shaker of something of his own. The black-haired beauty, Jean Kantke, was still there, alone now, her back to him.

Jimmy said, "Just as I pulled up, this great song started on the radio. I was going to hang a U-ey, keep on going. You ever do that?"

She turned. From across the room, she was pretty. From here, she was stunning. She brushed her hair away from her face. Up close, her black hair had a blue shine to it. She had green eyes, a bit sad. Her lipstick was some shade of fifties red, edged in black in a way you couldn't exactly see when you looked for it. Her arms were bare. And long. She laid a hand on the bar, struck a pose, but with her it looked natural. A line of little pink pearls followed each other around her pretty wrist.

As he took her in, in that long second, Jimmy had a thought he'd never say aloud, how a beautiful woman was like a classic car, the bold lines, the unexpected color, the *speed* of it, standing still. And the sense that its time was gone already, even as you stood there in front of it.

"I guess not," he said.

"I might," she said.

"I don't think so."

"Why not?"

"You're not the radio type."

"What was the song?" she said.

"It doesn't matter," he said.

She was drinking a martini too. Jimmy took her glass, dumped it, poured her one from whatever he'd made in the pitcher and one for himself. It was pink.

He dropped a thin green curve of lime peel onto the surface, like a professional, or an actor playing a bartender.

She started to taste it.

"Wait," he said. The lime twist was still turning in a circle on the surface.

She waited.

"OK."

She tasted her drink. "Wow," she said.

"Yep."

"What is it?"

"Manna."

"Manna."

"That's what *manna* means," he said. "In Hebrew. *Mannah. What is it.*"

He heard himself. *I'm trying to impress her,* he thought. It had been a while for that.

He came around the bar. "So, how smart are you?" he said.

"Pretty smart," she said.

She tilted her head to one side a few degrees, a look that was meant to be friendly, open the door a little further, better than a smile. Her skin was perfect, her face full of light. He wondered why he'd thought she looked sad before.

"I'm just here on a day pass," Jimmy said. "I know Joel."

They both took sips of their drinks. She was about to say something when he said, "So, how many languages do you speak?"

"Three or four," she said.

"English, French, Spanish, German . . ."

"English, French, Italian, German, a little Japanese. And I read Russian."

"Yeah," Jimmy said, "but do you know what you call that little thing on the tip of a shoelace, where it's wrapped?"

"In English?" she said.

She was at least as good at this as he was. He smiled, waited.

"Yeah, English."

"*Aglet,*" she said.

He touched his finger to the indentation below his nose, over the lip.

"OK, what's this called, the little dent?"

"The *philtrum.*"

"And the little thing that hangs down at the back of your throat?"

"The *uvula.*"

"This is kind of exciting," Jimmy said. "I had no idea."

She touched the lower part of the opening into her ear, above the lobe. It was as pretty and as perfect, at least tonight, in this light, as the rest of her.

"The *intertragic notch,*" he answered. And then, "Why do they call it that?"

"I have no idea," she said.

He offered his hand. "I'm Jimmy Miles."

"I know," she said.

But then, before the next line, before he found out how she knew who he was, there were two gunshots.

There was a beat and then a third shot, all from an adjacent room, too loud for the house, wrong for the scene. Everyone jumped, a few people screamed, but unconvincingly. Others laughed.

And they all moved off to investigate.

Jimmy stayed at the bar. Jean followed the others.

She looked back at him. There was a moment and then he followed her.

In the blond-paneled study there were floor to ceiling books—leather-bound, color-coded, looted from some Old Money family or bankrupt junior college—club chairs and ottomans, green shade lights and ashtrays big as hubcaps, for the cigars. Joel Kinser liked to tell people it was his favorite room in the house. The body on the floor had an effective bloody chest wound, still spreading. She was a woman in her twenties, brown hair, tight low jeans, black Gap shoes, one of those skimpy, navel-baring tees the kids called "a wife beater." If she was breathing it was very shallow. Here was another actor thinking this would do her some good. Her eyes were closed. She was cute dead.

Jimmy and Jean stepped in at the back of the crowd.

The man in the guayabera plopped down in the wingback chair directly over the body. He was an engineer at the Jet Propulsion Lab in Pasadena.

"Don't touch anything, Ben," a woman said.

"I wouldn't think of it, Deborah," JPL Ben said.

Joel was up front playing host. He stepped up onto the first rung of the library ladder.

"Well? Anyone?"

"She looks *dead,*" the TV comic said. They all laughed like it was the funniest thing.

"I talked to her," a young man said. He was tall, red-haired, still in his teens. He wore corduroy shorts down over his knees, Birkenstocks with white socks, a T-shirt with a word on it that made no sense. He had a squat brown bottle of Bohemia by the throat, propped against his leg.

"What did she say?" the woman asked.

The young man hesitated.

"Wouldn't you like to know," someone else said.

"What happened to the third shot?" Deborah said. "Give us *something* to start with, Joel."

Kinser was enjoying himself more than he should have been. "I will tell you this," he said. "She's a screenwriter."

"What's her name?"

"Rosie Scenario," the red-headed teenager said, very dry.

Ben bounded up out of the wingback chair. He had already made a discovery behind the couch, was just waiting to reveal it.

"So this would be her agent . . ."

The amateur sleuths gathered around the half-hidden second body, a young Latino in khakis and a white short-sleeved shirt, new running shoes on his feet, stage blood on his temple.

The gore was threatening to drip onto the off-white carpet. Joel lifted the lifeless head and put an *Architectural Digest* under it.

"What's in his hand?" one of the women said.

Someone opened the dead fingers. A computer disk.

"*Datum!*" Ben said.

The air was mock electric.

Joel stepped up another rung. "OK, listen, everyone, tonight we have with us a *professional* investigator, my friend, Jimmy Miles."

Everyone turned to look, but Jimmy was gone.

THE CUE BALL STRUCK THE FIVE BALL, WHICH clipped the eight, sending it into the side pocket.

"I meant to do that," Jimmy said.

Jean had stepped in. It was the game room. They were alone. He retrieved the eight ball and lined up another shot.

She waited, expecting him to speak. He didn't.

"We were hoping you might give us a fresh perspective," she said. "Some original ideas."

"The butler did it."

"Joel said—"

Jimmy took his shot, sank the ball. "I used to have original ideas," he said. "Then time and the world conspired to beat them out of me. Now I think the same thing as everybody else, only a little later."

He was still trying to impress her. He sank the three. It made a nice click.

"Kantke," Jimmy said. "Is that German?"

"Yes."

"Nice to meet you." He gave her a smile and offered her the cue.

She didn't take it.

"I asked Joel to invite you," she said.

In a beat, he changed, went cold, pulled inside. A familiar sadness overtook him, the way a cloud slides over the moon.

He went back to his game.

"I knew you and Joel were friends," she said, as he closed down. "I'd like for you to look into something for me. Joel said—"

Jimmy sank a shot and cut her off. "I helped Joel with something a while back and he's had the wrong idea about me ever since," he said. "I gotta talk to him about that."

"Please," she said. "I know all about you."

Now he gave her a challenging look.

"You only take cases every once in a while," she said.

He waited. He wasn't going to make it any easier for her.

"Nobody seems to know why you take the cases you take," she said, putting one word after another. "Money doesn't seem to be a factor—but I have money."

He already knew that. And he knew that she was used to people listening to her, doing what she said.

He put the cue in the rack.

"Are you in business?" he said.

"I own a company."

"I'm sure you know some investigators, security companies. There are some good ones."

"This isn't about my business," she said. "It's about something that happened a long time ago."

Each one of the words of that second sentence came hard for her. But he still just looked at her and smiled and left her standing there.

A Mexican maid was watching a little TV on the counter in the kitchen. On screen was a school picture of a Latino boy ten or eleven, an image that has come to mean "missing child" or "dead boy." The story was being told in Spanish. The picture of the boy gave way to a family crying in front of a little house, then an angle on a relative arriving, caught in the first moment he stepped from the car and got the news. On the L.A. Spanish stations the crime coverage was always more explicit, more theatrical, more frightening: *Monsters walk among us!* was the theme.

Jimmy came in. The maid tensed, but smiled. He opened a couple of cabinets until he found a glass. She watched as he filled it at the sink and drank it down.

She had a Band-Aid on her finger. He asked her about it. *"Te cortaste el dedo? Penso que era un* hot dog?"

She laughed and shook her head.

Then Jean came in.

She stopped under a bright recessed ceiling light, stood under its glare like a defendant in a sci-fi scene.

"In 1977," she said, "my father, Jack Kantke, was convicted of killing my mother and a friend of hers. In Long Beach. I was five."

There.

Jean looked at the maid. The maid looked at the TV.

Jimmy drew another glass of water and looked out at the backyard. A fog was filling the back of the canyon, rolling down from on high like a very slow waterfall. It was always sad when you heard what it was.

"My father was Assistant D.A.," Jean continued. "Mother was a dress designer. It was in all the papers, even *Time* magazine. There were appeals. He was executed in 1992. The gas chamber."

It was so matter-of-fact. So *repeated*.

"I know people say you shouldn't go back into the past," she said.

"I never say that," Jimmy turned and said.

"I just—"

"Were you there? When it happened?"

"No. I was at my grandmother's."

She'd lost some of her *force* from before. He liked her this way. This was the big hurt in her life. Most people, you'd have to know them for months or years to find out what it was. Maybe it was why he did this, *looked into things*. He liked knowing, even when in the end sometimes it tore him up.

"So what do you want to know?"

"If he really killed her," Jean said. "Killed *them*. He swore he didn't."

Jimmy said, "You know, innocent people don't get executed." He watched for some reaction to the word *innocent*. She didn't have one. "You would think it would happen and people like to talk about it all the time, but it really doesn't happen."

He looked at her until she nodded.

"It would be an enormous surprise if he didn't kill them," he said.

There was a long moment. She nodded again.

"So you just want to know how much to hate him?" Jimmy said.

"No."

"What then? What difference would it make? Everybody's dead."

He waited for some reaction to that word, too. To *dead*.

"I just think it would be better to know," she said.

Jimmy put his glass in the sink. "We could have a long conversation about that sometime," he said. "Sorry."

And he left her again.

Jean looked over at the maid, who was still pretending she didn't speak much English. Now on the TV there was a picture of the missing boy in a Cub Scout uniform. And then they were on to some other story.

AT THE END OF THE NIGHT, JIMMY WAITED OUT front surrounded by his new best friends, a circle that included Ben the JPL engineer and both murder victims, still in their bloodstained clothes. The fog had them all wrapped up. The TV comic was just hauling himself up into a caution-sign-yellow Hummer.

After Joel and the comic told each other they'd call, the Hummer pulled out and rumbled off to war down the drive. Joel came over to Jimmy's circle. He put his arm around the murder girl and kissed her on the cheek.

"Wasn't she good?" Joel said to everyone.

The actress smiled.

"You broke my heart," Joel said.

"I'm going to go get cleaned up," the girl said and started away. Joel looked hurt. She came back and kissed him on the forehead.

"She's going to be big," Joel said, once she was gone.

"You mean when she grows up?" Jimmy said.

"Funny."

"*Don't hate me because I'm promiscuous,*" Jimmy said.

"She loves me."

The valet brought up the Porsche, left the driver's door open. The engine growled low, warm and friendly, like a dog waiting for its master.

"Thanks for inviting me, Joel," Jimmy said.

"I never know when you're screwing with me," Joel said.

"I just said thanks."

"See?"

Jimmy got into the Porsche, closed the door, punched the gas a couple of times because he liked the sound. "You ever think maybe you were *too* smart?"

"Now I *know* you're screwing with me," Joel said.

Jimmy sped away. The radio came up, loud.

Jean Kantke stepped out of the house just in time to see the taillights disappear down the smooth curving drive.

CHAPTER 2

IN THE BELFRY OF THE HOLLYWOOD UNITED METH-
odist Church above Highland and Franklin, an owl
with luminous eyes scanned the scene below: the river
of taillights coming down from the Bowl, cop cars
and an ambulance, their red lights slicing up the night,
a body under a sheet, a cop drawing chalk rings
around spent shells. In the hills to the right was the
Magic Castle. Down from that, the façade of the Chinese Theater, seen from behind. This was inland and
there was none of the Malibu fog. The night was especially clear. The lights of the city south seemed to
crackle.

The owl took off. Hung on the side of the church's
tower was a fifty-foot AIDS ribbon. All the way down
below, a signboard announced this week's sermon:

"The Last Minute of Eternity"

Jimmy drove the Strip with the radio loud, the top down, past famous haunts, rolling eastbound. It was a Friday night so things were happening but everyone seemed to be headed in the opposite direction, headed west. From the looks on their faces they were happy.

He stopped on a yellow at Sunset and Crescent Heights. In the side mirror, the red neon sign for the Chateau Marmont shimmered. Jimmy looked back over his shoulder at the hotel on the rise above the Strip, its turrets and towers, the awnings on the penthouse patio, the roofs of the bungalows behind for the long-termers and New York actors and French directors. They'd just hauled down the tall Marlboro Man billboard who'd stood over the hotel for years, replaced him with a state-sponsored rant about secondhand smoke, a dolled up couple close enough to kiss.

"Mind if I smoke?" the guy was saying.

"Care if I die?" says the girl.

Then Jimmy saw him, a man in a Navy peacoat and watch cap. And this a warm night, too. He leaned against a wall next to a turquoise nightclub. This one was young, in his twenties. He drank from a bottle of water, his eyes on Jimmy, a sour expression on his face, a sour smile, as though remembering a sick joke.

They were called *Sailors*.

A trio of Valley teenagers walked past him, stopped

to read the names of the bands on the club marquee. The man in the peacoat ignored them, took another drink of water, kept his eyes on Jimmy.

There was an edge of blue light around him, at least to Jimmy's eyes.

"*I know you, Brother,*" he looked at Jimmy and mouthed.

Suddenly the passenger door opened and a girl plopped into the seat beside him, a very young girl in a very short skirt. She yanked the door closed, as if that settled something, closed the deal.

"Hi, what's your name?" she said, like she was thirteen.

Jimmy looked over at the turquoise nightclub. The man in the peacoat and watch cap raised his bottle of water in salute.

The light turned green.

"You'd better get out," Jimmy said to the girl.

"Let's just ride around," she said. "Just until it stops raining."

"It's not going to rain for four months," Jimmy said.

"It rained earlier."

"Bullshit."

"You're not very friendly," she said with a pout someone must have told her was sexy. The car behind the Porsche flicked its lights. Jimmy pulled out.

"I'll take you to the All American Burger," he said.

"Cool." She tugged at the hem of the skirt under her and changed the station on the radio.

"I hate this song," she said.

"I mean, I'll drop you off there," Jimmy said.

She ignored him, fumbled in her bag, found her cigarettes.

"Don't," he said. "Please."

She pouted another half second then closed her bag and turned in the seat to face him, to let him see her legs, if he wanted to look.

Jimmy looked up at the crossroads behind him in the mirror. The Sailor had turned away to walk back up Sunset. On the prowl.

"So. What do you do, Mr. No Names Please?" she said.

"Just drive around."

"Looking for trouble."

"No, I know where that is," Jimmy said.

She bit her lip and said, "I bet."

"You've been watching too much TV," Jimmy said.

He drove two more blocks, looking ahead. It was after midnight now and the night was coming into its own, shaking itself awake like a dog, the whores and their men, the hyper teens, pierced runaways on bus benches, their legs jumping, laughing and hitting each other, all of it looking like fun, for about the first ten seconds. The All American Burger was ahead, red, white and blue and way too bright.

"This car is cool but it's like older than you are, right?"

"It's a '64."

"And that's like older than you are, right?"

He laughed. "Yeah."

"I have a '99 Corvette back home in Ohio up on

blocks with only a hundred miles on it. I was a Gerber baby." She said it all in one breath.

"A *what?*"

"A Corvette."

"No, I mean—"

"A Gerber baby. In ads. In *Good Housekeeping.*"

There was something sweet about her lics, something that made him want to try to pretend he was her brother, take her along with him for a few hours and try to beat back the night.

But before they made it to the All American Burger they came up on a tricked-out pickup on the other side of the wide street. Another girl like this girl leaned in the window, talking to three teenagers wedged into the front seat shoulder to shoulder, El Camino High linebackers.

"Stop!" she said. "I know those guys."

Jimmy pulled to the curb.

She jumped out.

She threw the door closed and leaned all the way in. "You're sweet," she said in that way that doesn't mean anything.

Then she kissed him on the cheek.

She pulled back, *spooked.* She stepped away from the car. She stood on the sidewalk. She touched her lips.

Jimmy drove away, up Sunset.

When he looked up in the mirror, she still stood on the side of the street where he left her, watching him go, holding herself as if from a sudden chill.

* * *

ANGEL'S HOUSE WAS HALFWAY DOWN AN IMPOSSI-
bly steep hill in Silver Lake in a neighborhood of
Craftsman bungalows, some restored and almost *too*
neat, the rest of them peeling under all the sun the hill
took. Jimmy parked the Porsche, wheels canted to the
curb. You could hear the music from here. The moon
was still up. A couple made out against the fender of a
cherry Camaro. They ignored him.

The partiers spilled out of the house onto the ter-
raced backyard. Angel's place was never closed, his
friends and wards mostly Latinos with a few Cal Arts
types. Three people danced to ska under a string of
chili pepper lights hung in a grapefruit tree, its trunk
painted white. Somebody on the steps recognized
Jimmy as he came down around the side of the house
and threw him a beer.

Angel Figueroa huddled at a picnic table with a
skinny kid. Angel was in his forties, muscular, "cut,"
clear-eyed, un-tattooed. He wore starched wide-leg
jeans, stiff as cardboard, and a white T-shirt, a look
they called California Penal. He spoke Spanish to the
kid, fervent. The kid looked at the ground, nodding. In
Angel's lap was an open Bible with a homemade
leather cover.

Angel looked up.

"Ask Jimmy," Angel said. "Jimmy knows all about
Jesus but he won't accept the grace either."

Jimmy nodded hello to the kid, who looked embarrassed.

"I've been working on Jimmy Miles for years," Angel said. "Ask him. I don't go away. Jesus don't go away, I don't go away."

The kid's name was Luis.

"This is Luis."

Jimmy nodded at the kid again.

"Gimme some money," Angel said to Jimmy.

Jimmy dug in his pocket and took out a folded sheaf of bills. He handed it all to Angel.

Angel peeled off two fives and gave them to the kid. "Go ask that *chica* over there why she's been looking over here at you," Angel said. There was a pretty girl on the steps, drinking a Coke, as young as the hooker on Sunset. "Take her up to Tommy's. We all run out of food. Take my truck."

Luis went away to talk to the girl.

"I'm trying to get him in an Art Magnet," Angel said to Jimmy.

Angel shook Jimmy's hand and pulled him down onto the bench beside him.

"Tell me something good."

"I made the run to Tecate the other night," Jimmy said.

"You shoulda called."

"Stopped at that little fish fry place."

"I was probably busy."

"Next time," Jimmy said, to hit the ball back over the net.

"Yeah, *next* time."

Angel stood and put his arm around him. "I got something sweet to show you."

In the garage, a half dozen young men dressed like Angel and with beers in their hands gazed reverently upon a chopped and lowered '56 Mercury, a work in progress ground down to shiny steel.

Angel came in singing, *"Baby loves a Mercury, crazy 'bout a Mercury . . ."* He snatched a handkerchief out of the back pocket of one of the men, mimicked wiping off the hood. The men laughed. Maybe it was a joke about working in a car wash. Jimmy liked the people Angel drew to him, kids struggling to stay in school and men in their twenties and thirties and even forties struggling to stay in or out of any number of things. They looked like killers, but they weren't.

"What's the mill?" Jimmy said and ran a hand along the smooth fender.

"You don't want to know," Angel said.

Jimmy reached into the downturned mouth of the chrome grill and found the latch and opened the hood. There was no chrome on the engine. It was functionality writ large, wedged in its space like an iron fist.

The men stepped closer. Nobody said anything.

"A 427," Angel said. "Holman-Moody built it for Freddie Lorenzen in '66. Come by in the daytime, I'll light it up for you. It doesn't have very good manners."

One of the kids repeated the last in Spanish for the man next to him.

Jimmy lowered the hood, pushed gently until the latch clicked.

"You all right?" Angel said. "You seem a little down."

Jimmy didn't answer. He stared at the bare metal curve of the car, old and new at the same time.

"Come on," Angel said. "Say it out loud."

"You know how sometimes you forget about it?" Jimmy said.

Angel nodded.

"And then you *remember*."

"What happened?"

"A girl kissed me on the cheek," Jimmy said. "And she *knew*."

"What girl?"

"Girl on Sunset. A hooker. Jumped in my car."

Angel waited a minute and then he said, "They see a lot of dark shit. They get tuned in to it."

"Maybe she saw what's really there. You ever think about that?"

"Not about *you*," Angel said.

A few hours later, the moon had set, the women were gone, the men were lifting weights. Angel stood over the bench press spotting a fearsome man grinding out a last rep. Jimmy was up on the deck. The Hollywood Freeway was a half mile away and the traffic, even late, threw up a sound like the ocean. When you first heard it, it was exciting in a way, the sound of energy, of motion, of *intention*. But, like the kids out wild on Sunset, ten seconds later it felt like something else, something to turn away from before it pulled you down. He watched Angel and the men for a minute, listened to them teasing each other in Spanish, and then put down his beer, went down the steps to go.

He waved to Angel, started up the side of the house.

"Let's make a run to Tecate some night," Angel called after him. "Eat at that fish fry place."

Jimmy walked up the sidewalk alongside the white house. He brushed aside a branch of trumpet vine that arched overhead. He looked at his fingers.

Wet, from the leaves.

A LITTLE TV OFFERED UP THE FIRST NEWSCAST OF the morning. The sound was down but the visuals said enough: the school picture of the missing boy giving way to a live shot of helicopters combing brown hills somewhere in the Inland Empire, Verdugo or San Bernardino or Riverside. Jimmy sat at one end of the long table in the big dining room, eating toast, wearing the same clothes from last night.

The weather came on. Jimmy turned up the sound in time to hear, "A surprise trace of rain last night in parts of Hollywood . . ."

He left it on, walked away from it.

The bedroom was stark, a large room with expensive furnishings out of the past, huge pieces carved from some rain forest hardwood, dark, almost black. Jimmy stood at the tall windows, looking down at the backyard as the daylight burned off the dew. He yanked closed the blackout drapes and lay back on the bed, still in his clothes.

CHAPTER 3

JEAN KANTKE'S OFFICE WAS IN AN INDUSTRIAL
building just east of downtown on a street of rag trade
shops, down where they made bathing suits and neck-
ties, kiddy backpacks and knockoff men's jeans and
underwear. The office was on the third floor, the top
floor, and it was crisp and clean and high style, metal
frame windows, old-style wide silver Venetian blinds
dicing the morning light, and a desk that was silver
too, all curvy, looking like it came out of the purser's
office of an ocean liner.

An assistant showed Jimmy in.

Jean kept her eyes down, busied herself with some
papers on the desk. She wore a light blue suit, a blue
the color of iceberg ice.

"What changed your mind?" she said, still not

looking up. She was treating him like an employee. He was used to it. He understood it. People hated to need help, especially in daylight.

"My mind is in a constant state of change," Jimmy said. "Is that an oxymoron?" He was still trying to impress her. And still noticing it.

He looked around. "Nice office," he said.

"Perfume," she said. "I do very well."

"And you smell good, too."

Jimmy inspected a collection of perfume bottles from the past in a tall glass case, all the shapes and colors, cut glass and crystal. On the highest shelf, all by itself, was a black cat. Down low there was a shelf of goofy Avon cologne bottles, VW bugs and banjos and little businessmen with briefcases and black plastic stingy brim hats that unscrewed, a riff on the ordinary people and what they splashed behind their ordinary ears.

Jean was used to getting answers to her questions. "What made you change your mind?" she said again.

Jimmy picked up the black cat bottle. "It rained the other night," he said. "Somebody told me it did, and I didn't believe her."

Now she looked at him. "I don't understand."

"Me either."

Jean pushed back from the desk and stepped to a file cabinet. She found a folder, opened it, glanced at it, closed it. She offered it to Jimmy.

He didn't take it.

"You were five."

"Yes."

"Where'd they send you?" he said.

"What do you mean?"

"You were five. They sent you somewhere."

"I grew up in my grandmother's house."

"In L.A.?"

"San Francisco. Tiberon, actually."

"Is she still alive?"

"No."

"You said you had money. Did it start with her?"

"She had money. But I have my own."

"Any brothers or sisters?" he said.

"A brother, Carey. He lives in Arizona."

Jimmy didn't say anything else. Sometimes when you let silence rise up, people will fill it and some people will say things, sometimes more than they meant to say.

"I left my grandmother's as soon as I could," she said. "A boarding school in Atherton and then Stanford. When I was sixteen." She added the last with an impossible combination of pride and embarrassment.

"That doesn't sound like much fun," Jimmy said.

"I never thought it was supposed to be," she said.

"I didn't exactly make it to college," he said.

She didn't have anything to say about that.

"Can you tell?" he said.

"I don't really know what to think about you," she said.

"But that could be a *good* thing, right?" he said.

They both listened as "La Cucaracha" was played on the horn of a truck in the parking lot below. Jimmy went over to the window and spread the blinds. It was a lunch truck, chromed up, fancy. When you started your shift at five in the morning, you had lunch at ten-thirty. A Mexican man with a coin belt around his waist set up a folding table as the workers came out, all women as far as Jimmy could see. At least now she was talking to him like a person and not like a servant. Or a doctor. Or a priest. But he could tell she wanted this to be over, maybe was wishing she hadn't even thought of this, had never had these questions about her father and murder and a time out of time, or at least had not given in to them.

"Why me? Why do you want me to do this?" he said.

"I asked a few people to recommend someone. I asked Joel—"

He turned away from the window and looked at her. "Joel said he didn't put me up for this. He said you came to him, asking about me. Not about investigators. About *me*."

She just stood there. Whatever it was, she didn't want to say it.

He held out his hand. She gave him the file.

"Do you need a retainer or—"

"Kiss me on the cheek," Jimmy said.

She just waited.

"At the party at Joel's," he said, "before you revealed your ulterior motive, I thought you liked me a little. It'd be nice if it all wasn't just a smart girl's trap."

The phone buzzed. She didn't look at it.

"I don't see—"

"You have to kiss me," Jimmy said.

She kissed him on the cheek. There was a kind of defiance in it, as if she'd made herself believe that it was her idea.

She didn't recoil like the girl on Sunset.

Jimmy opened the file.

"One Ten Rivo Alto Canal," he said aloud.

THERE WAS A GUNSHOT STRETCHED OVER A LONG second and the flash that came with it, flaring in the white bedroom like lightning from a little localized storm. Elaine Kantke, late twenties, as pretty as a model, fell back onto the satin sheets on a circular bed, blood already leaking from the hole in her jaw.

Her silk pajama top fell open. She wore nothing else.

In the same second, a meaty blue-collar man named Bill Danko crumpled where he stood beside the bed as the same bullet which had passed through her tore away his cheek. He wore baggy suit pants and a loud shirt. There was a hi-fi on the nightstand, playing an LP.

Elaine Kantke was already dead. A second shot finished Bill Danko off, caught him in the V just above the bridge of his nose.

Jimmy wondered if they had a name for that.

He stood in front of the microfiche machine in the library at the *Long Beach Press-Telegram*. The killings were played up big, a four-column story and two sidebars. There were pictures of the two-story

Spanish style house on Rivo Alto Canal and interior shots of the bedroom, the covered bodies, the bed, the hi-fi. There were arrows and dotted lines and X's and hyperventilated text in the cutlines, all of it under a thirty-six point headline full wide:

TWO SLAIN IN NAPLES

Jimmy put in a quarter, hit the button, pulled a copy.

On the inside slop-over page, beside the rest of the story, there was an ad for a VW bug at $1,995. He smiled as he looked at it, that old familiar shape. He pulled a copy of that, too. He rolled through another week of microfiche. Time whipped past like a dramatic effect in an old movie.

He stopped on:

D.A. ARRESTED,
DENIES SLAYING WIFE, MAN

After a week or two, the evidence had been assembled. You took your time when your murderer was an assistant district attorney. The case they had against Jack Kantke was only sketchy at this point, at least what was in the papers, but it was enough to arrest, enough for another banner headline.

And enough for most people to make up their minds about Jack Kantke. There he was, if you needed something more, in a shot on the steps of the downtown Criminal Courts Building, his hands cuffed in front of him, an odd half smile on his face. One side of his mouth was grinning, the other wasn't. It was like those tragedy and comedy masks in one man.

He had short hair, shiny, combed left, a white tab collar shirt, a skinny black tie, a style more sixties than seventies. He looked a little like Jack Webb, not the face, just the gray suit and the ramrod backbone.

Or maybe Rod Serling.

They had arrested him at his office. Of course they knew where he lived—he was still living there, in the murder house on Rivo Alto Canal—and they could have done it yesterday, Sunday, when he was home, probably sitting in the sun out front, but they showed up downtown on Monday morning, came right in and walked past his secretary and opened the frosted glass door with his name in gold on it. They would have yanked him right up out of his swivel chair if he wasn't standing already, waiting for them, for *it*. Everybody knew this was high drama.

On down the page were the first pictures of Jack and Elaine Kantke in, as they say, *better days*, alive, smiling, chic, attractive. Party people, yacht clubbers. The shots were from what used to be called the *Soc* section of the paper, Society. *Where were the piña coladas?* One shot was from some official function, the assistant D.A. and his designer wife, Jack in a tux, Elaine Kantke in a black shoulderless gown wearing a loose watch with diamonds on it and diamonds at her ears. This being Southern California, they were probably overdressed.

And then there was a pretty picture of Elaine Kantke they hadn't used in the first go-around, a glamorous headshot with highlights in her hair and angled lighting, maybe a George Hurrell shot. It made Jimmy wonder if she'd been an actress, or had tried to be. When she smiled, at least for this, she smiled with everything. She looked young and happy and healthy. But she wasn't anybody's girl-next-door. She had what used to be called *sophistication,* not always meant as a compliment. She looked a little French. She looked like she smoked.

Jimmy tried to find something of Jean in her mother's face but didn't see it.

He didn't look for Jean in Jack Kantke's face. Jimmy didn't like him. *That didn't take long.* It wasn't the murder so much as the hurt he'd caused a little girl.

And that he couldn't seem to wipe the other half of that smile off his face.

Jimmy sped through to December, a year-end wrap-up, another banner headline:

1977 . . .
A MERGER   A MURDERER   A MONARCH

Cute.

JIMMY LOOKED OVER AT THE *QUEEN MARY* ACROSS the harbor as he drove down Ocean Boulevard. He was in his Mustang, a dark green 1968 GT 390 fastback. It was a big sky day, all blue except for a few clouds trying to build into something out over the shipping channel. The Catalina boat cruised toward the end of the breakwater, white as a wedding cake in the clear light.

Long Beach changed block by block, sometimes cleaned-up and rich and then the next street tired, sad, sorry. In one block, it'd be bright white BMW convertibles with blue tops, like they were little ski boats. The next block, left-behind grocery carts. Jimmy couldn't get the pictures of the murders out of his head. It was always like this. It always came to life right in front of him and stayed there until it was over. *Death came to life.* Funny. He tried to find something on the radio to splash a little light his way but it was all talk, talk about money and violence. When he was working, the world seemed made up of nothing but grief and greed and malice. Maybe it set him up to do the job, to see what he had to see, to go where he always had to go. He didn't like it, but when he wasn't on a case, there was something in him that missed it, wanted it. It put him at risk, body and soul, and there was something in him that wanted that because it made him feel more alive.

A narrow thirties-era concrete bridge humped up and over a twenty-foot-wide canal into the "Naples" area of Long Beach. That was what the real estate people called it, since the thirties when it was thought up and built, ten or twelve short blocks of big houses on narrow lots on finger canals, sailboats and harbor cruisers tied up in their "front yards." No abandoned grocery carts here.

Jimmy cruised down a skinny one-way lane. The houses had garages opening in the back onto the alley. It was a Monday but the neighborhood had more signs of life than most moneyed L.A. neighborhoods in the middle of the afternoon on a weekday. The people who lived here now were retired people or widows or people married to widows. You got a coffee and went by the broker's office in the village around ten, read the *Times* outside somewhere and then killed a couple hours before a late lunch. If you had a wife, she laid out your clothes on the bed in the morning, the bright slacks, the knit shirts, and sometimes they matched hers. You stayed away or out in the yard cutting back the bougainvillea long enough to keep her happy. The first drink of the day usually came at about four, unless you counted lunch.

There wasn't a 110 Rivo Alto Canal anymore. The ceramic plaques on the garages skipped from one oh eight to one twelve, probably more out of respect for property values than for the dead.

But there was the house.

Spanish-style, two-story, fading pink. It looked abandoned. *Could it have sat empty all these years?* Jimmy parked where the intersecting street dead-ended at the canal. Across the lane of water, a man hosed off a twenty-two-foot day-sailer. He was close enough to say something friendly, but didn't. A gull wheeled and dropped, threatening to land. The man flicked the hose in its direction.

An arica palm next to the house had a full head of brown fronds ready to crack off with the next real

wind, but the hedges and a bird-of-paradise were
hacked back and the little patch of grass out front was
green so the house wasn't abandoned exactly. Someone was dealing with it.

Jimmy stood before it a long moment and then sat
on the seawall. Spanish-style houses always had a
nice balance. There was a big picture window to the
left, an archway, a little portico, a heavy door behind
it, a door with black iron strap hinges and black iron
nailheads and a "speakeasy grill" to look out at the
Fuller Brush Man through, iron too, heavy and lacy at
the same time. That was Spanish. The walkway and
steps were painted red to look like tile or clay.

Jimmy looked up at the second-floor window, another picture window curved at the top to match the
arcs below. That was the front bedroom, where it hap
pened. One of the pictures in the paper had a uniformed cop standing at the window, looking out,
looking *up* for some reason, as if the murderer had
somehow flown out across the canal.

Jimmy walked to the picture window and looked
in. Dark drapes faded to green/gray stood open a foot.
It was the living room. There were a few pieces of old
furniture, what they used to call a divan, *Look* and
Life magazines on the coffee table, a couple of Klee
prints on the walls. It was like a museum of the mid-
1970s. Untouched. The table lamps were tall and bulbous, glassy gold dripping over aquamarine. The
carpet was white shag. The rotary phone was pink.
Over the fake fireplace with its dead and dusty electric
log "fire" was a pen and ink sketch of the Left Bank.

Off a dark hallway, a staircase stepped up through deep angular shadows to the second floor. If there were any kids in the neighborhood, maybe *grandkids,* they were sure to swap stories about ghosts. You wouldn't think so, but there were houses like this all over L.A., left-behind houses, *dead* houses. Sometimes it was about uncollected taxes. Sometimes it was about crazy. Usually it was about bad blood running through the constricted veins of bitter heirs. *If I can't have it, you can't have it.*

A spider stepped across the sill. Time meant nothing to it.

Jimmy stepped back. There was music from somewhere close, Abba's "Dancing Queen," more of the past pushing into the present. It was coming from the house two doors down, out an open upstairs window. The song ended and another Abba song started. It was an album. *Who listens to Abba albums?*

There was a sound from across the canal, a sound Jimmy was meant to hear, the sailboat man slapping the hose into coils on the dock. Jimmy looked over. The neighborhood watchman tested the valve again to make sure the water was off and then walked up the short walk into the house, stepped out of his Topsiders outside the door and went in. After a few seconds the white shutters in the upstairs window tipped open a crack.

Jimmy suppressed the urge to wave.

He walked down alongside the canal to the Abba house. A low stucco wall surrounded a small porch, a patio with Adirondack chairs and a little table for the drinks. He knocked on the door. He waited but nobody came. After a minute, the side ended. It was a record player. The needle lifted—you could hear it—and then a click.

"She was there a minute ago."

A young workman with his shirt off was sanding the dock in front of the next house down. He had KROQ on the box, the Chili Peppers.

"Try again."

"That's all right," Jimmy said.

"She was there a minute ago. She likes the sun," the workman said. He made it sound a little nasty.

"Is there still a Yacht Club around here?" Jimmy said.

The workman pointed down the walk.

Jimmy walked away from 110 Rivo Alto Canal but it stayed with him. He couldn't shake it. Instead of the sweet little walk under the trees beside the canal, he might just as well have been walking down that upstairs hallway toward that front room where it had happened, where the lightning had flashed.

He was already inside.

CHAPTER 4

THROUGH THE TINTED GLASS OF THE TALL WIN-
dows of the bar Jimmy watched the Hunters and
Catalinas and Ericsons motoring out toward the bight.
He drank his beer and swiped a few olives from the
tray.

The bartender was on a cell phone to his girlfriend.

"I know," he said every once in a while.

He was too young to know anything about the Kant-
kes. *Star Wars* was 1977. *Hotel California.* Elvis dy-
ing in August. *Car Wash. Saturday Night Fever. Roots.
Laverne & Shirley.* Foreigner's "Feels Like the First
Time" and K.C. & the Sunshine Band's "I'm Your
Boogie Man."

And *Abba.*

Jimmy got up, took his beer with him, and looked

at the pictures along one wall, the Long Beach Yacht Club over the years. In the old days, what you had was Old Money enjoying itself. The men wore yachting caps with a straight face, only nobody had a straight face. Then New Money started elbowing in. There went the dress code. The fifties were very black and white and the sixties were . . .

What were they?

The seventies and eighties looked even more confused and even drunker. The nineties saw a bit of a return to the old order, at least a stab at it, more contained hair, better clothes, straighter lines, a serious, unblinking *White* look, particularly on the two or three Black members who'd made their way in.

The current crowd in the latest pictures made no sense at all, like the rest of L.A. now, the only center being a lack of center. There were South Americans with ponytails like movie coke dealers shoulder to shoulder, drinks in hand, with USC frat boys and their old men, next to real life hippies in tie-dye next to leathery world-cruisers next to a lesbian couple all in white, she a little taller than *she*. Old salts, new salts, Russians, Armenians, Redondo car dealers, Indian ophthalmologists. And a dignified-looking Mexican man in a blue double-breasted jacket with gold buttons.

And Ernest Borgnine.

There was a picture labeled "Officers 1975–1976" but no Jack or Elaine Kantke.

A white-haired man and his wife came through the bar, dressed up. Jimmy smiled. They smiled back. A second couple followed the first. The second man wore a pink sports coat, the woman a dress the color of poppies with shoes to match and a pair of sunglasses that remembered the arched-eyebrow tail of a 1959 Chevrolet.

They said hello, too, and seemed to mean it.

"Something going on?" Jimmy said.

"Crabby Lewis," the white-haired man said.

Jimmy followed them into the banquet room.

Up front was a three-foot-tall picture of a tanned ancient mariner in blazer and turtleneck and yacht cap. Jimmy hung around in back. There were only ten or twelve of them, with four waiters.

When they'd finished their salmon and salads, the pink coat man got up and stood next to the picture.

"I remember when my boy Spence went sailing with Crabby the first time," the pink coat man began, his eyes on the big picture. "Spence was twelve or thirteen."

Everyone started nodding their heads. They knew the story. They weren't unhappy. They were too old. Too much had happened. Too many sailors had sailed off to Happy Harbor.

"When they were coming in, Crabby gave Spence a loose ten-foot coiled line, told him to stand in the bow, told him to get ready." *Here it was.* "Twenty feet out from the dock, Crabby said, 'OK . . . *Jump!*' Spence jumped in, still holding the loose line."

It got its laugh.

"That was Crabby. If you jumped when he said to, you were all right."

The people nodded. That was Crabby.

"Spence wouldn't ever do what *I* said," the pink coat man said. "Still won't."

One of the women daubed at the corner of her eye, but she might have been crying about Spence. Or her own Spence.

When it was over, Jimmy bought a round in the bar.

"Everybody liked Jack and Elaine," the pink coat man said.

Everyone nodded.

"His lawyer proved he was in Las Vegas," the white-haired man said. "At the Rotary convention." He and his wife were drinking tall club sodas. He'd sent the first ones back when they came without limes. "The prosecution had to admit there wasn't enough time to drive there from Long Beach after the murders were committed." He sounded like he was still mad about it. Or mad about something.

"The desk clerk testified," another man said. This one looked as if he'd literally stepped off the deck of a boat to be there, sawdust in his eyebrows and in the hair on the back of his hands. Teak. You could smell it on him. "There wasn't enough time."

The pink coat man shook his head. They all shook their heads. Everybody knew all the same things.

"Even with the time change," the sawdust man added.

"We're in the same time zone as Vegas, Ted," the white-haired man said. He was still mad.

"I don't believe so," the sawdust man said.

"Yes. Same. All of Nevada," the white-haired man said. "Including Las Vegas," he added.

"Well, I don't gamble," the sawdust man said.

"You probably *shouldn't,* Ted," the white-haired man said.

The sawdust man *could* have said, "Well, at least my boat isn't made out of *plastic,*" but he didn't. He just filed it away. And took a sip of his free beer.

"And there was the guy in the gas station in Barstow," a fourth man said, to bring it back around. "The gas station guy also verified the time line. Tell him about that."

"I believe you just did, Ev," the pink coat man said and traded a look with the white-haired man.

"What was his lawyer like?" Jimmy said.

"Harry Turner," the white-haired man said.

Jimmy waited.

"You don't know Harry Turner?"

"He's too young," the pink coat man said.

"I've heard of him," Jimmy said. "I didn't think he—"

"He *didn't.*" It was the white-haired man. "Harry Turner was behind the scenes. But everybody who knew anything knew Harry Turner was running Jack's defense. Well, *Jack* was running it but he had sense enough to know to go to Harry. But up front was . . . The guy at the table in the courtroom was . . . What was his name?"

"Upland. Or Overland," the sawdust man said.

"Harry Turner never lost a case," the pink coat man said.

"Still hasn't," the white-haired man said with a harsh little laugh.

"He's retired now," one of them said.

"Yeah, *retired*," the white-haired man said.

A silence rose up. They all knew something that Jimmy didn't know. Maybe someone would say it out loud.

"Up*church*," one of the women said. None of the wives had said anything until now, just sipped their G&Ts and traded looks while the men talked.

The men nodded. Up*church*.

And then things got too quiet again.

"None of you thought Jack Kantke did it," Jimmy said.

"Not then," the pink coat man said. "Nobody could believe it."

"And now?"

There was a long moment.

"Well, there's a system, isn't there?" the white-haired man said.

The woman in the poppy-colored dress took her sunglasses off. She smiled at Jimmy, a smile not connected to anything in the scene but which now made it about her. Her hair still had life to it and whoever had done the work around her eyes had The Touch. She knew what he was thinking and enjoyed it.

"So," Jimmy said, with a look that included all three women, "any of you in The Jolly Girls?"

On the microfiche at the newspaper library there was a sidebar on Elaine Kantke and her best friends. More importantly, *a picture*. Four vivacious, frisky babes at the selfsame Yacht Club bar, four of them on four stools, their hips stuck out.

That was what they called themselves, "The Jolly Girls."

The woman in the poppy dress was quick and apparently spoke for all of them.

"No."

JIMMY STOOD LOOKING DOWN INTO THE WATER beside a black-bottom pool in a spectacular backyard in Palos Verdes, a bluff overlooking the battered green Pacific.

"You're early," a voice behind him said.

Jimmy turned.

Vivian Goreck approached with a professional smile. She was another striking woman in her fifties. She didn't offer her hand, was from a time just before that. She wore a print dress, bright, tropical.

"You're the same color as the wall behind you," Jimmy said.

"All part of the plan," she said brightly. "Like a spider. Did you look inside?"

"Nope," Jimmy said.

She stepped back slightly and put a new smile on her face and he went where she wanted him to go.

The house was empty, high ceilings, blond floors, a lot of glass, Moderne. A man had lived here, alone, Jimmy could tell that right away. If a woman had lived here anything more than overnight she would have found something to take away at least some of the *edge,* to get the willful solitariness out of the air. A woman who cared about you, if you wanted her, alone was enough to do it.

There was an open kitchen with a pair of chrome sinks sunk in granite. Jimmy turned on the water, cupped his hand, bent and drank.

Vivian watched him. *You see it all.* Besides, she could tell he had money.

"The stove's a commercial Wolf," she said. "The fridge is Subzero. There are double Blankenship disposals, double Nero trash compactors."

Jimmy turned off the water. "Was there a murder or divorce in the house? I always heard people ask that."

She handed him a black dish towel. "They do. No, the house was owned by the builder and—"

Jimmy stopped the pretense. "My name is Jimmy Miles," he said. "I'm not your buyer, I just wanted to talk to you. Your office told me where you were."

She didn't even blink. She was solid. Secure. Jimmy wondered what had made her that way. It was something else you didn't see much anymore.

"Talk to me about what?" she said.

"The Jolly Girls."

She stood up straighter, almost laughed. "Really. Why?"

"I'm an investigator."

"I'm sure there's a statute of limitations on public drunkenness . . ." she said. Here was another beauty who still had her looks but kept reminding you of what had been, the way the fire must have flared once and how everybody, or at least the men, had gathered round to watch it. Jimmy liked her, wanted the time back when she was young.

"Gee, I sure hope so," he said.

"So what is it?" she said.

"The Kantkes."

"Really?"

Jimmy nodded. And waited.

"Who wants to know about that? Why now?"

Jimmy didn't answer.

She leaned back against the counter and crossed her still pretty legs at the ankle. "I used to always say I don't talk about those days," she said. "And now it's been ten years since anybody asked."

"We all used to be jolly," Jimmy said.

"You're a little young to be world-weary, aren't you?" she said in a voice, a *Mrs. Robinson* voice he could hear her using in a bar. "I have a daughter your age."

Then somehow she guessed it. Her mind had been working though she hadn't let him see it.

"Jean," she said.

Jimmy didn't say yes, didn't say no.

"I saw her picture in the *Times* a few years ago. The business section. She's very pretty."

He didn't deny that either.

"What does she want to know?" she said.

"*Who.* It's *who* she wants to know. Her mother," Jimmy said. "Or maybe her father." He hadn't thought of that angle until just that moment, that Jean was doing this to get closer to her father. Or close enough to never come close to him again.

Jimmy walked away from her and into the living room. It was big enough for jai alai. Except for a planter with a ficus in it, which looked brought in for the sale, there was no furniture, no coverings on the windows, nothing but a brass telescope on a mahogany tripod in front of floor-to-ceiling glass tinted the merest green.

The gas fireplace was lit, though it was summer and even here along the coastline there was no chill in the air. Jimmy stared at the stone logs, burning yet not consumed, like something in the Bible. *Like me*, was what he was thinking. He heard her follow him into the room, heels clicking on the wood floors.

"So," Jimmy said without turning from the fire, "did Jack Kantke kill them?"

"No."

Now he turned to look at her. If there was any pain in her memory of those days, of those people, she had found a way not to betray it.

"How do you know?"

"I knew him," she said. "Very well. We all knew each other very well." She gave the last line room to breathe, opened up a space for speculation. "Jack didn't care about Elaine and Bill."

"So he knew about the affair?"

"Of course."

"And he didn't care?"

"I don't think so," she said. "Does that shock you? Sometimes I shock my daughter."

Jimmy wasn't shocked.

"I think Jack thought Bill Danko was rather . . . *below* all of us," she said. "But Elaine enjoyed him. And Jack had other fish to fry, as we used to say."

"He had a girlfriend, too?"

She smiled a quick, complicated little smile Jimmy would think about later. "Actually," she said, "I wasn't referring to his love life. Jack was very ambitious. Ten years after the fact, he was still out on the New Frontier. I think he would have been governor eventually. Or he thought so."

She sat on the corner of the planter with her hip out. Jimmy thought again of the picture of the four of them, posing, full of themselves, at the bar.

"Was the Yacht Club The Jolly Girls' clubhouse?"

"Only in an emergency."

"Where then? Where did you hang out?"

"It's embarrassing to say."

"Where?"

"A place called Big Daddy's."

Jimmy remembered it. Marina Del Rey. A good forty-five-minute drive up the coastline, far enough away to see and be seen by a whole new crowd, and not be seen by people who knew your husband.

"That's where Elaine met Bill actually," she said.

"How close were you to her, to Elaine?"

"Not the closest of the group, but we were all close."

Jimmy said, "So who killed them?"

She said, "I have no idea."

There was a sound from the front of the empty house.

"It came out of nowhere, as so many things do," she said.

A man and a woman stepped in. The man had a phone to his ear.

It was Jimmy's cue. He touched Vivian's arm. "Thanks, the house is perfect," he said, loud enough for the prospective buyers to hear. "We'll talk."

She appreciated the gesture. "I'll be in the office until six, Dr. Miles," she said.

Nice touch.

Jimmy nodded to the couple and saw himself to the door.

Out front in the circular driveway was a cream-colored Rolls-Royce Corniche convertible with plates that read: "BUY BUY."

The potential buyers' Jag was parked behind it.

C H A P T E R 5

JIMMY DRANK A CEL-RAY SODA IN A BOOTH AT THE
window under a sign that said, "We Never Close."
Canter's was where John Belushi had spent some of
the last hours of his life. There was the deli and then
the bar in the other room, The Kibitz Room. There
had been a time when Jimmy collected *last hours*
facts, Belushi downing a pastrami at Canter's then going out to Westwood for a chocolate-dipped doughnut
at Dupar's, Janis Joplin shooting pool at Barney's
Beanery on Santa Monica before the drive up Highland to the hotel, James Dean stopping for a burger at
the diner in Saugus before the run to Paso Robles. But
the fun had gone out of it in time, after the list of the
famous dead got a little too long, or death a little less
of a gag.

The waitress came. She was young and Israeli. He didn't want anything else but he ordered a bowl of soup and another Cel-Ray. The place was empty for some reason and he liked her and it wasn't going to be much of a night for her.

He'd picked up a couple of tails, pale men in matching cheap suits, one tall enough to joke about, the other with a shock of bleached hair black at the roots in the style that had passed through the club scene two summers ago. *Sailors.* They were at a table for two in the middle of the room. They'd been down in Long Beach, on the bridge just as he was leaving Naples to go out to meet Vivian Goreck. After he'd left the house for sale, he'd stayed up on the cliffs at Palos Verdes until the sun dropped and then gone by Ike's, his hangout. They were parked on the street in a white Escort when he came out.

They weren't any good at this. Jimmy gave the tall one a look and made him knock over his water.

The second soda came and the soup, a pair of bagel chips speared by the handle of the spoon. The tails decided to pretend they were finished and they got up and left, pretending not to look over at him.

Jimmy slid a *Time* magazine out of a cellophane wrapper. He'd bought it at a collectibles store down in Long Beach. The cover was black with one little dim light, a candle, a hand cupped around it. It was from the week in July of the New York City blackout. He turned over the pages, stepped in. Here was another time capsule, images of 1977, the worries and frivolities of the day. Watergate hearings were grinding on.

Miss America Phyllis George married producer Robert Evans "under a four-hundred-year-old sycamore" in Beverly Hills. War between Ethiopia and Somalia. The Sex Pistols arrived in America, in New York, sneering in their *Wild One* black leather jackets, looking scary and silly, like something New Yorkers had found when the lights came back on.

The story on the murders was halfway through. This was just the kind of California story the East Coast loved. There were pictures of the house front and back and a smiling Elaine Kantke and a half-smiling Jack Kantke and a potato-faced Bill Danko.

The picture of Danko was a mugshot.

The overline read:

LA DOLCE VITA, RIVO ALTO STYLE

"Did I wake you?"

It was a hot night and Jean Kantke had the lights off. She wore a sports bra and three-stripe Adidas silks. She was in the living room in her apartment, the penthouse of a four-story building on a curving street in the hills above Sunset, above the Strip. She pushed aside the sliding glass doors—the apartment had a fifties feel to it—and walked out onto the deck with the portable phone. It was a killer view, the Strip below, the orange and yellow lights of the city stretching all the way down to Compton.

"I never know when people sleep," Jimmy continued. "I mean, regular people."

"Is that what I am?" Jean said into the phone.

"You have a job," Jimmy said. "An office. Hours."

She stepped to the south end of the wraparound terrace, went to the railing. It wasn't that late, a little before midnight. She could hear laughter every once in a while from the open-air cafés on the boulevard with their tables on the sidewalks.

"Are you alone?" she said.

"Yeah."

"I thought I heard something."

"I'm in the car," he said.

Jimmy was headed east on Sunset, past restaurants and bars with limos stacked up, even on a Monday. He'd lost the tails. They weren't around when he came out of Canter's. Or maybe they'd gotten better. He kind of missed them. The light ahead turned yellow. He gunned the Mustang and it leapt forward.

He turned left onto Miller Drive, up into Sunset Plaza, a neighborhood of houses and apartment buildings built like steps up the hills. Modest entrances, priccy vistas. On a quiet side street he parked in the shadows, turned off the engine.

He got out with his phone, leaned against the fender. There were old-fashioned bulbous streetlights on Corinthian stalks, *white* light, not the crime-fighter orange that colored most of L.A. Three or four houses up the hill, a dog nosed around a trashcan, looked in his direction, then plopped down in the middle of the street.

Jean looked south toward Long Beach, miles and years away.

"Was it cooler down there?" she said.

"Not much."

"At least it's clear."

She was full of longing, vague, undefined. She wondered if he could hear it in her voice.

"The house is empty," Jimmy said. "It looks like nobody's touched it since the murders. Inside, anyway. Is that possible?"

There was a hollow wind down the line a second or two.

"People keep telling me anything is possible," Jean said.

She had a water somewhere. She went looking for it, into the living room, then on into the kitchen.

"What do you know about The Jolly Girls?" Jimmy said.

"They were just Mother's friends," Jean said. "The papers made a lot out of it. They all covered for each other. That's what the papers said anyway."

"It's a funny name," Jimmy said.

Jean found her water bottle in the kitchen, but poured herself a drink instead. Vodka. She opened the fridge for some juice and some ice, left it open, standing for a moment in the cool wedge of white light.

"What was Bill Danko's story?" Jimmy said.

"He was teaching her to fly," she said.

She came back out onto the deck with her vodka and cranberry juice.

"I know, it's a bad joke." She watched the line of jumbo jets descending into LAX, the dimmest ones twenty miles out, almost to the desert, it was that clear.

"A couple weeks before the murders, he was arrested for 'drunken flying.' A police helicopter caught them strafing the house, looping around. The cops followed them back to Clover Field. My father kept it out of the papers, but everybody knew."

That would be Bill Danko's mugshot.

"I guess it was a wild time," Jean said. "Nineteen seventy-seven. Things were coming apart, getting a little crazy. Clubs and . . . polyester. And platform shoes. My father drove a Karmen Ghia. The papers called it a 'European sports car.' They all drank a lot, played around, I don't know what else. Loose but not yet *too* crazy. Just so it didn't get in the papers. Jerry Brown was governor. My father was about to be named to a judgeship."

She swirled her drink, took out an ice cube and touched it to her lips. Jimmy didn't say anything, let her walk around in her memories.

"I remember the seawall in front of the house," she said. "Trying to climb up onto it. But afraid."

"It's about two feet tall," Jimmy said.

"Daddy nervous, Mother laughing . . ."

A moment passed. Noise from down on the boulevard floated up again. Her longing had turned, as it does, to tiredness.

"I guess I'll go to sleep," she said. "Do you have anything for me?"

Jimmy looked up at the four-story apartment building across the narrow street from where he'd parked, the one with the terrace around two sides of the penthouse.

"You mean like a glass of warm milk?" He opened the door of the Mustang, got behind the wheel.

"I mean, can you tell anything yet?" she said. "I don't know how you work."

Jimmy started the engine. "This is pretty much it," he said. He put it in gear.

"Watch out for the dog," Jean said, over the phone.

Jimmy looked up at her. She was at the railing of the penthouse, looking down at him.

"That's Roscoe. He's blind."

"I'll call you tomorrow," Jimmy said into his phone, looking at her.

She stayed at the railing, watched as he pulled out of the shadows. He waited for the dog to move out of the way, drove up the hill, pulled into a stub of a driveway, turned around, came down past her, pulled onto Sunset, headed west, never looking up at her again.

She wondered how many cars he had.

She hadn't told him where she lived. She wondered about that, too.

THE MUSTANG WAS PARKED IN FRONT OF A TIKI bar on Pacific Coast Highway in Long Beach. There wasn't much traffic. The front door of the bar was propped open with a five-gallon can filled with sand and cigarette butts. The cleanup lights were on. You could smell the beer in the carpet from twenty feet away.

Jimmy opened the hatchback and lifted out the

frame of a bike, minus the wheels. He put it together, tightened the hardware, gave the wheels a turn. He was wearing a light-colored zip-up jacket. He took it off, folded it, put it over the rear seat and pulled on a black hooded sweatshirt. The moon was bright in the clear sky but ready to set. He closed the hatchback. He'd kept looking for the tails, the pale men, but they never caught back up with him. He was feeling all alone, so alone even some trouble would have cheered him up a little.

He rode the bike up and over the bridge into the Naples area, rode along the lane, along the backs of the houses, the row of garages, almost silent, almost invisible when he was between the streetlights. The cars in the alley were tucked into their covers. No one was out. A possum crossed the alleyway. There weren't even any free dogs to give chase.

Jimmy stowed the bike behind a hedge and came down the walkway alongside Rivo Alto Canal. He stood in front of the murder house, letting his eyes dilate all the way, now that he was away from the streetlights. A wind came up, rustling the dry, brown palm. The surrounding neighborhood was dark except for the dancing blue light of a television in one house across the lane of water.

Jimmy went to the backdoor, clicked on a penlight with a red cap lens. He read the lock in the knob. It wasn't much of a challenge, so old a good twist would probably open it. He shined the light on a ring of keys, the head of each wrapped in black tape to silence it. He made the match, put the key in and the knob turned. He wondered who the last person to touch it had been.

The door stuck, then gave way. He was in.

A few ancient dirt-crusted plates sat in the sink in the kitchen, a broken saucer on top. The faucet dripped into the center of an iron-stain circle. There was a single clouded water glass on the counter.

There was movement, a shape that turned out to be a cat darting away. Jimmy shined his red light on the window over the sink. There was a cracked-out pane, a tear in the screen.

In the living room, he crossed to the front window, looked out where he had looked in that afternoon. The blue light of the TV across the way was gone now. He turned, took in the room. On the wall by the front door was a picture of Jack and Elaine on a sailboat tied up out front. On the coffee table were *Reader's Digest*s, five or six or them spread out in a semicircle like a hand of cards. There was a *Life*. A chevron-shaped ceramic ashtray matched the lamps. All of it was covered with dust. The living room was unchanged from the newspaper photo taken the morning after the killings. All that was missing was the black-haired cop who'd stood beside the "fireplace" pointing at something that had nothing to do with the carnage upstairs. The wind drawn down the canal came up again. A bougainvillea scratched against the glass, like something wanting in.

There was a small bedroom downstairs. A boy's room.

Jimmy went upstairs. On the walls down the hall

were pictures of the family, pictures of Jean, a baby propped onto a silk pillow, a very little girl with a balloon, a four-year-old and her mother on the steps out front, Elaine in a light-colored sun dress with a full skirt, a cigarette between her fingers. There was one picture of Jean's brother, a sulking twelve-year-old in a suit that matched his dad's.

He shined the light into the bathroom: pink and green tile, a pedestal sink, dirty, a dimmed mirror. The plastic shower curtain was hard, cracked, brown. There was water in the toilet, which was iron-stained, too.

The door to the bedroom on the front of the house was closed. Jimmy tried the knob. It was unlocked. He stepped in.

It was full dark, shades pulled down over the windows. He swept the room with his light. There was the round bed, the black lacquered "Oriental" bedside table, the funny, overstyled clock radio. Somebody had cleaned the room and pulled the door closed and walked away. Jimmy knelt where Bill Danko fell. He unclipped the red filter from the penlight, scanned the white carpet for some trace of the bloodstain. Clean. He looked over at the floor-to-ceiling silver curtains where, the theory went, the killer had waited.

Jimmy stepped closer, reached out. The cloth had lost all of its life, turned to powder. His fingers went right through it. He touched the shade on the window. It rolled up, clattering and flapping like a window shade in a cartoon. He pulled it back down into place.

He came out, leaving the bedroom door open behind him.

At the other end of the hallway, a door stood open, a third bedroom. Jimmy hesitated. There was something bad still in the air in the house, riding in the molecules. He knew he was built to deal with the past, to walk though rooms most people couldn't bear, but this was creeping him out and he didn't know why.

At the end of the hall he clipped the red filter onto the light again and shined it at his feet, at the frayed carpet, worn in a path in the center. The dim red circle of light crossed the jamb, into the back bedroom. There was clutter just inside the doorway, stacks of magazines, folded grocery bags, a couple of empty flat cans.

Cat food.

He stepped in. There was quick movement somewhere, something the same color as the room.

Where was the wash from the streetlights in the alley?

Jimmy stepped to the bay windows that faced the back. There were heavy drapes, closed together, and lowered shades behind the drapes. He ran his fingers along the edge of the shade, felt something. He shined the red light: the shades were taped tight against the window with duct tape, blocking any light from outside.

Or maybe it was the other way around.

Jimmy was trying to make sense of it when a woman coughed and, in the same moment, a black-and-white TV flashed on.

He jumped half out of his skin, fell back against the windows.

The woman—she had stringy gray hair cut straight across the bangs and wore a faded dress and a sweater and slippers—had turned on the television manually. She now just stood there before it, blue/gray, dead-looking in its light.

She watched it a moment, stepped back, sat in a worn chair.

Jimmy was caught. There was no place to hide. He stood stock still in the pulsing light of the television.

Was it possible she hadn't seen him?

No, now she looked right at him, as if he had said that last thought out loud. A cat jumped onto the arm of her chair. Then a second cat and a third and a fourth came out from somewhere to rub against her. She still looked directly at Jimmy where he stood, eight feet away, against the windows, in the wash of TV light.

The red cap to his penlight fell to the floor. He bent to pick it up. She watched him. He looked into her eyes and she looked into his.

He took a step toward the doorway. She followed him with her eyes, her expression unchanged.

And then she looked back at the TV.

CHAPTER 6

ON THE OFFICE WALL WAS A COLORED PRINT OF Jesus sitting in his robes across the desk from a businessman in a gray suit.

Jimmy was across the desk from Angel.

"You didn't even see her, man?" Angel said.

"Not until she turned on the TV."

"And she didn't see you?"

"She looked right at me," Jimmy said. "She saw me, but I guess seeing someone standing there wasn't that out of the ordinary to her."

"So who was she?"

"I don't know. Nobody. A street person. Maybe just someone who comes in to feed the stray cats. It was easy enough to get in."

"Sad," Angel said.

Angel's body shop was downtown ten blocks south of the City Center. Through the windows in the walls in the inner office you could see men at work on expensive cars. It was a beautiful old wooden building, once a Packard dealership, with a high arched roof. The floors were slick white. This wasn't an insurance shop. You had to care about cars the way they cared about cars before they even let you through the door. *Clean* was about the highest compliment the men working here paid each other's work.

Luis, the skinny kid from Angel's backyard, worked alone in one corner of the shop, airbrushing a scene onto the tailgate of a chopped and lowered, scooped and stretched Ford F-150 pickup, an artful expressionistic rendering of the L.A. skyline, a pair of woman's eyes emerging from the night clouds, and a blue moon.

Jimmy got up from the chair. There was a picture on one wall in a black wood frame, a World War II-era bomber rolled out in front of a hangar. Huge block letters white across the roof said: STEADMAN. There were palm trees behind it in the picture, Santa Monica behind the palms and an ocean beyond that, suitably gray, since it was wartime.

"You know anybody at Clover Field anymore?"

Angel shook his head. "Nah, it's nothing but general aviation now, Wayne Newton flying in in his Gulfstar."

"I like Wayne Newton," Jimmy said.

"I think we all do," Angel said. "It's not Clover Field anymore."

"Yeah, I know. Everything changes."

Jimmy kept his eyes on the picture.

"So, you gonna tell me?" Angel said.

"Tell you what?"

"Tell me what you're working on."

"A couple of the dead," Jimmy said.

"Lucky stiffs."

Jimmy looked at another picture on the wall, next to the first, as he gave him the short version. "Double murder, 1977, guy killed his wife and her boyfriend down in Long Beach. He was convicted, executed."

"Kantke. I remember it."

"I'm working for the daughter. She wants to know if he really did it."

"What's the point?"

"I believe I asked her that."

"What's the connection to Clover Field?"

"The dead guy worked out of there. A pilot."

In the other picture, Angel Figueroa stood alone next to one of the bomber's fat wheels. The lettering said: "No. 2000 July 16, 1944." He had shorter hair now, a buzz cut, but Angel didn't look much different in the picture than he did here, sitting behind his desk.

"Good-looking guy," Jimmy said.

"I tell people it's Uncle Eduardo," Angel said.

"DISCO GOT A BAD RAP."

Jimmy was buying lunch at Vern's, a red Formica lunch spot out in The Valley on Lankershim Boulevard in North Hollywood, a half-gentrified art and

artists' neighborhood they were trying to talk people
into calling *NoHo*.

Chris Post drew musical notes on a three-by-five
card while they talked. They were at a table in the
window with a view to the street. He'd look out the
window and then say something else to Jimmy and
then draw another note on the card. He had a stack of
three-by-five cards with a rubber band around them
jammed in the pocket of his pocket tee. He was in his
forties. He had bad eyes and long hair thinning on top
pulled back into a ponytail. He wore orange jeans. *He
was skinny and tall, no ass at all.* That was a line a
lyricist friend had put to one of Chris's melody lines
once, presumptuously trying to turn it into a *song*.

Chris never spoke to him again.

He was a musician, a real musician, the kind of
shack-out-back artist who had twenty thousand dollars worth of computers and synthesizers and key-
boards—and a safety pin holding his glasses together.
To pay the rent, he played song demo dates and commercial jingles and the occasional session for a
Touched by an Angel, but what he really wanted to do
was . . . write atonal symphonies and then not play
them for anyone. A few years back, Jimmy and Angel
had encouraged him to apply for a grant from the National Endowment for the Arts and he did, scrawling,
Go Screw Yourself! across the application.

Surprisingly, he was turned down.

"Disco got a total bad rap. *Repetitive.* You want
repetitive? You ever listen to Vivaldi, or, better yet,
Ravel?"

Chris picked up a fork.

"What is this?" he said.

"A fork," Jimmy said.

Chris picked up a spoon. "What is this?"

"A spoon."

Chris started nodding his head. "Which is *better?*" he said.

"I hear you."

"You got a steak, I'll tell you whether a fork is better than a spoon."

"I get what you're saying," Jimmy said.

"Most people don't," the musician said. "Sadly."

Their food came. Chris got a bowl of soup the size of a hubcap, bean soup. Jimmy had just ordered a plate of steamed carrots. Chris picked up his spoon, wiped it off with a napkin.

Jimmy said, "I drove by there. Big Daddy's."

Chris slurped up the first too-hot spoonful of soup. He kept shoveling it in. He *ate* like a musician, like a musician who hadn't eaten in a week.

"How's the soup?" Jimmy said.

"It's all right."

Ten years ago when Chris's mother died, Jimmy had gotten him into an apartment and the first day he'd had to show him how to make canned soup. A week later, he introduced him to SpaghettiOs.

"So, I drove by there, Big Daddy's," Jimmy said. "Where it used to be."

"And it's a Starbucks now," Chris said.

"A Kinko's."

"But you get what I mean . . ."

Jimmy got what he meant.

"I don't get down there to the Marina anymore," Chris said. "It takes four buses." He took out a new three-by-five card and wrote a note to himself. "I'll burn you a CD. The stuff you should be listening to. You ever hear Cerrone?"

"*Love in C Minor.*"

Chris was impressed. "How *old* are you, man?" he said. "I've never been able to tell."

Jimmy let the question go unanswered. "Here's what I need," he said. "You know anybody who spun at Big Daddy's?"

Chris was to the bottom of his bean soup. "Could I get another bowl?"

"Sure."

Chris motioned to the waitress for another bowl, pointed to it like it was a Scotch and soda.

"I knew Slip Tony," he said. "But he spelled it with an *E* instead of a *Y*, like *tone*. Tone Espinosa. He was the best. He wouldn't say a word all night. He had all these imports. He was the first guy I knew of to use three tables. He'd throw something over something with something else underneath and you couldn't believe what you were hearing. Spoken word. He'd lay in a guy saying a poem or narration for a training film for air-conditioning repair. There wasn't anybody in L.A. who was a better DJ—except for maybe about a dozen gay guys in little clubs you never heard of playing tea dances on Sunday afternoons."

"Do you know where he is now?"

"Dead. It's funny," Chris said, then caught himself.

"Well, I don't mean being dead . . . He became a cop. He was on a gang unit, right down in there, Venice south. Shot dead. Two years after Big Daddy's, maybe by some slick who two years earlier was out on the floor, thinking how cool Slip was there in the booth, his head over sideways, half a headphone on his shoulder."

"You know anybody else from Big Daddy's? Anybody who's still alive?"

The second bowl of soup came. "I'd also like another one to go," Chris said to the waitress. He looked at Jimmy for approval. Jimmy nodded.

"Lloyd Hart. Lloyd-the-Void. He called himself *Popper* or *Rocker* or something but everybody called him Lloyd-the-Void. He was the DJ in the main room upstairs with the lights in the floor and the *Is-Everybody-Having-A-Good-Time?* jive. Slip Tone was in the *serious* room downstairs." He wrote something else on another three-by-five card and handed it to Jimmy. "I *guess* you could say he's alive."

Chris dug his way down to the bottom of the second bowl of soup and put his spoon aside. He looked out the window again and then drew one last musical note.

He handed the three-by-five card to Jimmy.

"I don't read music," Jimmy said when he looked at it.

Chris whistled an odd little twelve-note tune.

"You just wrote that?"

Chris shook his head, nodded out at the street.

"What?" Jimmy said.

"The palm trees. Other side of the street. Up and down, different heights. If they were notes on a scale, it'd sound like that."

Jimmy held up the card. "Can I keep this?"

"No," Chris said and took it back.

THE LOVE STORM WAS THE NAME OF THE OVER-night program at KLVV, fifth in the ratings for its time slot. The show had a cosmopolitan L.A. feel to it, slanting noir shadows and cigarette smoke curling out of your radio, but the studios were actually in a squat three-story box of a building on Van Nuys Boulevard in Van Nuys, the transmitter ten miles farther out in the Valley, almost to the mountains in a field of sun-flowers. This time of night, the flowers would be closed up tight.

Lloyd Hart was now Darren Price.

He was working alone. There wasn't even a janitor around. Jimmy talked his way in, past the squawk box down at street level. Price had said hello, had said something quick and sharp and funny actually, hope in his voice that it was some young girls out cruising around. When Jimmy said what he wanted to talk about, Price buzzed him up, another case of *"Now it's been years since anyone asked . . ."*

He was still good-looking, in a game show host way, and he had a good, deep, round voice and a way of putting the sound of a warm smile in every word he said. Jimmy thought he recognized the voice from a TV commercial for headache relief, the kind where you got the idea somebody really *cared* about you and your pain. He wore a velveteen running suit, almost purple, and perfect white shoes, Capezio *dance* shoes. He rocked back and forth in a chair that didn't squeak. His hand kept reaching for cigarettes he didn't smoke anymore, hadn't smoked for ten years.

"Hold on a sec," he said and lifted the cans off of his neck and up over his ears. He leaned to the mic. The song was ending.

Half of the show's audience were love-struck kids dedicating sappy songs to each other, to break up or to get back together or just to say to each other, and to the world and to ex-boyfriends and ex-girlfriends, that *this* love was real and would stand the test of time. The other half was people at work, at 7-Elevens with a portable on the counter they weren't supposed to have, people at bakeries and *tortillarias,* in emergency rooms, in factories where they chromed wheels or assembled meals for airlines, people cleaning offices, driving cabs, writing screenplays—and cops and suicide hotline answerers and dope-dealers and whores all waiting around for something to go down. There was a KISS station in town. Listeners were encouraged to call and repeat the money phrase, that they were "Kissing at Work . . ." At an hour like this, one other midweek night like this, Jimmy had heard a listener call in a request to *The Love Storm* saying he was "Storming at Work . . ."

A jingle played. A saxophone. A woman's voice. The sound of soft, rolling, distant thunder.

It made Jimmy wish it would rain, really rain.

"Andrea is up studying, studying for her nursing finals," Darren Price said, so close to the mic you could hear the breath going over his teeth. Jimmy felt like he wasn't there now, that it was just Price and Andrea and . . .

"*Carmen,* she just wants you to know that she's sorry she said what she said, sorry that it hurt you, and that she didn't mean it. And that the whole future is ahead for you two and she doesn't want to jeopardize that because she loves you more than anything. And she wanted to send this song out to you. She knows you're listening, too."

The song began, a song that didn't seem to connect to words said that shouldn't have been said or to "the whole future," but the song was good and the singer sounded as if he really had been hurt somewhere along the line, had *that* in his voice the way Darren Price had a smile in his

"I'm union. AFTRA," Price said as he pulled off the headphones and killed the music in the monitors. "We're all union." It was a way of saying he made good money, more money than he made when he was under brighter lights, when people knew who he was, when he was right there in front of them at Big Daddy's when Big Daddy's was the place to be.

There are all kinds of deaths, Jimmy thought.

"What was Tone Espinosa like?" he said.

Price squinted as if somebody had turned on the overhead lights. "This is about Tone?" he said.

"No," Jimmy said. "It's not."

"We got along all right," Price said. "He didn't ever really *get* it."

"Get what?"

"He hated it when *Saturday Night Fever* came along. That's just an example. When it got big, he said it was over."

Jimmy didn't say anything.

"Does that make sense to you?" Price said, real perplexity in his voice.

"I guess I know what he meant."

Price shook his head. "Well, I never did. He was about to get fired when he finally quit. They just ran cables downstairs and I played both rooms. I mean, I'm not glad the guy got killed or anything . . ."

The phone never stopped ringing. It was silent, just blinking lights.

Price punched one button.

"Yeah," he said.

"Hey." It was a soft little voice, up past her bedtime. "It's Andrea."

"Hey." Price looked at Jimmy.

"I just wanted to thank you for playing the song," she said.

"Shouldn't you be keeping the line open for . . ." Price looked at a Post-it note stuck on the mic stand. "Carmen?"

"I have call waiting," she said, sexy.

Price was still looking at Jimmy when he said, "I hope things work out for you guys."

"You're so sweet," she said.

"Not really," he said, as a sexy threat.

"Yeah-huh," she said.

"I want you to call me, whatever happens," he said. "On this line, OK?"

She said yes and he said he had to go and cut her off.

"I'm like a priest," Price said as her light went out.

"Yeah, I was just thinking that."

Jimmy told him who he was, what this was, a version that left out murders and executions and little girls orphaned, that almost made it sound like Elaine Kantke had lost her purse or one of her shoes like Cinderella and had hired Jimmy to get it back, all the way back from Disco '77.

"The Jolly Girls," Price said. He used a *slanted* intonation, like a comic. The *Jolly* Girls . . .

"So you remember them."

"There were three of them, *four* of them. They were babes. They were all older than I was. I was, I don't know, twenty-four. They were maybe thirty. It seemed like a real difference at the time, but they were still babes."

"And they always came to the club with their husbands," Jimmy said.

"Yeah, right, I remember that *distinctly.*"

"Who was the leader?"

"Elaine, I guess. I don't know. It's all kind of a blur, if you know what I mean."

Jimmy knew. "Did they do coke?"

"I wouldn't be surprised."

Jimmy had said *they* in a way that meant, "Did they do coke, too?" The DJ wasn't insulted. Lloyd-the-Void had tried to fill the void with one of the things you try to fill the void with. Step One was to accept that you were powerless . . .

"I wouldn't say they were the *biggest* Hoovers among the regulars," Darren said. "But then again, *that* bar would have been pretty high at Big Daddy's at that particular time."

"Did you talk to her much?"

"I talked to all of the regulars. It was part of the job. But I liked doing it. I was kind of a star. I got that kind of response from people, the regulars."

And he began to talk about the nights there. *I love the nightlife, I love to boogie.* He described each one of the lighting effects suspended above the dance floor, how they had been brought in from New York, how there weren't any lights anywhere else in L.A. like those lights. *Turn the beat around, turn it upside down:* He remembered the wattage of the sound system, the size of the big black bass cabinets that sat on the four corners of the dance floor so it came up out of the earth at you, too, how the floor was covered in fog, like a graveyard in a cheap movie. Talking about the past, he had a different kind of energy. He woke up. He had more words at his disposal and they were better words, words that put you there.

He interrupted himself when he needed to change a record or speak some words of encouragement to the heartbroken. An hour passed while he talked and the lovesick went to bed and the requests changed. Now it was more the people at work trying to stay awake, wanting something with a little more heat and a little less hurt.

He remembered what Elaine Kantke drank because he'd buy her and the other Jolly Girls drinks to make them feel special. *Long Island iced teas.* He remembered that she wasn't the best dancer of the four young women. That would be Michelle. Michelle would also be the biggest Hoover. Elaine would dance every once in awhile, but what she really liked was being at the bar, on a stool, facing the dance floor and laughing at her friends.

He remembered Vivian Goreck, a redhead. *Viv.*

He remembered Bill Danko but not by name, just remembered that for awhile there was someone Elaine seemed to meet, a blocky guy with his thick torso wedged into the requisite Nik-Nik pointy-collared polyester shirts and beltless, high-waisted flared pants. He remembered his name as *Wayne* or *Dwayne,* which is what you'd think, looking at Bill Danko.

He didn't know that Elaine Kantke was dead. DJs read *Billboard,* not the *Times.* He'd just assumed The Jolly Girls had found a new club or their husbands had finally gotten around to seeing *Saturday Night Fever* and had shortened their leashes.

"I learned two things about the bar business—and about life—when I was at Big Daddy's," Darren Price said.

Jimmy wondered how many times he'd said that line.

"The first thing, Big Daddy Joe Flannigan himself said to me personally. One night after we closed and we were all drinking kamikazes at the bar, he said to all of us, 'What business are we in?' Somebody of course said, the *booze* business, thinking that was what he wanted to hear. He had a white beard, looked kind of like Hemingway and wore these white shorts and a Kelly green shirt and he was big. Joe shook his head. Not the booze business. There were a couple more wrong guesses. He looked at me. I said, 'The *entertainment* business.' Big Daddy shook his head."

Price was going to make Jimmy wait for it.

Jimmy waited for it.

" 'We're in the *loneliness* business.' Not *loneliest,* loneli*ness* . . ."

Jimmy got it. He nodded his head.

"Buying or selling?" he said.

Darren Price didn't get it.

"What was the second thing you learned?" Jimmy said.

"Hats start fights."

They talked another half hour. Lloyd-the-Void looked disappointed when Jimmy stood up to go.

IT WAS ALMOST FOUR. THE KINKO'S THAT OCCUPIED the space where Big Daddy's used to be was open all night. They'd ripped off the two-story front and put in glass all the way up. It was a box of light in front of the empty parking lot. There were six or eight people in there under the ghastly bright lights, two guys behind the counter and one running the big machine that wasn't self-serve. They probably kept the reams of paper down below in what had been the *serious* room, Tone Espinosa's room.

They'd left the entrance the same, six steps up to what had been the main room of the club. Elaine Kantke and Bill Danko had climbed those steps, looking to do something about their loneliness, if you believed Big Daddy.

Jimmy sat on the front fender of the Porsche, the car he'd picked that morning from the line in the garage.

"Why do people need to make copies in the middle of the night?" he said, out loud, to no one. "What are they copying?"

A coughing VW bug came in, fast. A man with a belly and a colorless T-shirt the size that maybe fit him when he was twenty got out and charged in, taking two steps at a time, his fist clutching a thick sheaf of papers. There was one answer: it was open for the people up all night grinding their teeth at some grievance, consumer or governmental, assembling their cases, ready to by God *fire off* some papers in the morning.

It had been a long day. The days got longer when Jimmy was working, felt that way anyway. This story was at that early stage where everything was incomplete, sketchy, self-contradictory—and he had done this enough to know that a big part of what he was "learning" was just simply wrong.

A seagull landed on a light stanchion. Jimmy turned around and looked toward Marina Del Rey, the immense condominiums which stood over the wide channels and the hundreds of slips. The tops of the tallest masts were visible between the towers.

The light was odd, noncommittal. He wished the sun would come up, right now.

An LAPD sergeant's cruiser pulled in beside him. The cop was alone. The window was down.

"Saint Thomas," Jimmy said.

The patrol cars all had computer monitors hung on the dash now and a full-size keyboard where you used to put your coffee. The radio spoke, the voice female and not very friendly. You could tell the cop was a sergeant by the extra antennas on the roof.

Saint Thomas's last name was Connor. He got out. He looked to be in his fifties, handsome in that cops and firemen way, self-assured good looks, clear eyes, skin wrinkled not from worry but from being on the boat on the lake on days off, or on the sidelines coaching kids.

"You called?"

Jimmy nodded toward the Kinko's and asked if Connor had known the DJ who'd turned into a cop. And then a dead cop. It wasn't that Jimmy thought it had anything to do with the case, he was just curious. It was a good story, in that Movie of the Week way. Or maybe as a pilot for a cop show. Connor didn't know much about Tone Espinosa except that he'd been killed. Cops all knew who'd been killed, almost all the way back to the beginnings of LAPD.

"*Perversito,*" he said.

"What's that?"

"*Little Evil,*" the cop said. "That's who killed him, a gang banger. He went away for it."

Jimmy told him what he was working on, a version that left out almost everything *but* the murders and the execution and kids orphaned. Connor nodded.

They both looked at the nightclub-turned-Kinko's.

"Disco sucks," Jimmy said, but he was just quoting.

"I just remember getting laid a lot less for a year or so there," Connor said.

"You couldn't dance?"

"I guess not. Whatever it was, what I was didn't work for awhile there."

Sergeant Connor gave Jimmy a name or two, people who knew about the club scene back then, the drugs, the money. The bar business was a cash business and tended to have bad people around its borders, but Big Daddy's had been a safer, tamer, *brighter* version of the seventies club scene than some of the others.

Jimmy told him about the woman in the Rivo Alto house, asked the cop if he'd run a check on her, see if she had a history in the Naples neighborhood, in Long Beach. Maybe somebody had spotted her coming and going.

"You want her chased out?"

"No," Jimmy said, and then wondered why he'd said it.

And that was it. A ground fog started to come in around them. It wasn't cold but it *looked* cold.

Connor asked Jimmy how he was doing. Jimmy answered the question for real and asked the cop the same and listened to what he said. They both knew each other's story. When the radio called the sergeant off to something somewhere out there in what was left of the night, the two men stood up and embraced and held the embrace for a long moment.

Where was that sun?

CHAPTER 7

A CESSNA LANDED. BADLY. THE RIGHT WHEEL touched first, the plane bucked, then the left wheel hit hard. On the grass between the runway and the taxiway, four old men sat in white plastic lawn chairs. They took a minute then held up handmade cardboard squares with numbers, grading the landing as if this was the Olympics. They had all been fliers or had built planes. It was all very unofficial but the understanding was that the old guys had earned the right to rag on the youngsters. Every pilot who landed tried not to look over but all of them did.

This time the scoring fell somewhere between a four and a five.

Jimmy walked up.

"You look like an undertaker," one of the old men, Kirk, said. Jimmy wore a black suit.

He stuck out his hand.

"How are you?"

Angel had called Jimmy from his shop downtown at noon. He had come up with a name for him, somebody who might know about Bill Danko and what had been called Clover Field.

Kirk pumped the hand once. "I told Angel I'd come in to your office."

"Don't have one," Jimmy said.

"Well, let's do it," Kirk said, and then looked at his friends as he made a joke, "I don't have all day."

They walked down the taxiway. They were on the B-side of the airport, businesses in old wooden buildings and World War II Quonset huts, every third or fourth one vacant, airplane maintenance, radio repair, aerial photography, a skywriting company with one plane. Vines covered half the buildings. Most had peeling paint, gloriously neglected. Somehow, here in the middle of L.A. was a sizable section of the *unimproved*. There was probably an old person somewhere who'd so long ignored the men in suits with their Big Plans for the property that they'd stopped coming, now just waiting her out—it was usually a woman—waiting for her to die and get out of the way.

"Angel wouldn't tell me what this was about," Kirk said. "He said you were a private investigator. I guess one of my girlfriends' husbands is onto us."

They weren't headed anywhere in particular but

the old man walked at a good steady pace as if getting from here to there was something he'd be judged on.

"I told Angel, I got a photograph of your mother somewhere," Kirk said. "Autographed. I didn't understand those pictures she made over in Europe, but I sure liked *her.*"

It made Jimmy smile.

"Where do you know Angel from?"

"Big Brothers," Kirk said. "I ran a unit until I got too old to stand up to all the bullshit." He held up his hand as if testifying. "I mean, I'm not gay, but I can't prove it."

A sleek corporate jet took off behind them, screaming. The 10 freeway was less than a mile away to the north and the 405 almost as close to the east. The roars merged.

When it quieted, Jimmy said, "Angel said you were the guy to ask about the old days here."

Kirk said, "He said it was about the seventies. You call that the old days?"

"It's all relative, I guess."

"I was on the line for Steadman twenty-eight years," Kirk said. "I put Pitot tubes in ST-10s. Before the war, it was ST-3s. The 10s were built right over there"—he pointed to a massive hump-roof hangar, the biggest building at the airport—"and the 3s built in Hangar Nine that got torn down in September of '73."

Jimmy stopped to admire one falling-down building. They had walked almost to the end of the taxiway.

"So what's this about?" Kirk said.

"You remember the Kantke murders?" Jimmy said.

"Sure."

"Bill Danko."

Kirk nodded.

"You knew him?"

"I saw him around," Kirk said. "His outfit was up here behind what used to be the old Clipper Hangar. Everybody said he was an all right guy. That's what you're looking into?"

Jimmy nodded.

"I saw her once, the woman," Kirk said. "She showed up, waiting for Danko to come back from a photo job, a flyover. He had a Cessna 152. Red over white, mortgaged up. She had an old-fashioned hat on her head, tied under her chin with a ribbon, like as if they were going to fly off together in an open-cockpit Waco. She looked like a barrel of laughs."

The old man set out walking again and Jimmy followed him. Kirk talked fast and asked the usual questions, what they *all* wanted to know: what other cases Jimmy had investigated, the stories behind the stories, the moments when the flashbulbs flashed. Jimmy didn't offer much. He never did. He'd long ago figured out that nobody wanted to hear the truth. Death and sex, that's what most of it was about, sometimes money, but he didn't take those cases. A case was never what it looked like from the outside and when it was over, what was important was never the big plot points, the flashbulb moments. It was what was going on unnoticed in the corner of the frame, the ambulance guys rolling out a woman on a gurney, the cops talking to the people in the next bungalow—and a boy steps up across the street into a clot of strangers, just coming home from school. Maybe it was why he did it, to notice the unnoticed, to find meaning there. Or try.

They'd reached the last of the buildings off on a side taxiway. "There," the old man said.

It was a decrepit building, vacant, standing alone, barely standing, a faded Plexiglas sign on the end of it announcing Sunshine Air, a charter company. The sign hung half off. What was left of a painted sign was underneath: *Danko "Flying School"*—just like that, quotation marks and all, like it was a pretend flying school.

"He never could make a go of it, as far as anybody could tell," Kirk said, as if the look of the building didn't get that idea across. "And then Steadman Industries bought him out. For a good price, some said." The old man shrugged. He had lived long enough to see a thousand things he didn't get. "And then Danko was dead, before he could enjoy the money. Well, he bought himself a new plane right off, I guess he enjoyed that. And her."

Everybody seemed to understand how you could enjoy Elaine Kantke.

"You want to look around, go ahead," Kirk said. "Nobody'll hassle you. There's nothing back here now. Now in the old days, on the other side of Hangar Six was—" Another jet roared into the sky, drowning out the last of it.

Jimmy stood there thinking of her, Elaine Kantke in her hat, maybe standing right where he was standing now. He thought again about the detail he'd learned, how the bullet that had killed her, went *through* her, had creased Bill Danko's cheek. It had probably carried some of her to him, a last kiss.

Maybe Jimmy did this for the poetry.

Kirk walked away, leaving Jimmy there to knock around in the past. The front door was locked. He looked in through the dirty windows. The room was bare, cleared of everything but the old newspapers on the floor, a bed for somebody from the way they were shaped, and faded posters of Cabo and La Paz on the walls. On the back wall was an open rectangle where an air conditioner had been. Jimmy went around to the weedy lot behind the building and crawled in through the hole.

There was a small room off the main room. In it, a desk and a pair of chairs and a water cooler with a dusty glass bottle were stacked at odd angles up to the ceiling. There was a file cabinet. Jimmy opened it. It was empty except for rat droppings and a book of matches from a cocktail lounge.

The desk was on its end against the wall. It was as old as the building. He pulled it down, set it back on its feet, rolled over the wheeled office chair. The drawers were empty. There was a phone number written in pencil on the bottom of one, a number with a two letter prefix, from some business in the forties or fifties. Geologists had the right idea about history: it was just layers of sediment, one on top of the other.

And, given enough time, any sad piece of shit becomes precious.

Jimmy ran his hands along the underside of the wide center drawer and found a manila envelope wedged into a hiding place. He opened it. It was a bodybuilder magazine from the sixties, big-chested men preening on So Cal beaches.

In the ceiling was an access hatch. Jimmy arranged the desk and the chair, climbed up and pushed the square door up and over and stuck his head through to the crawl space. Screened vents at the two ends of the roof let in enough light to see. There were two cardboard boxes. He took off his suit jacket, folded it and put it over the chair back, climbed through the hatch and crawled toward them.

Both boxes were empty, but scattered among the ceiling joists were a few dozen pale green cancelled checks. With his head against the roof, Jimmy went through them. Ten or twelve were made out to "Beachside Market," each for five dollars, spending money, Danko's allowance. One paid the phone bill. There were rent checks. Steadman Industries owned the building. There were four to an aviation fuel company, three of them with notations about "Late Penalty ($10) Included."

And two to "Chip's Fashion House" for those Nik-Niks.

THE MUSEUM OF FLIGHT WAS ACROSS THE MAIN runway in a cavernous metal building, a new building.

A yellow biplane hung from wires from the ceiling, suspended over three open decks of displays, models and full-sized airplanes. Through the floor-to-ceiling glass on the backside of it you could watch takeoffs and landings, listen in on the radio traffic on a bank of headphones. It was the modern opposite of the old men in their lawn chairs on the other side of the runway.

Jimmy was in a sea of Cub Scouts surrounding a restored ST-10, the bomber in the picture on Angel's office wall. The boys jumped up and down below the wings, swatting at the undercarriage, trying to touch the teardrop tanks that hung down.

He went up to the top level.

Clover Field forty years ago. There was a wall of photos: the hangars, the workmen like Angel, the bombers coming off the assembly line.

It was also a history of Steadman Industries. As you walked along, the company moved into the fifties and sixties and then the seventies, props disappearing, wings angling back, nothing ahead but a bright, high-flying future. Or so said the PR.

There was a commotion behind Jimmy as half of the Cubs arrived. They pressed their faces against the glass of a display, the re-created Steadman boardroom of the sixties. Jimmy crossed the hallway and looked over their shoulders. It was complete: the original furniture—a great oblong mahogany table and leather chairs—Coke bottles, coffee cups, pads and pens, pictures on the walls, an ST-10 taking off outside a "window"—and ten wax figures seated around the table, their glass eyes fixed on the big man standing before them.

The plaque read:

WALTER E. C. "RED" STEADMAN
FOUNDER
1911–1973

He looked like the kind of man who could get his name painted in fifty-foot letters across the top of a hangar.

Jimmy thought he saw the old guy blink.

When he came back down to the first floor, his tails were back, the pale men who'd been at Canter's. Today, the short one even had on a peacoat and watch cap. It was easy to make fun of them, but there wasn't any fun in it today for Jimmy. Maybe it was all the scouts, all the innocents. He tried to make it through to the front door without them spotting him, but the tall one saw him and shot a look up at the second man on the higher floor. The two-tone blonde came down the staircase fast and joined the other, the two of them "hiding" behind a stacked rack of bombs, a pyramid of dummies.

Jimmy went after them. *Why were Sailors interested in this?* Maybe he could shake it out of one of them. The two of them tried to get lost in the crowd. They looked bewildered. When you were tailing someone, he wasn't supposed to come after you. They ducked behind planes, pretended to look at the shiny models of 747s and then at the mannequins of stews in pastel seventies uniforms. The Cubs had all descended from the top floor and made the two stand out all the more. Even the short one stood tall over them.

Jimmy kept coming. There was a flight simulator in one corner on the ground floor, a twenty-seater big as a bus mounted on hydraulic lifters. The two pale men cut in line, just making it through the simulator doors before they whooshed closed.

He got close enough to see the name of the ride: "Turbulence Over Tucson." The hydraulics sighed and then went to work.

Jimmy's '70 Dodge Challenger, painted school bus yellow, eight coats, hand-rubbed, was parked all by itself in the last row in the lot. He got in, buckled himself in, lit it up. It had a Hemi 454 V-8 under the bulge in the hood. At idle it made a sound a little like a tiger at the zoo in the middle of the afternoon, sleepy, not all that happy. There was a four speed on the floor. Jimmy backed around, pulled out. He eased up and over three speed bumps and moved onto the street, never spinning the tires once.

Westbound on Pico, he looked up in the mirror. Here they were, two heads in a white Ford Escort a quarter mile back. He slowed, let them close the gap. As they drew near, he pulled it down into second, punched it and hung a right.

They *tried* to keep up. Three blocks into a neighborhood of pastel Mediterranean houses with tender little yards, they stopped in the middle of the street. They'd lost him. The short one slapped the dash.

The tall one, who was driving, looked in the mirror. The yellow Challenger was right behind them.

Jimmy pulled around the dinky Escort, looked over as he came alongside, then gunned it, leaving a perfect pair of wide black streaks.

BUT THEY CAME BACK AND THEY CAUGHT HIM THAT night.

It started on Hollywood Boulevard. They were still in the Escort so for a minute it was still a joke. The traffic was light and Jimmy was a little down and almost glad for the company. He wasn't going anywhere, he was just *out,* knocking around in the present, or trying to.

He let them stay close behind him for mile or so and then took a quick right.

Where, it turned out, they *wanted* him to take a right.

When he came around the corner, the side street was blocked by a pair of black Chevys, nose to nose.

And four more Sailors. All of them had the blue edge of light around them, what you'd call *halos* if they were angels, which they decidedly weren't. The Escort came in behind Jimmy and closed the backdoor.

The new men got out of the Chevys and started toward him at the same moment the tall pale man and the one with the bad blond hair got out of the Escort.

Jimmy turned off the engine. He opened the door, but before he could get out, they pulled him from the

Dodge, rough, even though he wasn't resisting and they knew it.

Now he resisted. He tried to break away from them but there were too many of them and they were too sure of what they were supposed to do. When Sailors were involved in anything in L.A., it wasn't personal. They didn't act alone. A stray single one might throw a foot out to trip you going down the sidewalk of a night, say something sour behind your back, but when three or four came after you, got in your face, it was because they *meant* something by it. It was because they'd been told to. It was because you were in violation, *busted* in the part of dark things they ran. Jimmy assumed that it was about the Kantke murders, but maybe he was wrong. Maybe this was about the last one. The last case. Or the one before. Unfinished business. He upset people all the time.

But not ever *Sailors,* until now. They dragged him the half block down to the Roosevelt Hotel, nobody saying anything, right into the underground parking. There was an elevator there, and nobody to stop them from going where they wanted to go.

And then they were all on the roof. Sailors had a thing about roofs. High places, lookouts.

One of the four new ones was a foot taller than the tall pale man Jimmy had made fun of and weighed twenty pounds less. This one was like a tall stick in a suit, though his suit was a better suit than what the Escort boys wore. He had red hair. He had long, long fingers. He pointed one at Jimmy. And said nothing.

"I get it," Jimmy said. "You want me to stop."

Two of the other new ones, big ones who wore pea-coats and watch caps, took turns pushing Jimmy backwards. There was an ugly rhythm to it, almost like the three of them were dancing across the roof. They slammed him backwards into the base of an iron radio tower left over from what now seemed like a whole other age.

"You're the Disco Antidefamation League."

One of the big ones hit him in the face.

Long-fingers came a few steps closer. On his cue, the two big men yanked Jimmy up off his feet and carried him over to the parapet and stood him up there and turned him around and then leaned him out over the drop, holding him by the back of his black under-taker's suitcoat like a puppet. A wind blew up the side of the hotel, almost strong enough to hold him up if they let go. Almost.

Jimmy looked down, way down on the street, the people walking, the tour buses parked in front of the Chinese, a few cruisers out on the wrong night in their perfect lowriders, the lights. He thought of the line, from the Bible, *Cast yourself down.* But this wasn't the pinnacle of the temple and he sure wasn't Christ and Long-Fingers wasn't exactly Satan.

"Look down there," Long-Fingers said. "Can you see them?"

He didn't mean the tourists or the cruisers. He meant what was in the shadows, in the alleyways, be-hind the buildings. *Who.*

"Can you see them?"

"Yeah, I see them," Jimmy said.

"*You* want to walk around forever?" He said it again, the same words, as if he'd been told to say them, this time so loud the people down on the boulevard could have heard him. "You want to walk around forever?"

There was another kind of Sailor. *Walkers.* You've seen them on your streets, or at least in parts of your town. You've thought it was drugs or alcohol and maybe it *began* there. You've wondered why they keep moving, shuffling, how they went dead in the eye, where they could be going, where they sleep, where they go in the daytime. You wonder that, until the light changes, until your husband says something and you go back to your life, or you think of your wife and what's for dinner in the regular world, leaving them behind, like on the street below the Roosevelt Hotel in Hollywood.

"What do you want me not to do?" Jimmy said. "Give me a clue . . ."

The two big men received another silent signal from the tall bony one and they shoved their charge out over the abyss and then yanked him back, like this was a school bully's prank.

Jimmy didn't let them see the fear they wanted to see. But they saw something and the very tall one turned his back and started away, which meant they were finished, that *it* was finished. The two lifted him down. They didn't look at Jimmy again, just fell in behind the red-haired one with the long, long fingers.

CHAPTER 8

IT WAS LATE AFTERNOON BUT THE LIGHT WASN'T golden, just yellow, as it angled through the high windows of the lab at Jean's perfume company. It was a long room with black-topped tables and real-life blue flame Bunsen burners. Technicians in white smocks worked over chemical analyzers and beakers of liquids, swirling them, holding them up to the light, making notations, conferring with too-serious looks, like scientists in TV commercials.

Jimmy sneezed. One of the white coats looked over, annoyed. Jimmy waved his apology.

Jean stepped toward him from the end of the room.

They took his car, left hers in the lot. They went first to Ike's for a drink. It was Jimmy's hangout, a nouveau-*something* cave on a Hollywood street called

Argyle. The light was blue light from the flying saucer fixtures suspended over the bar. There was a Rockola jukebox and it was playing Marvin Gaye, "Come Get to This," the dead man's song still rocking, somehow *new* again, like the light of a burned-out star just reaching earth. It was early yet.

The bartender, Scott, brought Jean a cosmopolitan and then set *two* drinks in front of Jimmy, a martini and a manhattan. The drinks waited, spotlighted, on the bar, like something about to be beamed up into the UFO light fixtures.

Jimmy picked up the martini, took a sip.

"Has Krisha been in?"

Scott shook his head. He looked like he could have been an actor waiting for his break, too, tall enough and still young enough and good-looking in an obvious, immediate way, but Scott didn't want to act. He hadn't come to California for its show business.

"I guess you're still looking for her."

"I just haven't seen her lately," Jimmy said.

Jean wondered who she was, tried not to show it.

Scott stepped away to talk to a customer at the end of the bar.

Jean smiled at Jimmy. She didn't ask him about the case, his work. He wondered why. She had another cosmo and he had another martini and they talked about nothing, about the music and a solitary dancer on the floor.

And then they got up to go. She picked up her little purse on the bar. The manhattan was still there, untouched in its perfect circle of light.

It was almost nine by the time they got to the Long Beach Yacht Club. They'd driven by another place closer to downtown where her car was but the restaurant parking lot was too crowded for Jimmy and he changed his mind and waved to the valet parkers and made a loop through the lot and drove south. There wasn't any boat traffic in and out of the marina so the lights were left to reflect clean and still on the black water. The club was quiet. The early crowd had finished and left. The late crowd was still drinking somewhere else.

Jean ordered a steak. The waiter took her menu.

Jimmy handed him his. "I'd just like a plate of tomatoes," he said. "Bring it when you bring her steak. And another bottle of water."

The waiter nodded and stepped away.

"I don't think I know any women who still eat steaks," Jimmy said.

"Yeah, I'm strange all right," Jean said. She was making fun of him. She took a sip of her drink.

"What happened to your eye?" she said. He had a cut over his right eye from the business with the men on the roof on the Roosevelt Hotel, a little bandage.

"I got falling down drunk last night," he said.

An older couple was shown to the next table. The man held his wife's chair and she smiled at him as he sat down to her right instead of across from her.

Jean watched them. She wondered what her parents would look like if they were still alive. *What would be left of the young faces in the old pictures?* She looked around, the yacht clubbers, the polished brass ship's fittings, the photos on the walls, the hurricane flags hung over the long bar.

She wondered how much like her mother she was.

"Is it all right, being here?" Jimmy said.

"Of course," Jean said. "I'm not sentimental . . . and I don't believe in ghosts."

"Your parents aren't in any of the pictures."

She wondered if he knew *everything* she was thinking.

"You've already been here," she said, not as a question. She moved her drink so the light from the candle floating in the bowl lit it up, made it even prettier.

"You wanted to know how I worked. This is how I work."

"Tell me what that means," she said.

"Everything carries its own history with it," he said. "You do. I do. Objects do. Places. Whatever happened in this room is still here in a way. If you want to see it. If you let yourself see it."

He didn't look away from her. "So there *are* ghosts," he said.

"Are they sentimental?" she said and smiled.

"Some of them," he said.

She didn't want to talk about ghosts.

"Have you ever been here before?" he said.

"There are pictures of me with my parents here."

"But you haven't been here since?"

She shook her head. "Why would I?"

"You must have always wondered the things you wonder now, whether he did it, who she really was."

"No."

"So what makes you want to know now?"

"I don't know," she said, but it wasn't true.

Someone dimmed the lights. It was nine o'clock.

The linen of the tablecloth was so white, the marigolds in the clear vase so bright and perfect. He breathed in her scent. It filled his head. Starting from when they were at Ike's he was saying more than he usually said, letting her see more. *I'm falling for her,* he thought, and thought again how good a word for it it was, *falling,* wherever it led, whatever happened now.

"What are you wearing?"

"It doesn't have a name," she said.

"Your own concoction?"

"Do you like it?" she said.

"I don't know if that's the word," Jimmy said.

She smiled again and looked away. Maybe she was falling, too.

"What is perfume made out of?"

"Oils, mostly. And alcohol."

"How did you get into this?" he said.

"A woman taught me the business."

"How does it work?"

"The business or the perfume?"

"Perfume."

"The molecules of the scent activate receptors in the nose and the mouth, which excite certain areas of the brain."

She drew her drink across the table closer to her, turning it in her fingers. "That's the simple explanation," she said, as a way of teasing him.

"A minute ago," Jimmy said, "I remembered a day

with my mother. On Point Lobos. Carmel and Monterey. Out of nowhere. I thought maybe it was your perfume."

"Were there flowers?" Jean said.

"I don't think so. I don't know. I remember the cypress trees." He knew he was telling her more than he should.

"It's not supposed to work that way," she said. "That's called 'a headache.' It's when a scent—" She broke off. "How much of this do you really want to know?"

"More," he said.

"A basic, low-quality scent acts directly on the limbic system in the temporal lobe of the brain. It calls up what are called 'moment memories.' It's better for a scent to be more general. The smell of cotton candy reminds you of a trip to the carnival when you were six. A good perfume reminds you . . ." And here she paused, because she knew how it would sound. "Of being in love."

The ghosts in the room leaned closer.

"Mixing memory and desire . . ." Jimmy said.

She knew the line, but didn't remember what it was from. "What is that?"

"Freshman English. T. S. Eliot," Jimmy said. "'April is the cruelest month, breeding lilacs out of the dead land, mixing memory and desire, stirring dull roots with spring rain . . .' *The Wasteland*. I read it—and quit school."

She laughed. "You just stood up and walked out?"

"I waited until the end of the day," he said.

Even when he lied he was telling her too much.

THEY WALKED ALONG THE CANAL, PAST THE HOUSES. Jean had taken off her shoes. It usually cooled down at night in L.A., particularly on the water, but this night was as warm as the afternoon had been and the canal stank a little. Every once in a while there would be a flash of white over their heads, a gull reeling. Maybe they fed at night. Most of the living rooms were open to the walkway, drapes drawn back, shutters open. People read in chairs or watched TV. They would look up at the movement outside, unconcerned when they saw that it was a young man and a young woman. Some of the houses flew their own bright flags on angled poles, pictographic statements about the people within, crests and flowers and boats and too many rainbows. One banner brushed across their heads as they walked under it, like a magician's scarf.

"When I was a little girl," Jean said, "I used to wonder what it would be like if your footprints could be seen everywhere you'd ever gone. A path of them. My little footprints would be up and down this walk, I guess. It's almost too much to bear."

They passed three more houses. The wind changed direction suddenly and the temperature dropped ten degrees, a gift.

Somewhere along the way, she took his hand.

A rat watched them from under a painted cement mushroom.

"This is odd," she said, "letting someone into your life so quickly. You already know things about me no one else knows. And you're strange."

"I think you said that already."

"What did you think when you first saw me?"

"That you were beautiful."

He thought better than to tell her his idea about a beautiful woman and a beautiful car, how its time was gone already even as you looked at it.

At this moment, she seemed very *present*.

"That's what men always say," she said. "I guess it gets the desired response."

"I also thought you looked sad," Jimmy said. "In the eyes. Maybe from thinking the same sad thing over and over."

He thought she would let go of his hand but she didn't and they walked on without either of them saying anything. Steps climbed up and over the haunches of a bridge and there was just another short block.

And then they were in front of 110 Rivo Alto Canal.

Now Jean let go of his hand and held herself, like the girl on Sunset after she'd kissed Jimmy and felt a chill run through her. The watchful neighbor across the canal was away or asleep and the house of the Abba neighbor was dark, too. They were alone, or at least as alone as Jimmy's worldview allowed.

She was about to say something, to fill the silence.

"There's a woman living in the back bedroom," Jimmy said.

Jean didn't look away from the house. Even in the dim light he could tell she was trying not to react, or at least not to show it.

Jimmy said, "I don't know if she lives there all the time or just comes and goes."

Jean turned away from the house.

"Have any idea who she is?" Jimmy said.

"No." Then she said, to try to put a period on it, "It doesn't matter."

Jimmy wasn't going to let it go. "Gee, it seems like it would," he said. "Maybe she bought it after—"

Jean looked at him.

"I own the house."

He really hadn't thought of that.

"It sat empty while my father was in prison during the years of appeals. Then it went to my brother Carey and he didn't want to have anything to do with it and needed the money, so I bought it from him."

"Why?"

"He needed money."

"Why did you want it?"

"I don't know. I guess I thought the answers were there. *Here.*"

"When was this?"

"When I was at Stanford."

She made herself turn and look at it again, or to let him know she wasn't afraid to.

"What's it like inside?"

"You've never been back?" Jimmy said.

She shook her head. "My business manager pays the gardeners, the electricity."

"It's like a museum, like a World's Fair exhibit from 1977."

Another chill ran through her.

"A little creepy," Jimmy said. "So who is the woman?"

"I said I don't know. I guess a transient. I should sell it, tear it down."

Jean stared at the dark face of the house for a long moment.

"Are your parents alive?" she said.

The question knocked him off balance.

"No," he said.

Her eyes were fixed on the house, as if waiting for the front door to open, as if she'd knocked.

"If I could see my mother's face, at the moment it happened," she said, "I'd know everything."

"Or your *father's* face," Jimmy said.

Jean turned her back on the house again. This time he took *her* hand. He drew her to him, held her like a dancer. The wind came up again and it made the tackle on the mast of the sailboat across the canal clang, like a signal that something should be starting or ending.

She touched his forehead, where he'd been cut, knew somehow that it was part of this, that he had already given up something for her.

After a moment, she said, "I have trouble getting close to people."

"I don't know anybody who doesn't anymore," Jimmy said. "Maybe my friend Angel."

"Why is that?" she said. "Do you know?"

"No."

"We should go," Jean said.

They were next to the seawall.

"Stand up on the wall," Jimmy said.

She took his hand and stepped up onto the low wall, like the little girl who had lived in that house and been afraid. She walked along, balancing dramatically, happy again for a second, and when she stepped down she went into his arms and kissed him, both of them out of the reach of the past for another second, even though they were this close to it.

CHAPTER 9

THEY PULLED UP TO HER APARTMENT. THE RADIO was on low.

"Can we just keep on going?" Jean said.

He looked at her.

"I like this song," she said.

So that was how they came to drive up through Benedict Canyon to Mulholland and then along the crest of the mountains, the lights spread out first on the right, the Valley, then on the left, Hollywood and West Hollywood. They came all the way out to Bel Air, over the 405, dove right down onto Sepulveda, on through the tunnel. Now the hills were dark, the road winding, and the grid of Valley lights only occasionally flashed through gaps in the trees, or the half-moon.

Jimmy steered right into a wide curve where the

two lanes became four, just past the first cluster of houses, moving from one pool of orange streetlight onto another.

The radius of the curve opened and then eased into a left. They had the road to themselves and, it seemed for at least a few more seconds, the night.

The windows were down. "I love that smell," Jean said.

"Manzanita," Jimmy said.

They were just another man and a woman, falling. Out on a date on a weeknight, all the time in the world.

"You know how sometimes you forget about it?" *Jimmy said.*

Angel nodded.

"Then you remember."

And then there was a kid covered in blood right in the road in front of them. Jean called out a wordless sound like a frightened sleeper. Jimmy saw the boy and braked hard and skidded off the road.

He was sixteen or seventeen, in a bright blue snowboarder's knit cap. He seemed oddly calm, flat, somewhere else already, gone. The blood was from a cut at his hairline and it was still coming, covering his face and now the neck of his Notre Dame High School T-shirt. He just stood in the middle of the street, oblivious to the threat of traffic, slack, careless, as if the worst thing had already happened.

The white Honda Accord was on its roof on the shoulder in a sparkling bed of broken glass, the wheels still turning. Jimmy and Jean got out and

Jimmy walked purposefully toward it, left Jean behind beside the Dodge.

She stepped toward the kid still standing in the road.

"Don't touch him," Jimmy turned and said to her, calm. "He's all right."

She didn't understand but she did as she was told. There was something about the way he said it that froze her in place.

"Call," Jimmy said.

The driver was crushed in the frame of the window, hanging half out of the overturned car. Jimmy knelt, put fingers to the boy's neck, felt for the carotid. He stood. On the passenger side in the front seat another teenager hung upside down in his shoulder belt, covered in blood, too, but moving, alive.

The bloodied kid still standing in the road came out of his daze. He looked at Jean as she got her phone out of the Dodge. He started to say something, but then shook his head and turned away from her.

He walked stiff-legged toward Jimmy and the Accord.

He saw the boy crushed in the window, the dead driver.

"Whoa. Sean? Shit, man, I hit my head . . ."

He saw the front seat passenger, moving, alive.

"Oh, shit, man, Sean and Calley . . ."

Before Jimmy got to him, the boy knelt in the broken glass to look into the backseat where there was a third body, another face covered in blood.

Jimmy yanked him to his feet.

"What's your name?"

"I was—"

"What's your name?" Jimmy said again.

"Drew."

Jimmy started walking him away from the wreck.

"We were just—" the kid began.

"The driver is dead," Jimmy said. "The other guy is hurt. An ambulance is coming."

He wrapped his arms around the teenager as if he was nine years old.

"I'm messed up . . ." the kid said. He stared at the half sphere of the moon through the trees, looking like the blade of a Gothic ax.

"I . . ."

Jimmy now put a tender hand to the side of the boy's head and spoke into his ear. Anyone close enough to hear would have understood even less by knowing more, would have said later that the words sounded like Latin, like a liturgy from another country or another century. And then that person would have shrugged.

Jean came closer, stopped a few feet away.

"They're coming," she said. "There's a fire station at the top of the hill."

Jimmy spoke a last line to Drew and then turned him and walked him past Jean, toward the car.

"They're coming," Jean said again.

"I know," Jimmy said to her. "Get in the car."

Jimmy opened the passenger door, put Drew in the backseat. The siren could be heard now, coming down from Mulholland, howling as it passed through the tunnel.

Jean said, "I don't understand—"

"They'll take care of the others," Jimmy said. "I have to take care of him."

"Were they—"

"One's dead, one's hurt. Get in the car." Jimmy got behind the wheel and the engine roared up.

Jean got in. She looked at Drew in the seat behind her.

"My head is messed up," Drew said.

"It's not as bad as it looks," Jimmy said, just eyes in the rearview mirror.

"No, I want the ambulance," Drew said. "This is wack. I'm not—"

Jimmy turned and fixed him with a look.

"I'll get you to a doctor."

There was something in the look or in the words or in Jimmy's voice that made the kid relent, lean back against the seat. With balled fists, like a little boy, he wiped the blood out of his eyes. He looked at it on his hands as if embarrassed by it.

"I'm messed up," he said.

Jimmy steered around the wreckage, the Challenger's tires cracking on the glass frags, and drove on down the hill as the red lights of the ambulance pulsed through the trees above them, behind them.

Jean looked straight ahead through the windshield.

THEY WERE IN THE KITCHEN. JIMMY STOOD AT THE sink drinking a glass of water. Behind him, a pair of hands looped the last two stitches in the cut at the kid's hairline. Drew, now dressed in a clean shirt and pants, had his eyes open but wasn't looking at anything.

The doctor daubed at her handiwork, then sorted through her bag for a bandage.

She was Krisha. She had dark brown hair, pulled back, a serious look like a poet in college. She wore a running suit. She'd been running the loop around the Hollywood Reservoir when Jimmy called.

She smiled at Drew.

"All right?"

Drew wouldn't look at her. Maybe he was imagining her, imagining all of this.

Jimmy had taken Jean home, left her standing in the street with a look on her face that was hard to read, more confusing than confused. She hadn't asked any questions on the drive back from the scene of the accident, hadn't said much of anything. Maybe she had put together an explanation for herself that was sufficient for now. Or maybe there wasn't one, ever, and she knew it. She had stood watching as Jimmy backed down the hill to the next intersection, turned around, drove away.

Jimmy walked the doctor to the door.

"He's OK," she said to Jimmy. "I'll come back in a few days. If his ribs keep hurting, you can bring him in to the clinic after hours. We'll X-ray."

"All right."

"What did he see?" she said.

"I don't know. Not everything."

"Are you OK?"

"I wasn't in it," Jimmy said. "I was just driving by."

"I mean, are you OK?" she said.

"Yeah," Jimmy said. "How about you?"

"I'm keeping busy."

It was a line they used. They said good-night and Jimmy thanked her. He watched from the open door until she got into her car and drove away down the long driveway.

Jimmy turned.

Drew was standing in the doorway to the dining room.

"You people are messed up," he said. "This is some weird shit that is happening because—"

In Jimmy's eyes, the boy glowed with the blue edge, like the Sailor on Sunset Boulevard and the men who'd hauled him to the roof of the Roosevelt, but brighter than them. Vibrant, undeniable, otherworldly.

Drew had stopped in midsentence because now, too, that was the way he saw his host.

Jimmy picked up the blue snowboarder's cap from the table in the foyer and tossed it to the kid.

"Let's go for a ride," he said.

A FOG HAD COME IN. DOWN BELOW AT LEAST. THEY were on an overlook off Mulholland, above the city. Jimmy had brought him up here to tell him. They leaned against the hood of the car, the yellow Challenger, pointed out at the sea of white. An ambulance far, far below pushed up La Brea, the light throbbing red under the cloud, looking like a fissure in the surface of the earth.

Drew said, "I don't know why I'm going along with this bullshit."

Jimmy knew the answer to that. "Because almost everything in you is telling you it's true," he said. "It can't be, but it is."

"You're the same as me?"

"Yeah."

"When did it happen to you?"

"A long time ago."

"When?"

"Nineteen sixty-seven."

Drew looked over at him, the youth still in his face. *How could it be?*

"How did it happen to you?"

A solitary car came past on Mulholland.

"People get to tell you that when they want to," Jimmy said. "I was about your age. A little older."

"Why were you there, at the wreck?"

"I was just there," Jimmy said. "I was out driving around."

"That woman who was with you, is she—"

"No."

"What would have happened if you weren't there? If you hadn't come by."

He was smart, asked the right questions. Jimmy remembered when *he* had had all the same questions himself, all at once. It was like this was a foreign country and, somehow, here you were, standing in the midst of it.

"You would have walked away," Jimmy told him. "Into the woods. Wandered around for awhile. One of us would have found you or you would have found us. Maybe in a hospital. Maybe a cop, a night watch-man."

"Are we angels?" Drew said.

"No."

"Ghosts?"

"No."

"What, *vampires?*" Drew said.

Jimmy looked across at him. "You feel like a vampire?"

Drew said, "No, what I feel like is once I got some blunt down in Huntington Beach that was messed up and I was stupid for three days. I *saw* myself in that backseat."

"What you saw was what was left."

"I don't get that."

"Something they can bury."

Drew looked like he was going to be sick.

"I don't get that."

"It's just the way it is. Something's left behind and yet you're here."

"I don't get that."

"I don't either."

"What is the blue shit about?"

"It's how we see each other sometimes," Jimmy said. "Sometimes it's there, sometimes it isn't. It comes and goes." Suddenly Jimmy was tired, tired of this night, tired of all the times it had been re-peated.

"This is bullshit," Drew said.

"Yeah, you already said that."

When they came down off the mountain, it was after three. The man in the peacoat and watch cap was
back at his post on the corner in front of the turquoise
nightclub at Sunset and Crescent Heights, now joined
by another Sailor dressed the same. Their eyes
tracked the passing Challenger.

Drew looked over. There was the blue flash.

"So they're the same as us?" Drew said.

"No," Jimmy said, a little too abruptly.

"What's the difference? I kinda like the coat—"

"There are two ways to go. That's the other way."

Since they'd come down off the mountain, Jimmy
had been thinking about himself, not Drew, and he
had gone to a dark place inside. Dark and quiet.

By now they were on Santa Monica. Jimmy looked
over as he drove past one square, blockish building.
Clover. It was closed up tight now, a row of razor wire
around the lip of roof showing silver in the street
light, like a crown of thorns.

Jimmy thought how it *had* been like his church
once. In a twisted, dead-end sixties way.

And then he was driving past Chateau Marmont
again. It was something they all did. *Returning.*

Looking up at the roof again.

A cop car cruised along beside them. The cops, a
shaved head East Islander and a Latina woman,
looked them over good but it was mostly the car, the
paint job, the clear-coat, the way the reflected lights
rolled off the rear deck in perfect *Os*. The two cars,

the Challenger and the cop car, stopped side by side at the next corner, at the light.

"Take me home," Drew said. "I want to go home." He had a whole different voice suddenly.

"No," Jimmy said.

"I want to see my mother."

"No."

"I'll get out then. I'll go to them." He was talking about the cops next to them.

"I meant you can't. It won't do any good," Jimmy said.

"I want to go home."

IT WAS A QUIET STREET IN A RESIDENTIAL NEIGH-borhood in the Valley, an area called Studio City. There were large trees and sidewalks, old-style white streetlamps, cats watching from under parked cars, artificial Ohio. Jimmy killed the headlights, slowed to a stop. A half-block ahead, there was a cluster of cars around a house, the only one with all the lights on. A dog in a fenced yard next to the car barked three or four times, then stopped.

With the windows down, you could hear the soft roar of the 101 freeway a half mile north, that sound like the ocean, but nervous. Jimmy opened the glove compartment. There was a bottle of water. He snapped the top and handed it to Drew.

Drew was staring at the house.

"How long?" Jimmy said.

"My whole life," Drew said. That defiant voice was gone. He was a little brother again.

Jimmy just let the engine idle. The sense of the neighborhood was heavy in the air. The trees leaned over to hold it in. They knew the boy here. Drew had probably learned how to ride a bike on this street. Before that, the joints in the sidewalk had made a beat to sing a song to as his father or mother pushed him in a stroller around the block. Maybe the yard in front of that house had carried a balloon sign, now almost too sentimental to think of, that said, "It's a boy!"

Everything carried its history.

Now it's a *dead* boy.

Someone was arriving, a shiny duelie pickup, probably someone who worked at the studios, a gaffer, a grip, a carpenter. They liked duelies. The man got out and rushed toward the house.

"It's Terry," Drew said. "My mother's—" He didn't finish it.

The front door of Drew's house opened, throwing an angle of light onto the lawn, and a man from inside stepped out of the doorway and opened his arms to the man coming up the walk.

The front door closed. Shadows crossed on the drapes.

"You could look in the window," Jimmy said, "but you don't want to carry that around with you, seeing them this way. You could walk in, but they wouldn't know you and it would only add to their pain."

Drew looked at him. "I look the same. How can that be?"

"They wouldn't know you. To their eyes you have a different face. It's something that happens inside their heads, the people you leave behind. They have their boy. They're going to put him in the ground in a day or two."

Jimmy could hear the breath catch in Drew's throat.

"But you're here, in the flesh," Jimmy said. "With us. To be this second version of yourself."

"This is wack," Drew said, his eyes on the house.

"It's just the way it is," Jimmy said. "I didn't design this. I don't know who did."

Now Drew was crying.

"You're here for as long as you're here, until whatever unfinished business you have is finished. You can try to do some good—or you can be one of those people we saw on the street back there, on Sunset, here to do wrong."

He didn't tell the boy that there was a *third* thing you could be. *A Walker.* Dead to the world, this world and the other.

"You have a new family now," Jimmy said, flat and unsentimental, looking straight ahead at the grayed-out trees in the next block.

He heard the door open as Drew bolted from the car.

Jimmy went after him, as once somebody had gone after him.

He caught up to him on the lawn, on the black grass.

"Leave me alone!"

"I'm telling you, there's nothing you can do," Jimmy said, loud enough to wake the neighbors. "I know."

Drew had stopped.

"Come on," Jimmy said.

The door opened. The man, Terry, had heard the noise, the voices. He came out onto the front step. He tried to make sense of two strangers standing there ten feet away.

"Don't say his name," Jimmy said.

Drew turned toward the man. With the door open, there was light on the boy's face.

"Don't," Jimmy said.

"What are you doing?" Terry said.

A woman stepped into view behind him in the doorway.

"Who is it?" she said with the saddest kind of hope.

AS THE SKY TURNED PINK, JIMMY YANKED CLOSE the blackout drapes in the bedroom at the end of the hallway in his house. Behind him Drew was on his back on the black covering on the bed, eyes open.

CHAPTER 10

IN THE MORNING PAPER THERE WAS AN ARTICLE about last night's accident, a picture of the overturned Honda, a headline:

TWO DEAD, ONE CRITICAL
IN CANYON CRASH

There was a school picture of Drew, probably from two or three grades ago, a straight-faced, trying-to-look-older pose. His last name was Hastings. The other dead boy had been a runner, had held some state record so he got more ink. And a *smiling* picture, taken from the sports pages of the Notre Dame High School paper.

An adjacent article showed the same photo they

were using of the young Latino boy lost in the brown hills out in what they called the Inland Empire and, now, a picture of a man in handcuffs, a Mexican man who looked as if he'd never smiled.

"The news is always the same," Jimmy said. "It just happens to different people."

Angel came into the dining room from the kitchen with a cup of coffee.

"I almost drove him down to The Pipe last night," Jimmy said. "Maybe he should see that *first*."

"He'll know about it soon enough," Angel said.

Jimmy picked up a phone and dialed the number for Jean's office. She wasn't expected in all day. Jimmy called her apartment. After three rings, the machine picked up. Jimmy hung up.

"She was with you?" Angel said.

Jimmy nodded.

"What's her name?"

"Jean."

"What's her last name?"

"I told you, Kantke."

"What did she see?"

"A car wreck," Jimmy said.

Angel took a sip of his coffee, waited for Jimmy to remember who he was talking to.

"I don't know what she thought," Jimmy said. "She didn't say anything. I took her back to her office to get her car and then followed her home."

Jimmy went into the study. Angel followed him.

"So she's the Long Beach thing. The murders."

"Yeah."

"So it's more than the case. With her. For you."

"I guess it was getting to be. I don't know what it's going to be now."

Jimmy sat behind the desk and pulled the keyboard closer and rewound the digital machines that recorded output from the security cameras that ringed his property. Between midnight and one, the pale men and the big men from the other night on the hotel roof had made an appearance at the back gate, testing the iron bars, hanging out for twenty minutes.

Jimmy put the picture onto a flat screen monitor on the wall.

"You know these guys?"

Angel looked at the screen and shook his head. Jimmy froze the image and clicked a few keys and the printer printed out a hard copy.

"Maybe they were selling magazines," Angel said.

"I played a little road tag with the two on the left the other day. They were in an Escort."

Angel got the joke.

"Lon and Vince," Jimmy said, looking at their pale faces. "And then the other night I met the other two and a leader, a guy close to seven foot. They showed me the view from the Roosevelt."

"And that has to do with *this?*" Angel said.

Jimmy didn't know. Or wasn't ready to say. He shrugged.

Drew was in the game room playing pinball, a bottle of Dos Equis sitting on top of the glass. A TV was on, big screen, street luge skaters ripping down a too steep canyon road somewhere, crisscrossing, losing it, spinning out, crashing into hay bales. Drew apparently didn't get the connection or he would have turned it off.

Jimmy stepped into the doorway.

"I have to go somewhere. You want to go with me?"

"Go where?"

"I'm an investigator. I'm working on something."

"A what?"

"An investigator."

"What's the point?"

"You'll feel better if you do something, if you go out there and try to find some answers to the questions that there are answers for. Like I said, there are two ways to go."

"Yeah, I know," Drew said. "Everybody's gotta believe in something. I believe I'll have another beer . . ."

Jimmy turned to go.

"Let me ask you something," Drew said to stop him, not looking up from his game. "Can I die? I mean, *again?*" Maybe he *did* get the connection between the crashing luge skaters and what had happened to him on the canyon road.

"You can get hurt," Jimmy said, "*bad,* but you won't die." Here was another chance to tell the kid about the *third* thing that could happen, about how your spirit could die and you'd be left with even less, how they could take your spirit away, the thing they'd hauled him up to the roof for, just so he'd remember it. "You're here until it's time for you to go—"

"Yeah, I know . . ."

"But you can't bring it on yourself and nobody else can bring it on you."

Drew threw his weight against the machine to force the steel ball uphill.

"Even if like a bullet went through my head, I wouldn't die."

"No."

"If I was shredding down a mountain and pulled a full-on Sonny Bono, I wouldn't die."

"No. You could get messed up, but you wouldn't die."

The pinball machine clattered wildly. Something had happened.

"The pathetic thing is I don't know if that's good news or bad," Drew said.

Jimmy said, "That's why there are—"

"Yeah, 'two ways to go . . . '" Drew said. "'Use The Force, Luke.'"

JIMMY KNEW MOST OF THE STORY AND A PHONE call to a friend in politics brought the rest. Harry Turner was a "kingmaker," one of the men—or, depending on whom you talked to, *the* man—you went to if you wanted to be governor or a federal judge. Or, if you believed everything you heard, the anchorman on the local news in Santa Barbara where one of Harry Turner's five big houses was. It was one of those stories that over the years got better and better. To run things in California, you had to wait in line. The man at the head of the line, hand on the gate, for

the last twenty years anyway, was Harry Turner. He'd
been the real lawyer who ran Jack Kantke's defense,
behind the scenes, behind *Upland* or *Overland* or *Upchurch* or whatever his name was, the Long Beach
lawyer whose name nobody could remember but who
had to sit at the table next to defendant Kantke and
take the loss when it came. When Harry Turner
stopped practicing law himself, "retired" in the
nineties, he still kept his firm open with a half dozen
lawyers angling to be his favorite, his heir, the son he
never had. He went even further behind the curtain.
He was on a dozen boards of directors. He owned car
dealerships. He owned a chain of smog inspection stations. He owned billboard companies. He held patents
for devices he couldn't point to on a table, for "pro-
cesses" he couldn't begin to explain. He owned a
restaurant. He owned *airports*. He made money while
he slept.

And twenty years ago, with a new dogleg in the
aqueduct to bring in water from the Colorado, he became one of the "visionaries" turning green the
Coachella Valley out past Palm Springs and Indian
Wells. Desert into farmland. He had a thousand acres
of winter lettuce and another five hundred in table
grapes.

He was eleven feet tall, on the back of his horse.

He rode, not that fast but steady, out of a block of
date palms planted in rows and then along the edge of
a field of something so green it clashed with the sky.
He rode without changing his pace right straight at the
black pickup with the ranch logo on the door, came up

fast enough to make them all turn their heads aside. He wore chinos and short brown Wellington boots and a long-sleeve white shirt. He stayed in the saddle, all eleven feet of him.

Jimmy had been hand-delivered by a pair of robust cowboys who made the Sailors on the roof of the Roosevelt Hotel look anorexic. These men were Basque, real cowboys. They'd stopped Jimmy even before he made it to the gates of the ranch, sixty seconds after a black helicopter had overflown him in the Mustang on the mile-long road in off of the highway. They'd shown him where to leave his car in front of one of the very clean outbuildings. One of them nodded toward the front seat of the black truck and then got behind the wheel and the other man climbed in back and sat against the tailgate and rode that way all the way out into the fields.

They were strong and their suspiciousness was industrial-strength, but they weren't smart. Jimmy had told them he was the mayor of Rancho Cucamonga.

Harry Turner looked him over, looked at his sissy shoes, his Prada suit, and smiled a little sourly.

"Mr. Mayor," he said. He had a walkie-talkie hanging off his wide brown belt. They'd called ahead.

Turner climbed down out of the saddle and took off his hat, a flat-brim Stetson that made him look like a mounted cop. His hand came out and Jimmy thought it might be the start of a handshake but Turner was just reaching for a kerchief he kept tucked up his left sleeve. He wiped off his forehead, even though he wasn't sweating.

Jimmy still hadn't said a word. It was the right thing not to say.

"You had lunch?" Turner said.

He didn't wait for an answer, just walked past Jimmy toward a black flagship Mercedes S600 that hadn't been there thirty seconds ago. Another Basque man now stood beside the pickup. Mexican men in jobs like these always looked at the ground when you weren't talking to them. These men looked at *you*. One of them retrieved an automatic rifle from the trunk of the Mercedes before Turner got behind the wheel and they left.

They drove for a mile between two fields and then turned right and drove another mile. All the roads were paved. They had them to themselves. There were tumbleweeds and burger wrappers blown against the chain-link fences. They came out onto the access road and then onto the highway, Interstate 10, headed east through the brown and the green, all of it as flat as the top of a stove. They drove and drove. The Chocolate Mountains on the other side of the valley were getting bigger in front of them.

Maybe they were going to Phoenix.

The green glass in the window beside Jimmy's head was an inch thick. He tipped his head over to where he could see the side mirror. The black pickup was a half mile back, three of the Basques shoulder to shoulder in the front seat.

Turner didn't say much of anything, beyond naming the crops in the fields alongside the interstate as they passed, three kinds of *summer* lettuce, "baby's breath"—which he sure enough made sound like a *product*—jojoba and sod. The sod farm was out the window for a long minute at eighty miles an hour, an expanse of lawn with no big house behind it, unsettling, *wrong*.

They passed a section of planted date trees, *Medjool* dates, Turner said.

"Dates are too sweet." Which meant they were somebody else's dates.

Jimmy didn't disagree.

Just as he was settling into his seat, thinking they *were* going to Phoenix, or at least Blythe, they came up on a big new gaudy Morongo Indian casino with a hundred-foot sign out front and a name that didn't say anything about Indians. Turner looked over at it with a long look that made Jimmy figure he owned that, too, or a piece of it. And he took the brand-new exit just past it.

But they weren't going to the casino. They took another road, another *paved* road straight south for five or six miles and then there was a big white box of an aluminum building, nothing else for miles, with three Lincoln Town Cars and a pickup and a new Cadillac in the lot in front. It didn't have a sign.

There was just one long wooden table inside but it was covered with white linen and the tableware was silver, though a plain pattern. There weren't any flowers. There weren't any windows either. It was about sixty degrees, a hundred and nine outside.

A single waiter in a plain-front white shirt and black pants stood next to the kitchen door. There wasn't any music, just six or seven men talking. They were all dressed like field hands. In four-hundred-dollar boots. None of them were young.

"We waited, Harry," one of them said. The plate in front of him had a pile of bloody bones and a last smear of what looked liked creamed spinach.

Turner slapped the man on the back.

"Don't get up," he said, since the man wasn't moving.

He shook the hands of two of the other men. One of them introduced the man beside him he'd brought as a guest. Turner knew the rest of them. He didn't introduce Jimmy and the other men didn't ask.

"Looks like it's lamb," Turner said as he and Jimmy sat down across the table from each other at one end, away from the others.

Jimmy nodded.

"It'll be good," Turner said. "Americans don't know how to slaughter lambs." The way he said *Americans* made Jimmy wonder if maybe Turner wasn't his real name. A lot of the farmers and ranchers out here were Armenian. "Most Americans *think* they've eaten lamb and most of them think they don't like the taste. You butcher it wrong, you let any part of the meat touch the layer of fat just under the wool and the lanolin turns the meat, gives it that *lamb* taste."

The waiter came with two plates, put them in front of the men, and filled their glasses with red wine.

"But maybe you already know all about lamb," Turner said.

"I didn't know that," Jimmy said. "I even thought I

liked it." He picked up a lamb chop and chewed off a bite.

It was the best lamb in the world, the lamb of kings.

Or king*makers*.

"Guess I see what you mean," Jimmy said.

"You know how to eat it," Turner said. He picked up a chop with his fingers, too, out of the puddle of blood.

Turner said what Jimmy had already figured out, that a group of them in the Valley had gotten together to make this place, a private dining hall, built it, built the road out to it, hired a chef away from some hotel.

"French," Turner said. "But he's all right."

Jimmy ate his spinach. From that first *Mr. Mayor* out in the fields under the nonstop sun, he knew Turner was onto him. He also knew that was the way to get in to see someone like Harry Turner. You lied to *him* in the right way, in this case the smart-ass way.

You sure didn't come in trying to flatter him. A man like Harry Turner had stood before a line of flatterers stretching away to the horizon. You didn't bow and scrape. Even the waiter knew that.

So Turner was onto him. The question was how much.

The waiter stepped in to top off Turner's wineglass. Turner looked at him.

"We'll do that."

The waiter left the bottle and backed away. The wine was a Jordan Beaujolais.

"I understand you want to know about my brilliant defense of Florence Gilroy in the poisoning death of her third husband," Turner said.

So they'd radioed out to the fields that the mayor of Rancho Cucamonga was there to see him. And Turner had said *bullshit* and told them to call in the plate on the Mustang. Then who knows what other calls he'd made, even before he started riding in from the date palm oasis. Whomever he'd called, Harry Turner knew everything he needed to know. Or thought he did.

"I *do* want to know. Sometime," Jimmy said.

Turner wasn't in a hurry to eat. It made Jimmy know that this was more important to him than it could have been, maybe even than it *should* have been.

"Did you look up Barry Upchurch?"

Jimmy shook his head. "Is he still alive?"

Turner said, "You know, I don't know." It was a lie.

The last three men left together. One of them, the one who'd introduced his man to Turner, put a hand on Turner's back as he passed and leaned in close and said something, three or four sentences, into his ear.

Turner nodded. And then shook his head no.

"That's what I said," the man said, loud enough to hear.

Then they were alone. The waiter even disappeared.

Turner said, "Where were we?"

"You were saying Jack Kantke couldn't possibly have done it because he was talking about the Dodgers with the gas station guy in Barstow at eight-fifteen and the time of the murders was determined to be between eight and midnight."

"*Six* and midnight," Turner said. "They couldn't peg it any closer, not then. 1977. Maybe today."

"Six and midnight," Jimmy corrected. "Still . . ."

"He drove fast," Turner said.

"I thought of that," Jimmy said.

"You like to drive fast."

"I just like to drive. I even like to sit in cars in my driveway."

Turner ate a good half of his meal before he said anything else. There were linen napkins. He wiped the blood off of his lips onto one.

"I never understood why the other side didn't say that," he said. *"He drove fast."*

"People hate math," Jimmy said.

Turner nodded. He thought he was being likeable.

Jimmy tried to come at it from another angle, got out a few words of a question, when Turner cut him off.

"We *bought* the guy at the gas station in Barstow. Six hundred dollars, as I recall. And I think he asked for a pair of Dodgers tickets, his idea of a joke. He's dead now."

"But not because he had a bad sense of humor," Jimmy said.

Turner gave a little hint of that sour smile again.

The waiter reappeared without being called, put a cup of black coffee beside Turner's left hand. He was left-handed.

"So what time *did* Kantke stop for gas?" Jimmy asked.

Turner said, "About two hours after he shot and killed his wife and Bill Danko."

Just like that.

There it was.

In case Jimmy didn't get it the first time, Turner said again, "He drove fast."

"It would have been rush hour," Jimmy said.

"It was a Saturday," Turner said. "But you knew that."

Jimmy did know that.

He put his fork and knife on top of his plate.

"So," Jimmy said. "What's for dessert?"

"None of us eat dessert," Turner said, looking straight across the table at him. "Vanity. Young wives."

"Did you see him executed?" Jimmy said, right back to his eyes.

"You make it sound like an obligation."

Jimmy didn't know how he was supposed to take that.

"You lose the case, you have to watch the man die?" Turner said.

"I guess it's a long way up to San Quentin."

"Jack Kantke and I weren't friends," Turner said. "I was just a lawyer trying to help a fellow member of the California Bar."

" 'In good standing . . . ' "

"All of us," Turner said.

WHEN JIMMY CAME OUT OF THE DINING HALL INTO the glare of the sun, into what was now the hundred and *ten* degree heat, his Mustang was sitting there waiting for him.

And Jimmy had the keys in his pocket.

He looked up at the utterly clear sky. There wasn't even a daylight moon. He hadn't seen Turner come out behind him and hadn't heard anything, but now the black Mercedes pulled out of the lot and onto the road, followed by the men in the pickup in their black *txapela* Basque berets.

And then Jimmy was alone out there.

CHAPTER 11

WHEN JIMMY STEPPED OUT OF THE FARMERS' AND ranchers' private dining room in the middle of their made-over desert and looked up at the rich blue of the empty sky, for some reason he remembered something he'd heard a NASA scientist say once on a television program, that space wasn't all that far away, *that if you could drive there in a car, you'd be there in an hour.* And he remembered something else from the program, that way way out, a few billion miles past that first edge of space, sometimes they would identify a body by the *negative* evidence, know something was there because everything pointed away from it, because there was a too clear expanse of nothing.

What Harry Turner had said—and what he hadn't—had turned Jimmy's mind. Turner had stated outright that Jack Kantke had killed his wife and Bill Danko, then driven hard and fast out of L.A. to cobble together an alibi. What Turner had said, had *confessed* on behalf of his client, was meant to convey the same message to Jimmy as the trip to the roof of the Roosevelt Hotel with the Sailors. *Nothing to see here, move right along.* . . . Harry Turner had read Jimmy Miles as wrong as the tall bony redheaded Sailor and whoever had sent him. What was meant to drive him away only drew him in closer.

Maybe it was just the look in Harry Turner's eye.

Whatever it was, Jimmy now guessed, just for himself, that Jack Kantke *hadn't* killed his wife and her lover. He didn't know who did, didn't know *why,* but, just for himself, he was all but sure it had been somebody else standing with the gun behind the wisp of a curtain in the white front bedroom in the Rivo Alto house and that they'd gassed the wrong man.

If you still believed in the notion of right and wrong men.

CALIFORNIA 74 WAS A WINDING, CLIMBING TWO-lane road highlighted in the AAA tourist guides as something special, *the Palms to Pines Highway*, slithering its way up off the desert floor into the San Bernardino Mountains, toward Mount San Jacinto, "from a desert oasis to snow capped mountains." And, though it was June, almost July and the valley behind him was baking, there *would* be snow on the sides of

the road when he got to the higher elevations, up to
the top, into the evergreens, eight thousand feet.

But he wasn't there yet and he was enjoying the
drive. He came to the first of the tall stick trees and
pulled off the road and got out. The air smelled cool
and green, like the world wouldn't mind if you lived
another day or so. That was the way it was in the
mountains. Back down behind him in the desert, Nature didn't much care if you were there or not, re-
garded you the way a tortoise looks at you, *Are you
another rock?*

Jimmy opened the hatchback and pulled the soft,
worn red plaid Pendleton shirt out of the grocery bag.
He was alone on the highway, hadn't seen another
soul for twenty minutes. He took off his white silk
short-sleeved shirt and then the T-shirt underneath it.
It wasn't cold at all but the air made his skin ripple.
He pulled on the stretched-out Sears undershirt from
the bag and unbuckled his slacks and dropped them
and slipped into a pair of faded, patched-at-the-knee
Levi's. He folded his suit pants and sat on the rear
bumper and changed his socks and put on a pair of
black hightop Converse All Stars.

He'd bought the clothes at the Salvation Army in
Palm Springs. Everything came to a couple of bucks
less than what he'd paid for the socks he walked in
wearing. He wasn't in any hurry, knew where he was
going next, so he spent some time talking with the
woman behind the register. She had that look in her
eye, that *recovered* look, a little shaky but she was go-

ing to be all right, had managed to get in the present, to just read the page in front of her. Maybe she could tell Jimmy how to do it.

The shirt felt good. He wondered about the man who'd worn it last. Angel had told him about a preacher who made a thing of only wearing the clothes of men in his congregation who'd died, clothes bundled up and handed over by widows and grown children, after they'd buried their faces in the shirts one last time. Jimmy buttoned up the plaid shirt and closed the hatchback. Clothes with a history, it fit.

In Idyllwild, he bought ten dollars' worth of gas and paid cash. The attendant, a high school kid, looked him over good, though he didn't get up out of his plastic chair to do it. The Mustang was a little too cherry to really match the driver in the knockaround clothes, but the kid and the locals walking by didn't seem to notice, didn't seem to be thinking much of anything when they looked at Jimmy. Which was the idea.

Idyllwild was a collection of log buildings on both sides of the highway on the flat part of the summit. A pair of Alpine A-frame gift shops, almost identical, stood across the road from each other, each with an eight-foot redwood bear out front, chain-saw carved. There was a restaurant. There was an ice cream parlor. There was a bar. There was a little brown wood church up the highway. And a "creekside" motel with cabins.

Jimmy drove across the highway from the gas station to the restaurant and parked the Mustang and got out. A slice of a giant sequoia, taller than he was, was leaned against the wall on its edge, like a big coin. It was polished, the rings clear. Events in History were marked with little flags on pins, nine hundred years of history, if they had it right, fires by blackened rings, droughts by thin rings, Columbus setting sail, Lincoln dead, Kennedy dead, a man on the moon.

It was late enough in the day that Jimmy decided he'd stay over, go at it in the morning. This was where Barry Upchurch had retired, probably moved into what had been a weekend place before. Jimmy had found the lawyer's name listed in a "Mountain Areas" city directory in the library down in Palm Springs. Then he'd found an article in the microfiche about an Idyllwild *No Growth!* committee Upchurch had served on when he first came up the mountain ten years ago. Retired So-Cal lawyers seemed either to go to the mountains or the beach, the size of the house and the acreage determined by just who you kept out of jail or bankruptcy. The lawyers who put people *into* jail, when they retired probably just stayed in their houses in the Valley or out in Santa Monica, grandfathered in.

Upchurch wasn't a government lawyer but from what Jimmy had heard and read he hadn't had a big client practice either. His house was likely a cabin on one of the roads heading up into the low hills above town, nothing fancy, a couple of bedrooms, or maybe a glass-fronted A-frame, if the seventies had made a bit too much of an impression on him. Jimmy had an address but he wasn't just going to walk up to the door, at least not yet.

There was snow on the shady side of the cabin, a short foot of it banked up against the stone foundation. Each cabin had a cute wildflower name. The key to "Star Lily" had a green plastic fob, old style. Jimmy opened the door. There was red carpet, fairly new but an old-fashioned pattern.

There was no TV, no phone. An empty fireplace, gingham curtains somebody had made by hand, a bed spread picking up the same reds and greens. There was a kitchenette. Jimmy tried the faucet. There were two jelly glasses in the cabinet. The water was cold and sweet, better than anything in a bottle with "mountain" in the name.

But the cabin was too lonely to stay in, with the light dying and all in among the tall trees, and Jimmy turned around and walked out. Better to be out with people, even strangers, than in with himself.

He went next door to the Evergreen Club. It was dark, but in a good way. There were antlers on the wall and pictures of "Early Idyllwild" and an over-sized electric train running on a track up just under the rafters.

And Barry Upchurch was at the bar.

Probably.

Twenty years, not ten, were added to the face from the picture in the microfiche of the *No Growth!* Committee. Maybe there had been too many nights here drinking what looked like bourbon in a rocks glass. He had a *mad* look to him, in his eye, in the way he sat hunched over, protecting the space in front of him. And he smoked, too.

Everybody Jimmy had been meeting lately looked like they were trying to get over something.

The barstools didn't swivel so Upchurch and the three or four regulars beside him were using the mirror over the bar to watch the young woman shooting pool behind them.

She was traveling, alone. She had a backpack, a real backpack, not an *accessory*, stowed against the knotty pine-paneled wall, worn hiking shoes, a tan that wasn't from a UV lamp. She was German or maybe Swiss, tall enough to be a model. Short, dark red hair, cut different lengths, like a Beatle, good for the trail. She was laughing at herself between missed shots and drinking a dark beer. The kid from the gas station was her partner.

He put his stick back in the rack, shaking his head. "I gotta go," he said.

"Sorry," she said, heavy accent. "I'm terrible! Please not to be giving up on me, I am *trying*." She laughed between every other word and touched his arm.

"No, it's all right," the kid said. "I just gotta go. You're OK. Really. It was nice to meet you . . ."

He held out his hand.

"Greta," she said.

He shook her hand. "Enjoy." He left.

She racked up the balls again while the regulars at the bar poked each other in the ribs. Your turn. But it was too early and they were all too sober, or too old, to make a move.

Jimmy took a stool. The bartender was a woman past sixty, maybe past seventy. She had a cigarette going, too, lying in an ashtray swiped from a fancier place than this.

Jimmy ordered a dark beer. A *German* beer.

"Good luck," the barmaid said.

But Jimmy wasn't going to make a play for the girl. Now he was there to watch Upchurch, maybe close the distance of the three stools between them, talk to him before he *talked* to him. He hadn't meant to get into this tonight but sometimes *The Case* had other ideas, its own sense of timing.

It turned out one of the other men was a lawyer, too, and still had a practice going down in Palm Desert. This one was twenty years younger than Upchurch. Upchurch listened to him go on and on about a case, more detail than anybody wanted or needed, another murder but this one more immediate than the Long Beach murders long ago, this one about a meth lab in a double-wide too many miles up an unpaved road.

Upchurch just nursed his drink and nodded every once in a while. This gang had probably all heard *his* murder story too many times. Or maybe he wasn't a talker.

When the beer clock said *seven,* Upchurch got up and stepped back, steady, not the least bit drunk. His pants leg was hiked up. He slid it down, over the little Colt Detective Special .38 in an ankle holster stuck in the top of his black socks.

Upchurch picked up the change that had been sitting there all along and pushed two singles across to the trough. The barmaid palmed them straight into the pocket of her jeans and somehow made the whistle on the chugging electric train toot.

Jimmy waited a minute and followed him out.

Upchurch came out of the town store across the highway with what looked liked a thick steak wrapped in pink butcher paper. Jimmy was in the shadows alongside the gas station. It closed at nightfall, lights out. Upchurch walked back across the empty blacktop, not in any hurry at all, apparently not having any idea someone was watching him. He glanced at a Jeep CJ-7, old style, open on the sides, parked in front of the bar, walked past it, started up the easy hill, walking in the middle of the gravel road.

Jimmy waited, followed him.

A woman in her fifties came out to poke at a charcoal fire in a steel drum smoker out behind an A-frame all by itself next to a dry creekbed in among a good stand of trees. There was an owl somewhere, hooting. She searched for it with her eyes. Then she went back inside. Jimmy watched.

And then the barrel of the tidy .38 was behind his ear.

Upchurch didn't say anything smart or sarcastic or even nasty, just had Jimmy walk the rest of the way up toward the house, toward the light so he could get a better look at him, his gun now down at his side.

When they got into the light, Jimmy told him who he was, what he was there for.

Upchurch dropped the .38 into the pocket of his chinos but didn't shake Jimmy's hand or anything.

The woman, Ellie Upchurch, stepped out onto the

deck, surprised to see anybody, her hand going to her breast.

"He's here about Barry," Upchurch said.

Maybe he was schizophrenic.

But then they went inside the house and the first thing Jimmy saw was a portrait of the *real* Barry Upchurch, under a brass-plated tube light. Maybe a client had painted it, "in partial payment for services rendered." The Upchurch in the painting was older than he would have been at the time of the Kantke trial and he was better looking than his big brother, probably always had been. But the eyes, the face had the same *slapped* look.

The other Upchurch, whose name was D. L., stepped past Jimmy without looking at him and took the pistol out of his pants pocket and put it in a drawer in a table with a Tiffany-style lamp on it and a vase of pretty purple mountain wildflowers called nightshade. Ellie Upchurch came over and took D. L.'s hand and kissed him on the cheek, something Jimmy guessed she always did when someone was looking at the portrait of her first husband.

D. L. grunted something that could have been, *I love you, too.*

The A-frame was nicely furnished without a lot of references to the past, his or hers or *his,* except for the portrait. There was an oval "rag rug," on top of pine flooring, a Kennedy rocking chair, an over-and-under shotgun on pins on the wall, nothing too fancy, a Browning. There was a big leather chair in front of the stand-alone black Swedish fireplace, a healthy fire, a *National Geographic* bright yellow on the ottoman. It was all one big room, with a bedroom upstairs, a loft.

"You can go on," D. L. Upchurch said and walked toward the open kitchen. He meant that his wife could talk to this stranger about her first husband, his brother. He took the wrapped steaks from the counter and put them in the fridge. He got himself a Bud Light in a can and then dug around in the back of the icebox until he came out with a bottle of beer, dark German beer. He handed the Beck's to Jimmy after he wrenched off the cap with his bare hand—it may or may not have been a twist-off—and then he went outside, left them alone.

She sat in the leather chair and Jimmy stood beside the fire and she gave him a version of the intervening years. Barry Upchurch had practiced law in Long Beach another twelve years after the Kantke trial and then he retired and they moved up the mountain and he died two years after that.

The short version was he'd never gotten over it.

"*Doctors* are like that, some of them," Jimmy said. "They keep it to themselves but it rips them up when they lose one."

She sat with her legs crossed, her hands in her lap. "That wasn't Barry's problem," she said. "He had no problem losing a case."

She probably didn't mean the twist of bitterness in the way she said the line.

"It wasn't that," she said.

And then she went into it in great detail, the days and weeks of that time, of 1977, starting even before the trial began. She never referred directly or even indirectly to Harry Turner setting things up, running things from behind the curtain, but he was as *present* in the story as if she had named his name or he was standing there in the room with them. They'd disagreed from the start, Barry Upchurch and "the others," until Upchurch finally got the message and shut up and stopped having ideas, or at least stopped saying them out loud.

And then came the verdict. And then the appeals. And then the execution.

"His practice picked up after the Kantke case," she said, this time intending every bit of the bitterness she laid onto the words. "It was quite remarkable. Some of the finest criminals in Long Beach were suddenly Barry's."

Jimmy asked her the question he already knew the answer to.

"No," she said. "Jack Kantke was innocent. Completely. And Barry knew it. And knew how to prove it."

She laid it all out. It had to do with the killer behind the wispy curtains in that front bedroom, waiting, and the angle of the barrel of the .45 in that hand, the trajectory of the two bullets, the *height* of the shooter.

And the fact that Jack Kantke was an inch over six feet.

"They wouldn't use it," she said. "Barry went to the mat but they wouldn't use it. And it killed him."

She heard what she had just said.

"Killed *both* of them I guess."

"You never knew why," Jimmy said. "Why they wouldn't use it."

She shook her head and then looked at him as if maybe, now, *he* was going to tell her. When he didn't, she said, "So I guess losing *did* take its toll. Or maybe it was seeing the ways things really are."

Jimmy would remember that last line.

She invited him to stay for the steaks but he just shook her hand again and looked again at the portrait and went out the way he'd come in.

D. L. Upchurch was watching the fading charcoal fire.

"You can stay," he said. "Eat."

Jimmy looked at that face in the red and orange light. What would come to him in a minute was starting to come now.

"No, that's all right," he said.

"Up to you."

Jimmy said, "Sorry about the creeping around. I really meant to come out here in the morning."

"Old habits," D. L. said. Maybe it was an apology, too.

Then Jimmy got it.

He stayed put in front of the man.

"She tell you about the trajectory?" D. L. said.

"Yeah."

"The angle. The shooter behind the curtain."

"Yes."

"Bill Danko's *wife* killed them," D. L. said, straight ahead, eyes down. "She was five-foot-one."

D. L. Upchurch was a cop. One brother's a lawyer and his big brother's a cop, like something out of an old Warner Bros. movie.

And not just *any* cop, a Long Beach cop, the Long Beach uniformed cop in the newspaper picture looking out of the murder bedroom. Looking *up*.

JIMMY WENT BACK TO THE EVERGREEN AND DRANK dark beer until they closed and then he was in his cabin with the tall German girl. They kissed and that's all they did and only that because the day and the work with its tricks and surprises and reversals had gotten to him.

And because they were both so far from home.

CHAPTER 12

A CAT RUBBED AGAINST HIS LEG AS JIMMY STOOD in the middle of the back bedroom in the murder house. It was late afternoon. Needles of light shot through pinholes in the shades taped against the windows. There was a second bathroom off the bedroom. He hadn't noticed it the first time. She was in there. The water was running.

She came out, saw him. She was startled, but again accepted the apparition before her, even as she tried to ignore it. He did see her hands shaking a little this time.

She walked past him and sat in her chair, looking at the TV, which wasn't on, *not* looking at him.

"My name is Jimmy Miles."

"Not funny," she said.

"I didn't mean to scare you. I knocked. On the backdoor."

"OK, I'm not going to talk to you," she said. "I'm not going to talk to you because then it'll be you *and* the others."

She was only in her forties, maybe even her thirties. The other night, Jimmy thought she was older. She wore the same worn dress, faded roses, a sweater over it, slippers on her feet. He made a harsh judgment: she'd never been pretty, except maybe to her daddy.

"I know you see people," Jimmy said gently, "but I'm really here. I'm real."

"The beat goes on," she said to the blank TV.

"I just want to ask you about this house."

She still wouldn't look at him. Jimmy took an apple from his pocket. He took a noisy bite. She didn't look at him but the smell of it suddenly filled the room.

"Any of them ever eat an apple before?" he said.

She glanced at him. He took another bite. From his pocket he produced another apple. He put it on the TV tray beside her chair, the way you put down food for a dog you just rescued and then step back.

She watched the action, then tried to shake it off.

"The beat goes on," she said, staring ahead again.

Jimmy sang a line of "The Beat Goes On."

"Any of them ever *sing* before?"

She gave him a quick look, a flash of impatience.

"Yes . . ."

"Take a bite," Jimmy said.

She hesitated, then reached for the apple on the TV tray. She took a bite.

"It's one of those new Fuji apples," he said. "How do you think they did it? How do you get a brand new apple?"

She took another bite. "You didn't knock," she said. "You said you did."

"I knew you wouldn't answer. What's your name?"

"I can be here," she said. "I've got a right."

"I have nothing to do with that. What's your name?"

She looked at him. "Rosemary. Rosemary Danko."

Jimmy already knew it, before she said it.

"You look like your dad," he said.

"I've got a right to be here. This is where they killed him. I'm not leaving."

He stepped back, leaned against the wall.

"Where do you get your food?"

She straightened herself in her chair. "Two a.m., I go to the Ralph's. It used to be a Hughes. They cash my checks and they take my stamps."

"Are you on medication?"

"They think I live at the other place, over in Garden Grove," she said. "Sometimes I have to go over there on the Six Bus, to keep them thinking that."

A cat jumped into her lap. She looked at it a moment, as if she wasn't sure what it was. Then she relaxed.

"They won't kill me here," she said, as much to the cat as to Jimmy.

"Who wants to kill you?"

She said something that he couldn't understand, something mumbled, swallowed up.

"Say it again," he said.

She suddenly looked at his feet. "I like your shoes. Most people don't wear those."

"Who wants to kill you?" he said again.

She looked at him hard, suddenly angry. "Who are you? What does this have to do with apples?"

"Who killed your father?"

"I know what I know. That's why I don't live over in Garden Grove."

Jimmy nodded as if he understood.

"They knew his weakness," she said. "They were waiting in the closet."

Maybe it was *the pretty people*—maybe that was what she had said.

Jimmy asked her again who *they* were but she just ate her apple. Every bit of it, stem and seed.

"I've never seen a picture of your mother," Jimmy said.

"She comes on Sundays."

Jimmy waited.

"And I go there Mondays. When she comes here, I know the next day is Monday."

"What does she say about you being here?"

"We don't talk," Rosemary said.

"What does she say about you being here where they killed him?"

"That's what she doesn't talk about."

"What day is today?" Jimmy asked.

She got up out of her chair.

"Did you ever hear the record they were playing?" she asked, her face opening up a little, "Daddy and that woman?" She didn't wait for an answer, opened the front of a nightstand, an old humidor cabinet, and took out a 45 record in its original sleeve. She stepped over and put it on a turntable with a fat center post, a teenager's record player. It clicked, the arm moved over, it began.

It was Streisand's "People (Who Need People)."

"It was still playing, again and again, when the police looked in the window. They left it here. They had no idea how it fit in . . ."

They both listened to it. When it ended, it started again and Jimmy left her there.

AFTER DARK, ABOUT NINE, WHEN THE NEIGHBORS would all be inside with their prime-time TV or their murder books and their third or fourth drinks, she came out. The streetlight over the alleyway behind the house was out. She pulled the door closed behind her and started away, nothing in her hands. One of the cats came out of the broken kitchen window and watched her go from the sill.

The Number Six bus was crowded with domestics headed home from the beach neighborhoods, a funny name for the cleaning women since most of them were illegals. They carried plastic bags of the supplies they preferred, pungent disinfectants, Day-Glo green. Since it was the end of the day, they didn't talk to each other.

Rosemary Danko was in the sideways seat behind the driver. Jimmy sat in the last row, against the window. When she'd sat down, one of the cleaning women moved away. Rosemary knew Jimmy was there, had turned to see him at a stop where a man with no shirt had gotten off the bus. She had looked right at him. He thought for a second she was going to lift her hand to wave.

The bus took her all the way into Garden Grove, a twenty-minute trip straight east on Westminster. Away from the water, it got hotter by the mile. Jimmy could feel it coming through the glass of the closed window. Inland, it hadn't gotten any cooler when the sun went down. It was another reason the women didn't talk.

She got off at a big cross street and walked north two blocks and then over a block. When she passed through a section with the streetlight shot out or burned out, she quickened her pace.

It was a ground-floor unit in a building of ten apartments. She knocked at the door and waited for almost a minute before she knocked again. Then, impatient, sighing, she took the key from the black mailbox beside the door. She wiped her feet on the mat.

Estella Danko had died fourteen months ago.

Jimmy stood in the dining room at the round white Formica table and went through the mostly unopened mail. She had died somewhere out of the house. She had died suddenly. There were quarterly dunning letters from a nursing home but Estella Danko hadn't died there. She had worked as a nurse and had left without turning in her uniforms. Died inconsiderately, without giving them notice.

There were government letters referring to Rosemary. She was on disability. Her utilities for the apartment were being paid direct by some agency. With the death of her mother, she'd gotten a bigger check. She had been an L.A. Unified School District teacher, ninth and tenth grade math, a school in Diamond Bar. Her middle name was Marialinda. Rosemary Marialinda Danko.

Jimmy looked in on her. She had gone straight into one of the bedrooms, her mother's bedroom. She was watching television, sitting on the end of the stripped mattress. It was one of those dating shows. She looked over at Jimmy, waved him away.

In the living room he found a cabinet full of old pictures, the next best thing to living witnesses. He turned on a floor lamp and pulled it closer and sat on the end of the coffee table. There were boxes of photos, loose and in leather albums. The Dankos liked cameras.

There had just been the three of them. They'd had a house somewhere for most of the time, had lived in other apartments in the early years after a wedding in what looked like Rosarito Beach, down over the border on the way to Ensenada. Estella was Mexican. She had been a beauty but she was the size of a child.

Every picture except the wedding had the baby in it. And then the baby grew. There was one of Rosemary at four or five on a pony at the rides in Griffith Park, her smiling father sitting on the rail as she passed behind him staring straight ahead, a scared look on her little face.

Jimmy slipped it into the pocket of his shirt.

Almost every other picture of Danko had him beside one plane or another. There was a framed photo in fading colors of a four-place Cessna, red over white, Danko standing with his hand on the tip of the wing, the world headquarters of the Danko "Flying School" in half-focus in the background.

"Dancing Queen" was painted on the engine cowling.

Jimmy took that one, too.

And he found the picture of Estella Danko to take. It was from an open-air bar somewhere, sand on the floor and the beach in the background, probably down in Baja. Three blond girls, probably college kids, more *pretty people,* were grouped behind Bill Danko who sat on a silver beer keg, his legs open, wearing shorts and *hurraches,* his elbows on his knees, aviator glasses, a big grin on his face, a bottle of beer in his hand. Estella was off to one side, away from the others, not happy, as if the girls had waved her into the shot.

It was hard to imagine a .45 in the empty little hand at her side but not so hard to picture a murderous look in her eye.

There was a sound from the kitchen.

Rosemary stood in front of the microwave.

"Three zero zero," she said, more than once.

It dinged. She opened the door and took out a package of macaroni and cheese. She pulled back the covering and set it on a plate to cool. She held her fork in her hand and waited, like she was counting seconds in her head.

She did all right with numbers. She just didn't know what day it was. She had a broken sense of time and she didn't know who was dead and who wasn't anymore.

Jimmy felt a certain kinship.

IT WAS A ROUGH NIGHT ON THE STRIP, ODD AND ugly and edgy for some reason. Young men who'd all stripped off their shirts ganged in front of The Roxy, spilled out onto the sidewalks between a pair of shows for some metal band come round again. They were like natives on the banks of a river. Some of them were trying to get a fire going in a trash barrel to complete the picture. Ninety degrees at eleven o'clock and they're starting fires.

Jimmy rolled past, Streisand's "People" still looping in his head from the weird afternoon, making the scene all the stranger.

He slid in the CD his musician friend had made for him, the collection of disco music Chris thought he should be listening to. The first song was lush, symphonic, with a sexy chorus, women singing the same three words over and over. It was romantic, dramatic. It was soundtrack music, for the movie playing in the heads of twenty-somethings on the dance floor, overriding, at least for part of a Saturday night, their ordinary lives.

One of the Roxy natives jumped out from the others, slowly and deliberately flipped him off as he cruised past. Maybe the kid could hear the disco music.

Or maybe he just didn't like Fords. Jimmy was in the Mustang. After spending the early part of the night with Rosemary in the house in Garden Grove, he'd taken a cab back to Naples where he'd left the car and then driven up from Long Beach on Pacific Coast Highway, the slow way, trying to sort it out. Estella Danko was dead but that didn't make much difference to him, to the case. Now he'd *met* her. He even had her picture in his pocket. Dead now or not, there was a good chance she was the one who'd done the killing. Jealous, left-out wives pulled triggers in bedrooms all the time. D. L. Upchurch thought she had done it and he had brooded over all this more than Jimmy had or ever would.

She was five-foot-one.

And she wasn't her husband's Dancing Queen anymore.

So Jimmy thought he was getting closer to certainty, to an end to it, closing in on something he could take to Jean.

Your father didn't kill anybody. She did.

He'd gone by Jean's apartment. There was no answer downstairs, no lights in the penthouse. He still hadn't seen her or talked to her since the night they'd come upon Drew. He wondered how *gone* she was.

Jimmy thought he was closing in on certainty, but what he *didn't* understand was what this particular piece of old history had to do with Sailors. His tails were back, Lon and Vince, still in the subcompact Escort, almost bumping into him when he slowed.

And now there was another one.

At least this one had better taste in cars. He was in a black 745 iL BMW, smart because it blended in in most parts of L.A. better than a basic Ford. And this driver knew what he was doing, stayed two blocks back and turned off onto side streets just a half second before you really noticed he was there, making you think maybe you'd imagined it.

But Jimmy knew how to do this, too, and had caught a good look at the car twice, once on PCH and once when he was coming back down onto Sunset from Jean's.

It was then that he got a look at his face. When the driver knew he'd been seen, he'd turned into the space in front of a restaurant, had even gotten out to meet the valet, very cool. He was tall, skinny, in an expensive black suit, slicked-back hair. He was too far away, but maybe it was Boney M, the tall one with the long fingers from the rooftop of the Roosevelt.

Jimmy figured he'd never see the man again, though that didn't mean he wouldn't be there.

It was their mistake. If they'd stopped following him a week ago, he probably would have ended it by now, told Jean it was over, that there was nothing worth knowing that he could tell her. After the night in the canyon when they'd come upon the overturned Honda, everything in him had wanted to wrap up the case, tell her whatever he could tell her, and then see if there was any way to salvage things with her.

But they hadn't quit. They were back, following him, nosing around, keeping it alive, accomplishing the opposite of what they wanted, making *the black clear space where the answer was* a thing he could never turn away from now.

He looped around and cruised by Jean's a third time.

The lights were still out and this time he didn't go to the door. The song on the CD lasted all the way there and halfway back to his house down Sunset, the singer telling him she loved the nightlife but sounding a little sad, like she was trying to convince herself.

CHAPTER 13

IT WAS AN OLD LINE PRODUCER'S OFFICE, BAD ART, big furniture, a slab of chalk for a coffee table. Jean was alone, on the pink couch. She picked up a book, smiled when she read the spine. Behind the couch was a wall of photographs, the *Everybody-Knows-Me-Wall*, pictures spanning twenty years, marked by the changing hairstyles of Joel Kinser, who was in every one, his head an inch too close to the head of each famous actor or politician, Gerald and Betty Ford among them. So Kinser had spent a little time at the Betty Ford Center out in Rancho Mirage. It was a big club.

Jimmy was in one group shot, three or four nobodies, Joel and a star. It was recent. They all looked like themselves. But a few rows over was a picture from the past, Jimmy and Joel and an actress. Joel had a blown-out eighties look, from another time, but Jimmy didn't look much younger than now, much changed, unless you noticed a brightness in his eye then that now was gone, or at least dimmed.

Joel came in. He kissed Jean on the cheek. "I'm sorry," he said. A movie star out of the limelight lately was a step behind him.

"Do you know_____?"

"No." Jean extended her hand.

"This is Jean Kantke," Joel said. "We're in Mensa together."

Jean still had the book in her hand.

"Where did you find that?" Joel said. "I've been looking for it."

Jean handed it to him.

"Catullus," Joel said.

The fading star waited a moment, nodding, and then said, "I gotta roll outta here, Joel." He told Jean it was nice to meet her and left.

"Are you doing something with him?" Jean said when he had cleared the frame.

Joel leafed through his phone messages.

"Hollywood has two speeds," he said. " 'Screw you' and 'Yes, Master!' Is the commissary all right?"

There were only ten tables in the Executive Dining Room, blond chairs, skylights, a Hockney on the wall, waiters who *didn't* want to direct.

Joel nodded to a man taking a table alone across the dining room. The man gave back less.

Their food had just come.

"What did Jimmy do for you?" Jean said.

"Found an actress who didn't want to be found," Joel said. He was staring at his fish.

"Where did he find her?"

"Mexico."

"You aren't going to tell me who it was?" Jean said.

"_____. We were in the middle of shooting and suddenly she's gone. Tuesday, she's there. Wednesday, she's not. I put three other guys on it, regular guys on it. Nothing. Then Jimmy found her in like a day. How, I don't know. It took another day for him to go down there and talk her in. Following Monday, we're back rolling."

He stared at his fish.

"The picture never worked. We could never get the third act right. It did all right foreign. I always assumed Jimmy had a thing with her, but he said no."

"Look at this piece of salmon," he said in the same breath. (He pronounced the *L*.) "A little *parsimonious*, isn't it?"

"Try putting some salt on it," Jean said. "What else do you know about him?"

He poked at the piece of fish, as if it could change. "Fairly bright. Locked in a Peter Gunn kind of thing with his clothes, but he has taste."

"Has he ever been married?"

"Don't know. Is he gay? I don't know. So, I assume he's working for you. He took the job."

Jean nodded.

"And you want it to be something else."

"No . . ."

He waved the waiter over. "I'd like a bigger fish," he said and handed him his plate.

He looked at Jean. "That salt thing. Funny."

She waited for him to answer her questions.

"Everybody loves Jimmy," he said. "He works that Little Boy Lost thing. I could never pull that off."

"He's not lost," she said. "He knows exactly where he is. He just isn't telling."

"And this for you is a turn-on?"

Jean didn't answer.

"You know who his mother was, don't you?" Joel said.

DARREN PRICE DROVE UP JIMMY'S LONG GRAVEL driveway in a fifteen-year-old Mercedes convertible with a vandal's cut in the top patched with duct tape.

Jimmy was waiting for him on the steps that led up to the tall dark front door. It was the afternoon but he got the idea that the DJ hadn't been to sleep since his overnight shift. He got out of the Mercedes wearing the same velveteen exercise suit and white Capezio dance shoes from the other night.

Lloyd-the-Void stood with his mouth open, looking at the house. He looked back down the long driveway to the iron gates and then back at the house and the motor court and the four-bay garage. All four garage doors were open. In separate stalls were the black Porsche convertible, the Mustang, the yellow Dodge Challenger and in the last garage, covered by a tarp, something with high poking fins and bright wide whitewalls.

"Holy shit," Price said. "Your house has a *name?* I'm in the wrong business."

Jimmy took him inside, through the house, past the living room, into the office, the room with the chromed racks of security gear and electronic equipment.

"Holy shit," Price said again.

Jimmy sat behind the desk and put his feet up. He was barefoot. He was waiting for Price to get over the money around him and to say why he was here, why he'd called.

"You want anything?" Jimmy said.

"I want a house like this," Price said. "And four cars." He sat in the leather and chrome chair in front of the desk. He put his feet up, too, like Jimmy, like they were new best friends. "What's the one under the tarp?"

"I'm afraid to look," Jimmy said.

Since Price apparently wasn't going to start, Jimmy decided maybe *he'd* go first. "Did you ever see Bill Danko's wife at Big Daddy's?"

"He was married?"

"Yeah."

Price shook his head.

"Five-foot-one. Spanish."

The Xeroxes, the newspaper articles of the case were spread out on the desk. Jimmy slid a few papers around and found the picture of Estella Danko.

Price looked at it, handed it back. "I never saw her. Or didn't know I was seeing her if I did. I didn't even think about anybody being married. It wasn't about that."

"You said you remembered something," Jimmy said.

The kid Drew came into the room, looking like he just woke up. He stood a foot inside the doorway. He ran his hands through his hair, standing there, and then shook it out. He wore it in a long, shaggy skateboarder's cut.

"My hair stopped growing," Drew said.

Jimmy nodded.

Drew glanced at Darren Price, then walked out again.

Price tried for a second to fit this new piece into the Jimmy Miles puzzle, then gave up.

"Do you want to hear this or not?" Price said.

"Sure."

Price woke up a little more. "OK, I was telling this girl about how I was working with you on something, on the thing," he said.

Jimmy let that pass without comment.

"She wasn't even *born* then, but she said something that made me think of something."

Jimmy just looked at him. He liked him better in the middle of the night. He guessed that almost everyone did.

"Anyway. This girl, I told her about that time, what we talked about, and she said, 'Four girls wouldn't be friends.'"

Jimmy didn't have much of a reaction.

"The Jolly Girls," Price said, said it the same way he'd said it at the radio station, The *Jolly* Girls.

"OK."

"Then I remembered. *Michelle.*"

"The one who did the most drugs."

"Yeah. Did I tell you that?"

"Yes." Jimmy waited. "What about her?"

"Michelle hated Elaine—and, you know, *not* in that way girls are. *'I hate you!' 'I love you!' 'You are* so *my best friend!'* " He said it in a funny voice-over voice, good enough for a cartoon. "There at the end, Michelle really hated Elaine Kantke. It was real."

"Why?"

Price took a beat, knowing he had something.

"Bill Danko. Michelle liked Danko. I couldn't see what the attraction was with him but, anyway, they both liked him. And, *sorry Elaine,* Michelle saw him first."

"Maybe he was with both of them," Jimmy said.

"I don't think so. He was love-struck by Elaine from what I saw. He stopped dancing with Michelle. That means something, or meant something then."

Jimmy found the copy of the shot of the four Jolly Girls on the stools at the Long Beach Yacht Club.

"Which one was she?" he said.

Before he answered, Price said, "This was before Slip Tone, before they hooked up. You knew they were married, right? Michelle and Tone?"

Jimmy didn't. "When?"

"Right when he quit. To be a cop. And then she died, after like only a year."

"Died how?"

"Swimming. At Mothers' Beach. Right there in the Marina."

Price bounded out of his chair and came around and looked over Jimmy's shoulder at the picture, standing too close.

"The short one. That's why she *loved* platform shoes."

THERE WERE TOO MANY DEAD.

Coming back from the desert and the mountains, Jimmy thought it was pretty simple. He'd find Bill Danko's short little jealous wife. Maybe she'd be a nurse somewhere, estranged from her daughter, wondering where she was, and Jimmy would be able to tell her, after she'd let him see her guilt about the murders without ever exactly admitting it. But now the Estella Danko story had come and gone, felt like it anyway, like time-lapse film footage of a storm out over the desert, arising out of nowhere, building fast into something dark and big and full of heat lightning, and then dissolving away again to nothing, as quickly as it had come. Estella Danko was dead, past admitting anything, even with her eyes. And now there was Michelle. He wished he was driving across town to meet *her* now, wished she had a store somewhere or was a decorator or a lawyer or somebody's mother or a school administrator, straight-arrow and proper, even square, giving nobody in her life now any reason to suspect she'd once been a disco dolly in tall shoes with a tingling nose. But she was dead, too. He wasn't going to get the chance to look into her eyes either and ask about those old murders.

Sgt. Tom Connor coached a kids' soccer team. It was late in the day but there was still another hour of daylight left. They were practicing in a city park in Van Nuys. He came over to the sidelines as Jimmy stepped away from the yellow Dodge Challenger.

Walking up to him, Connor said, "What I like about soccer is that most of the fathers don't really know anything about the game." The kids kicking goals behind him were nine or ten. Even the goalie would laugh when they scored on him. "I think that's what they like about it, too. The boys, not the dads."

Connor went right to it. Jimmy had called him, filled him in on what he'd learned about Michelle Espinosa.

"Homicide detectives came in, but they didn't end up with anything," Connor said. "On paper, it was a drowning. She went out, pretty deep, out into the channel, in among the sailboats in the slips. There wasn't anybody around her. It was a little cold. Nobody else was in, all of them up on the beach with their kids, in the shallows or digging in the sand."

Jimmy knew there was something else.

"But . . ."

"But she was a swimmer and diver in school," Connor said. "USC on a scholarship. And it was a *marina*. It's not like there were waves or undertow or anything."

A ball came over. The cop kicked it back.

"What about drugs?"

"Supposedly she had cleaned up her act," Connor said. "She and Espinosa were married by then but he wasn't a cop yet."

And then he was a *dead* cop, Jimmy thought, somebody else he wasn't going to get to look in the eye.

"She was pregnant."

Connor let that hang in the air for a minute.

Mothers' Beach.

They both thought about the name.

"Maybe losing her was what made him want to be a cop."

There were too many dead.

"Did you check on the Kantke thing?" Jimmy said.

"I did. A guy's still alive who was the second lead detective on it."

"And . . ."

Connor shook his head.

"They had their killer. And they were good cops."

Jimmy thanked him, was ready to go.

"You think what?" Connor said. "This Michelle did it? Shot dead her ex and her ex-friend?"

"I don't know."

"And then, *what?* Someone drowns her for that?"

"I don't know," Jimmy said.

"You're forgetting something."

Jimmy waited.

"Jealousy wasn't that big around then," the cop said. "Remember? *If it feels good, do it.*"

"I think that was the sixties, Tom."

"The sixties was weed. The seventies was blow.

But same difference. *'Oops, I screwed your girlfriend. Sorry.' 'No problem.'* "

Jimmy nodded.

Connor said, "I guess there could have been some other motive."

"For which one?" Jimmy said. "For Michelle murdering them, or for someone murdering her?"

CHAPTER 14

JIMMY RANG THE BELL DOWNSTAIRS AT JEAN'S
and waited.

Nothing.

Just as he turned to go, it buzzed open.

He rode the elevator up. It was unlocked right into
the penthouse, opening onto a foyer, the living room
beyond. Jean wasn't there, wasn't in the living room
anyway. The sun was just going down and the light
looked like tea, made the room look like something
out of an old magazine. The elevator doors closed behind him. It was quiet enough to hear the gears and
pulleys as it took itself all the way down to the first
floor.

"Where are you?" Jimmy said.

She didn't answer.

On the desk were a dozen books about Hollywood, *new* books, open. He got the idea they were meant to be seen. He clicked on a light. There was his mother's face under his fingers, black-and-white, high-glam portrait more shadow than light. The other books were opened to other pictures of Teresa Miles, with a famous French actor, with a famous American director, slant-back wooden chairs on a round rock beach somewhere in the South of France. She had close-cut blond hair, eyes that looked away in every shot, that very commercial, very exploitable look that said *Save me* and *I'm too much for you* in the same moment.

There was a Xerox of a fan magazine article from the late sixties with the headline:

TERESA MILES' TRAGIC BREAKDOWN

and a paparazzo's photo of the actress coming out of one of the bungalows at the Chateau Marmont, shaken, eyes on the ground.

In the background was a teenager in bellbottoms.

There was a reprint of the newspaper obituary:

MILES' DEATH REVEALED

Fifties "New Wave" film star Teresa Miles died two weeks ago in Twenty-Nine Palms, Calif., it was revealed Saturday. She was thirty-eight. Cause of death was listed as "emphysema."

Miss Miles' former manager Len Schine

confirmed that the actress, star of such films as *Marina* and *Morning at the Window* (*Le Matin a la Fenetre*), was buried at an undisclosed location following a private service.

She had no survivors.

Miss Miles, twice nominated for an Academy Award, two years ago suffered a nervous breakdown and retired from . . .

Jimmy tossed the obit into the desk. It was covered with papers and books. It was like his desk only *he* was the subject under investigation.

He heard something above him.

He stepped out onto the patio. Jean was up on the sloped roof overlooking the deck, sitting with her knees drawn up to her, with a glass of wine, looking out at the pastel haze.

The way up was to step onto the low wall around the patio and then walk along it to where you could step up onto the roof.

Jimmy joined her, silent for a long time.

"I came by a couple times. Called."

"I know," she said.

"I'm sorry. I mean, if I hurt you."

"Is that what you think happened?"

She kept her eyes on the streaked sky. It looked like it had been painted by a child.

"I don't know. I'm only inside *me*," Jimmy said.

She looked at him, for the first time since he sat beside her. And she smiled.

"What happened to that kid?"

"He's staying at my house."

She waited for him to say more.

"He's all right," Jimmy said.

That was all he was going to say about it. An ambulance screamed up Sunset. They listened until it faded.

"Why the books? In the living room."

"Just trying to understand," Jean said.

"Understand what?"

"You. This."

He wondered what all she meant by *this*.

"It isn't supposed to happen, is it?" she said. "Getting involved this way."

"I don't know," he said. "It happened. I'm happy."

"You don't look happy."

"It's my facial structure," Jimmy said.

She stood. She offered him her glass of wine.

"You look like her," Jean said.

He took the glass of wine, took a sip. It was as warm as the air.

"I remember what you told me in my office," she began, "that first day, that maybe it wasn't always better to know everything."

"You *can't* know everything so it doesn't really matter."

"I don't care about the murders anymore," she said firmly. "I don't want to know. I don't need to know."

"The woman in the house is Bill Danko's daughter," Jimmy said. "Her name is Rosemary."

"I don't care."

"She was nine or ten when he was killed. Her mother died a year or so ago. Maybe that pushed her over the edge, sent her looking for the house in Naples."

"I want this to end," Jean said. "This is my choice. I don't need to know any more."

"I don't think your father did it. Your mother was probably just in the wrong place with the wrong guy. There's a woman who may have done it, one of her friends. Actually, there were *two* women who may have done it. Bill Danko had a wife."

"Stop."

"There's some link to now, to today."

"Stop it."

"To the people who run things. But I don't know why."

"*Stop!*" Her fists were clenched.

But he wasn't finished. He wanted to *tell her.* He wanted her to know *all* of it.

But he stopped himself.

SHE WANTED TO GET OUT, TO COOL OFF, TO RIDE somewhere, so they were on the streets of Hollywood in the yellow Challenger. It was after nine and still hot. They rode out Sunset, east, into East L.A. Jimmy pulled up into the corner lot where there was a Tommy's burger stand, the original Tommy's. A *paletero,* a Mexican ice cream man with his *triciclo,* a cart on rubber wheels, was supplying dessert for the crowd sharing the white-painted picnic tables. Jimmy bought Jean a cup of shaved ice doused in blood-red watermelon syrup so sweet it made your teeth hurt.

They doubled back on Sunset Boulevard in East
L.A. The traffic was heavy but easy going. A real-life
lowrider came past them in the other lane, bass notes
thumping, echoing off the faces of the storefronts and
second-story apartments that made the street a canyon.
Maybe everyone was just trying to cool off, nowhere
to go, to forget about what they would have to remember tomorrow.

Jean looked out the side window, a girl on her
front steps, reading a book by streetlight. They were
on Franklin now, one edge of Hollywood, in a neighborhood of single houses with no yards, sidewalks
right up to the windows, rental houses, Russian fam-
ilies in this block, and a few busted actors.

"Who was it?" Jean said, still looking out the window. "Which friend of Mother's?"

Jimmy thought, *No one can look away. Everyone
has to* know.

"Michelle. Michelle Simmonds. She became
Michelle Espinosa."

"One of The Jolly Girls."

"Yes."

He told her about the *five-foot-one* angle.

"Have you talked to her?"

"She's dead a long time."

Jean nodded, still not looking at him. She thought
that was all there was. She felt strong for asking.

"I think someone killed her," Jimmy said. "But it
wasn't down as a murder. She drowned. In the Marina."

Jean turned and he saw the sudden hurt on her face,

the *world-pain.* Jimmy kept forgetting that most people didn't see the world the way he did, the way he had for most of his years, full of treachery and death and dark motives. Most people thought almost everyone was good.

"Maybe I'm wrong," he said. "I have to watch myself."

"What do you mean?" She didn't feel so strong anymore.

"Always thinking the worst," he said. "People die all the time. Natural causes."

They had passed into Los Feliz, a richer neighborhood of thirties and forties apartment buildings on streets sloping up toward the low hills, the backside of the Hollywood Hills below Griffith Park.

After a ways, Jean said, "You said this was somehow connected to other people. Who?"

Like an answer, there were headlights in the mirror.

They were back. They'd been behind them all the way from before Tommy's, through four or five rights and lefts, a white Taurus, two heads haloed by the lights behind them.

Lon and Vince had traded in the Escort for a Taurus.

Now they were closing. Fast.

Jean looked over at him, saw him with his eyes on the mirror.

"Put on your seatbelt," Jimmy said.

She turned around to look. "What?"

On the next side street, a second car, the black BMW 745 iL, waited at a stop sign—with a man in a peacoat and watch cap standing beside it.

"What's the matter?" Jean said. "Who are they?"

Jimmy gunned it and the Challenger streaked away, blowing past the BMW on the side street, leaving the Taurus to try to catch up.

She put her seatbelt on.

The man in the peacoat next to the BMW stepped back and the driver pulled it into gear and spun into a U-turn and roared up the hill.

Jimmy was already two blocks away. He'd taken a hard left off of Franklin, onto Vermont, rolling up the rising straight street with the Taurus closing on him.

"Who is it?" Jean said.

"They've been following us."

"What do they want?"

He was very cool. "We'll lose them up here," he said, as if it was an answer.

The speedometer popped up to seventy. Jimmy went through a red light at a cross street called Ambrose and the Taurus stayed with him.

But didn't make it.

A Jeep coming fast through the intersection tagged the left rear panel of Lon and Vince's Taurus and sent it spinning, a pair of quick 360s in the middle of the X.

Jimmy watched it in the mirror, the hit and the spinout. He was already at the next corner. This time the light was green.

But then the black BMW came at him from the intersecting street, Los Feliz Boulevard, trying to T-bone him, or at least be there when somebody else did.

Jimmy stood on it and cranked the wheel, sliding

sideways to avoid him, then sped up the hill as the BMW skidded to a stop inches away from the nose of a fat beige Lexus.

The two Sailors in the Taurus recovered and went after Jimmy, front wheels smoking.

The BMW had stalled out. The driver lit it up again, backed it into a hard J and went after them, fishtailing for a second before the big powerful car got into the groove.

The three cars—Challenger, Taurus, BMW—blew into Griffith Park on a straightaway on a boulevard through a canopy of trees, blew *one, two, three* past a sign nobody had time to read:

OBSERVATORY GOLFCOURSE ZOO MERRY-GO-ROUND

The Taurus was falling back, outgunned. Jimmy was at eighty, leading the thing. Jean sat with her hands on the dash in front of her, like it was a roller coaster.

The first climbing left into the higher parklands was coming up fast. Just as they went into the hard curve, the BMW came up on their right, door to door. Jimmy dropped down a gear and the Challenger and the BMW took it together, mirror to mirror.

Jimmy looked over to see the driver. The BMW eased off and fell back in behind him, then rolled over onto Jimmy's left, moving up. They went like that through a pair of *esses,* a chicane. Jimmy would surge ahead for a moment, but the BMW would gain in the corners.

"I might have brought the wrong car," he said.

Jean was wide-eyed.

"*Stop, please,*" she said.

The two cars banged fenders as the BMW driver tried to shove them into the outside rail. Jimmy got his first good look at him, but didn't have time to process it.

The Taurus was back.

The three cars came around a corner, three wide, and there was the Griffith Observatory, lit up, green-domed, as sudden as an explosion. The turn was a hairpin and the screeching tires made people look, tourists and teenagers crossing over from the parking lot.

The BMW sideswiped a van and spun into the parking lot and the Taurus rear-ended it. They were stopped.

Jimmy pulled away.

It was all downhill now, a straightaway down the backside of the low mountains. He wasn't slowing.

Jean looked back.

"*Stop,*" she said. "*They're gone.*"

But as soon as she'd said it, she saw the two pairs of headlights coming after them. She looked at him, at the look in his eyes. He was all the way into it, given over to it. It was frightening.

They roared past two men standing close by a tree. Ahead was a cluster of cars, lights out, pairs of men leaning against the fenders, others sitting atop picnic tables, eyes bright dots in the Challenger's headlights.

Jimmy braked hard and stopped. Stopped dead.

"What are you doing?" Jean said.

"Get out. I'll come back for you."

She didn't want to get out.

"Get out."

Jean opened her door.

"It's all right," Jimmy said, but he was still that same man, changed and frightening and too full of purpose.

She got out and he sped away, the power slamming the passenger door closed.

Jimmy looked up in the mirror at the paired men and Jean, a couple of them stepping toward her.

Ahead he had a clean straight run through a corridor of tall, dusted eucalyptus, a bridle path on one side. The speedometer, dim and green, touched a hundred. The Challenger was made for this.

He smiled.

In the moment he thought *he* was made for this, too. He shifted up a gear. The engine sucked in boost. Ahead, the mouth of a gentle curve. Jimmy barely slowed as he steered into it.

Horses. *Horses.*

Suddenly there were *horses* alongside the road, six horses, empty saddles, tied together and led by a mounted cowboy. All in the same second, the cowboy turned two silver reflecting eyes toward the car howling down the straightaway at him and the last animal in the line reared and leapt sideways into the road, and then the next in front of it followed.

Jimmy yanked the wheel. The Challenger skidded and smoked and screeched and then slammed against the stout trunk of a eucalyptus.

He was thrown against the window, knocked out.

The first minute passed.

The Hemi engine raced, roaring, then died.

The horses whinnied wildly, all of them rearing now, shredding the air with their front hooves in the wash of the Challenger's headlights still burning through the stirred up dust.

The BMW was first to arrive. The driver got out.

The cowboy fought to gather and control the six horses and himself.

"He was—"

"Yeah," the BMW driver said, cool and calm. "Go to the phone. Get some help." She had an accent.

The cowboy did as he was told and let go of the spooked horses and pulled himself into the saddle of his own horse and rode away down the path. The trail horses tried to scatter but were still lashed together and pulled in different directions so that none of them escaped.

The wrecked, smoking Taurus arrived. Lon and Vince. They got out, pumped up, ready to hurt someone but Jimmy was bloodied and looked dead.

Another minute passed.

A black Lincoln Town Car pulled up. Lon and Vince straightened, almost came to attention.

The backdoor opened.

Jimmy had started to come around. He was bleeding from a cut on the side of his face. He tried to focus, the headlights, the images through the shattered glass, through his own blood which streaked the window: the cars, one white, two black, *figures moving*.

He saw the red-haired man with the long fingers, Boney M, get out of the back of the Lincoln Town Car. And, with the door open, another man in the backseat, under the spot of the reading light, a big man, familiar.

Then someone was walking toward him.

It was the BMW driver, the man in the expensive suit, slicked-back hair.

But it was a woman in a dark expensive suit.

It was the German girl from the Evergreen Club, from the dark beer, from the kisses in his cabin. He even heard her voice, her accent, as she said something to Lon and Vince.

But then things got darker and faded out.

CHAPTER 15

THE SUN WAS JUST UP, THE AIR SMOKY WITH A warm fog.

Jimmy was backed against a tree, sitting in the eucalyptus leaves and brown grass. It looked like deep woods. You couldn't see the road from here, or anything else. It was like he was in Australia, or wherever it was that eucalyptus trees came from.

There was blood, dry and almost black, all around him, so much of it that he wondered how it could all be his.

He thought of Jean. He got to his feet.

Everything ached. One eye was sealed shut some way he didn't want to see. A finger was broken. A few teeth felt loose.

"Let me ask you something," Drew said. *"Can I die? I mean, again?"*

"You can get hurt," Jimmy said, *"bad, but you won't die."*

"Even if like a bullet went through my head, I wouldn't die."

"No."

"If I was shredding down a mountain and pulled a full-on Sonny Bono, I wouldn't die."

"No. You could get messed up, bad, but you wouldn't die."

They'd pulled him out of the car and dragged him away and worked him over, Lon and Vince and maybe even the German woman, hoping for maximum mayhem, hoping to mess him up good, to try to make their point another way.

Or maybe they did it just because they enjoyed it.

He came out of the trees and found the straightaway road and then the scarred trunk that told him where he'd crashed, the skidmarks on the pavement and the furrows in the leaf-covered ground of the bridle path.

The yellow Dodge was long gone, but his shoe was there.

And the scars from the hooves of the trail horses.

He thought maybe he'd dreamed them.

He found the tracks where the black Lincoln had stopped and then turned around to go back up the straightaway. Somewhere in the fog, he'd decided the big familiar man glimpsed in the backseat had to be Harry Turner.

But maybe he'd dreamed him.

* * *

JIMMY AND ANGEL WENT FIRST TO JEAN'S APART-
ment.

Angel waited behind the wheel of his truck, the
one with the blue moon over the city and the woman's
eyes airbrushed on the tailgate.

There was no answer. Jimmy came back and got in.

"She wasn't there?" Angel said.

Jimmy shook his head. Angel pulled out.

"She had a phone," Jimmy said after a minute.
"She probably had somebody come get her."

He called her office. She was in a meeting.

Jimmy tossed the phone onto the seat between
them. Angel looked at him.

"She's all right."

Angel stopped at the bottom of the hill. "Where do
you want to go?"

"Home. I'll get a car."

They rode along in silence another four or five
blocks, then Jimmy said, "Maybe you can run down
the Dodge, take it to the shop, see if you can put it
right. I guess the cops towed it."

Angel nodded. "How bad is it?"

"Bad."

Angel turned right. "You might want to get cleaned
up a little, too."

Jimmy dropped the visor on his side and got his
first look at himself in the mirror. He flipped the visor
back up. It was better not to know.

"So what's happening with this lady?" Angel said.

"I hadn't talked to her since that night we picked up the kid," he said. "She was spooked then. I don't know what she's thinking now. Maybe she's figured it out."

"I doubt that," Angel said. "She's still around."

Jimmy fell silent.

"It was the same Sailors?" Angel said.

"The goofy guys and the leader from the thing up on the roof of the Roosevelt. And there's something else going on. There's a man in the middle of it, too, not a Sailor but maybe a kindred spirit."

"Who?"

"His name is Harry Turner. The lawyer behind the scenes in the murder trial. He put a tail on me. He might have been there last night."

Jimmy wished again he'd gotten a better look at him, at the big man in the backseat of the Lincoln. *If I could be sure.* It was how Jimmy knew he had passed over into the land of the secret, the territory of the unknown that always came in the middle of the case, when he heard himself saying, again and again, *If I could be sure.*

"She was there, the tail. In a 745 BMW. She's German. She's not a Sailor either. Neither of them are."

"She's the one ran you into a tree?"

"No, I did that all by myself."

"How do you know this guy hired her?"

"I saw him in the morning and she was there the same night. Up in Idyllwild."

"Tailing you?"

After a moment, Jimmy said, "Yeah, very close."

Jimmy thought about her lips, about the way she'd put her hands over his eyes when she kissed him. He didn't have to wonder what he'd said to her, what he might have revealed. He hadn't said much of anything. And neither had she. She was good. In that bad kind of way.

Harry Turner had read him right. Jimmy remembered Rosemary Danko's line, *They knew his weakness*.

"Why does this guy still care about some old settled murder case?"

"That I don't know," Jimmy said.

They rode along another block.

"God had his hand on you," Angel said.

Jimmy nodded, never looking at him. They were on Sunset now, going past Tower Records yellow and red and then The Whisky and then the Hustler store full of tourist shoppers. In daylight. *Was there any more secular place on the face of the earth?*

Jimmy had a decision to make, to go toward it or away from it.

"So what are you going to do now?" Angel said, just as Jimmy was wondering the same thing.

CHAPTER 16

SOME THINGS LOOK LIKE WHAT THEY ARE. JIMMY and Jean were heading north on California 1, the coast road, approaching the southern end of Big Sur. This was the edge of a continent and it looked it. The road was just now climbing into the high section, coming up off of the grasslands and cattle ranches past Hearst Castle and Cambria. The massive mountains, long and brown and only crowned with evergreens at the highest reaches where the fog was, broke off jagged into the ocean, ending big.

It had cooled off as soon as they'd rolled over the mountain from Thousand Oaks into Camarillo, Oxnard and then Ventura. They had the windows down. If you knew what to listen for, what to separate out, you could hear the wind off the ocean, singing, constant, blowing through the dull leaves and the slick red trunks of the manzanita covering the foothills.

Jimmy dropped it down into second as he steered into the first tight climbing curve. They were in the Mustang. He went in hotter than he could have, the C-force snugging him into the bucket seat. At the first switchback, there was already a hundred-foot drop-off to the rocks below and the very blue water.

Jean looked over at him for a long moment, as if the look and the time were needed before she said something, but she didn't say anything, she just studied him. When he'd come to her office just before noon, he'd told her that she should get away, that she should go off to hide someplace. She'd said no. Then he called it something else and she'd said yes. In the end, it turned into this, going north with no set destination, no time frame, the two of them. She'd come straight from the office. She was wearing a suit.

He was wearing a clean white shirt and a clean white splint over his ring finger on his right hand, the hand resting on the gearshift. He was bruised and butterfly-bandaged, now with two cuts on his head, over his eyes.

She was still looking at him. Anyone else would have turned to look at her.

"It's good to get out of the city," she said.

"What do you want me to tell you?" Jimmy said.

Now he looked over at her.

He kept surprising her. Being with him meant things moving at odd speeds, sometimes coming out of nowhere, sometimes *not* coming when they were expected. And only now was she beginning to be able to read his tone. His abruptness meant only that he was ahead of her.

She could have asked him what she really wanted to know, what she *suspected* about him, about this, but she didn't. The answer, if he'd given it, would have brought her all the way into it, into an idea she thought she might not be able to accept. Not yet. Do you ask a question when the answer might be that the world is not what you've always thought it to be, that everyone else thinks it to be? That there is something in between what you believed were two absolutes, *the* two absolutes, that the dead, some of them, are somehow here?

"What happened after you put me out of the car?"

"I crashed, went home." He enjoyed his joke even if she couldn't.

The two-lane road was rising so steeply Jimmy double-clutched and downshifted into first. The engine and the gearbox sang a warm low note. On the shoulder on the opposite lane was the first of the Big Sur hikers, shorts, tanned legs with braided calf muscles, a day pack, a wide floppy hat. He was in his sixties. He carried a gnarled walking stick that came up to his chest and he kept his pace even as the path angled up under him.

"I came by, where the car was," Jean said. "My assistant came and got me. We drove on down. I saw your car smashed against the tree. There was a police car there and a tow truck and a man on a horse, but nobody else."

He didn't say anything.

"The men in the two cars came right past me. They must have been there when you crashed."

"They pulled me out."

"What'd they do?"

"Dumped me in another part of the park."

"Who were they?" she said.

He looked at her. "It's probably about another case, something out of the past."

He wasn't going to say anything else about who they were. Jean rolled up her window. It was almost cold.

She waited a beat.

"Why didn't they kill you?" she said.

Jimmy looked at her. Maybe she *was* going to ask it. She'd seen Drew walking away from the turned-over Accord. Maybe she'd also seen his bloodied crushed body in the backseat as they drove away on down the hill. Maybe she'd read the papers the next day. That night and afterward she hadn't asked the right questions.

And she was afraid, but not as afraid as she should be.

Why was that?

She knew more than she was letting on.

"They were just trying to scare me off," Jimmy said.

"Did they?" she asked.

It was a good question.

"I think *I* know enough right now," he said.

It was a good answer.

After a minute, she said, "We seem to take turns trying to talk each other out of this."

He didn't say anything for another five minutes as the road climbed higher and then leveled off, tracing with every turn and switchback the fingers of land that broke off above the ocean.

That was another way he was different. He could say nothing.

THERE WAS A GAS STATION, A PULL-OFF RIGHT AF-ter a blind turn. The gas was thirty cents a gallon more than it had been twenty miles behind them but everyone stopped anyway. It was the first place to get out, stretch, and let the full view fill your head. There was a sleek tour bus four shades of purple, with a glass front, top to bottom. Germans. All of them were out of the bus, smoking. Gulls floated overhead, facing out to sea, staying in the same spot by riding the updraft off the cliff face, angled heads watching the tourists below, occasionally calling with a cry that sounded unsettlingly like screeching tires.

Jimmy topped off the tank and cleaned the windshield. He kept an overnight bag in the back, one in every car. He unzipped it and took out a soft Patagonia shell, a pullover. He put it on. The heat of L.A. was far behind.

One of the Germans came over to admire the Mustang. He walked around it, careful to keep a respectful distance. He nodded at the hatchback vents high on the rear quarter panel, the "gills," then went to the front and squatted before the shark's mouth grill, as if to see what it would look like swallowing you whole.

He stood up. *"Bullitt,"* he said.

Jimmy nodded.

The man smiled and made an up and down motion with his hand, like a porpoise diving and surfacing in the surf, the "Bullitt" Mustang flying up and over the streets of San Francisco.

Jimmy nodded. *"Ich versuche zu, zu mein Mustang auf dem Boden behalten,"* he said. *"I try to keep my Mustang on the ground."*

Jean was in the little store. She took a Martinelli's sparkling apple juice from the cooler, twisted it open and drank it while she walked the aisles. She picked up a bag of trail mix called "Big Sur Sunshine" and a candy bar, looked through the rack of T-shirts and sweats and found a hooded sweatshirt with a minimum of decoration. She got a few more things and went to the register. On a shelf behind the clerk was a flock of souvenir ceramic seagulls floating over redwood blocks on wire stalks. When the door opened, the draft made them dance.

Jimmy came in to pay for the gas.

"Do you want anything?" Jean said.

Jimmy saw her things on the counter. There was a toothbrush and toothpaste.

"No."

"And the gas," Jean said to the woman behind the register and handed her a credit card.

"And this," Jimmy said. He took an atomic fireball from the bowl on the counter.

They drove on through the afternoon. Another fifty miles and they passed into the first of the massive trees the drive was also famous for. Orange poppies flashed in bright sunny patches where the road cuts were. A rocky creek ran alongside the road, glimpsed now and then through breaks in the green. The air had that evergreen smell that made the whole day seem like morning. The trees grew taller, closing in on the swath of bright blue overhead.

Then the light began to change, and quickly.

Just in time, the road broke back out into the open, to the coastline, and they stopped at the first motel.

The room was paneled with redwood, diagonal. Jimmy came in alone, left the door open behind him. He tossed the overnight bag onto the bed. He opened the drapes, slid open the sliding glass door. The wing of rooms was on a pad high above the surf, a hundred yards above the rocks and the water, but the glass door was still grayed with ocean spray. There was an hour or so of daylight left.

In among the trees, it would already be dark.

Jimmy cracked the seal on a bottle of water and lay on the bed with his head against the bag. He looked at the redwood ceiling, the redwood beams, the redwood walls. People came here for the big, tall, indomitable redwoods, to literally put their arms around them, put their cheeks against them, and they also wanted their rooms and their restaurants paneled with rough-sawn dead redwood.

He looked out the open sliding door. There was a patch of grass and a pair of white plastic chairs and then a row of cypresses at the cliff's edge.

Cypresses.

Jean came in. She carried a paper bag, another raid on a gas station store. She emptied it of bottles of juice and sunblock, a bag of sunflower seeds, sweatpants to match her sweatshirt and a pair of pink canvas shoes she'd never wear at home.

"Look," she said. She lifted out a cheap tape player. And a cassette tape. "Reggae." She said it with an exclamation point.

Jimmy sat up against the headboard, watched her as she fit the C batteries into the machine and then went to work on the stretch-wrap around the cassette.

She said, "In the gift shop they had tapes of 'Sounds of the Sea' and 'Sounds of the Big Trees.' *Relaxation* tapes." She slotted the cassette into the machine.

"No Woman No Cry," she half sang, before it began.

"It bothered you that I said you weren't the type who drives around the block to hear a song on the radio," Jimmy said.

"I hardly ever think about it," Jean said.

She smiled and the music started, a crack of a high hat and then a rolling rhythm. It wasn't "No Woman No Cry," but a song that began:

I don't want to wait in vain for your love . . .

But neither of them thought the song was about them, or at least about this. She turned it up and fiddled with the bass.

From the very first time I rest my eyes on you,
my heart says follow through . . .

"I got two rooms," Jimmy said.

She didn't say anything, went into the bathroom
and changed into her new sweatpants and cheap pink
shoes. When she came out, she smiled at him and
walked past him out the sliding door to see if she
could see the water.

She went all the way out to the edge. She turned
and looked back at him through the open door, happy.

SHE TALKED HIM INTO TAKING THE RAGGED PATH
zigzagging down the cliff-face to the rocks and the
water. It took thirty minutes down, from the warning
sign at the top to the sweet little cove and improbable
beach below perfectly littered with driftwood, and almost an hour back up, the last half in the dark with
Jimmy going ahead and Jean holding his shirttail and
laughing.

They drank a bottle of Liebfraumilch over dinner
at the seafood place next to the motel and then another. They took what was left in their glasses out to
the cliff's edge and listened to the wind and the surf
far below that they couldn't see except when the
biggest waves blew out white against the rocks.

Jimmy pulled back the cover on the bed.

"Can we leave the sliding glass door open?" he
asked.

It was chilly, but she nodded.

The lights were out. The moonlight lit the walls. He realized what the bias-cut paneling on the walls had reminded him of when he'd first come into the room: recording studios. There was a time when they all had walls that looked like this, diagonal redwood paneling. He'd spent hours in those rooms.

"People come to look at the trees and then sleep in redwood-paneled rooms," Jimmy said.

"And come to the ocean and eat seafood," Jean said. She was drunker than he was. She put on a funny voice. " 'Let's go someplace beautiful—and eat it!' "

There was a silence. She kissed him. He touched her neck. Her breath in his face was sweet and warm, the last drink of the night.

"*You proceed at your own risk,*" she said, laughing too much.

HE WAS UP EARLY, BEFORE THERE WAS LIGHT. HE sat in a chair and watched her sleeping. It had been a while since he'd been with a woman. As he watched her, as he listened to her breathe, he felt sorry for himself. It had been a while for that, too.

He showered. After he shaved, he dried his face and looked at himself in the mirror. The sunblock Jean bought was on the counter, a pink bottle, sunblock for kids, *no more tears*. He squeezed a white circle of it into his palm, rubbed his hands together, spread it across his forehead, nose and cheeks. The smell of it hit him, summers on the beach or on a sailboat, way back. That smell and the memories it brought with it, the Liebfraumilch last night, *Mother's Milk,* the cypresses, this road into Carmel and Monterey—he knew already what the day was going to be about.

And wished he'd gone south instead of north.

Two hours later, he was on Point Lobos. There was a thin fog. Jimmy stepped out onto the point. Here the cypresses were gnarled, arthritic, almost bare but still alive, their roots reaching down to find unlikely nourishment in cracks and crevices in the rock. Lace lichen bearded the branches of understory trees. Cypress Cove and Pinnacle Cove were to his right, Bluefish Cove beyond. There were prettier places all around him, where the trees were fuller, where there was more color, but this was where he'd stood with his mother all those years ago.

He was sixteen. An hour earlier, in the car, after she'd gotten out, as he sat listening to the radio, he'd laid a tab of acid on his tongue.

"It's a shame to shoot color," Teresa Miles had said.

She had a Leica on a leather strap around her neck. On her, it looked like jewelry. Her hair had just been cut short and she kept running her fingers through it, what was left of it. She was flying away in a week for a movie. She wore a thin sweater that buttoned up the middle, buttons made of abalone. She had perfect breasts, full for a woman as thin as she was, and always wore French bras that offered them up with a little less self-consciousness than Playtex or Maidenform. It was another thing Jimmy resented about her, the way his friends looked her over when she stepped into the room, and the way she pretended not to notice.

"It doesn't matter," Jimmy said. He leaned against a cypress. His mother was out in the open. It was overcast, a world of grays. "It's going to look like black and white anyway."

"No, it won't," she said. "It won't have the *drama* of black and white!"

"Drama." Jimmy repeated her word.

"Why don't you play your guitar?" she said. "Get it out of the car. Play me one of your songs."

No. Because you asked me to.

Nothing was happening. Jimmy wondered if the acid was bad, or not acid at all, a trick played on a rich kid in the lot behind The Troubadour.

But then a rock flared at his feet and then another.

She brushed his hair out of his eyes. It was 1967. His hair was long, as long as The Beatles' and The Beatles' was getting longer with each LP.

She walked away across the rocks.

He'd been up all night and she didn't know it, had come back at four or five from hanging out at Clover. It was the recording studio on Santa Monica Boulevard in Hollywood, a low-cost place, one main room and a booth for vocals, the control room, an "artists' lounge" with a pinball machine, which was just the first skinny room you came into off the dirty street. A singer/songwriter had worked all night on one track. Nobody. Jimmy knew the producer, who was older than sixteen but just a kid, too. It was that time when hits could come out of anyplace, any*body*, so almost everyone was cutting tracks and getting paid for it.

And The Beatles were on Blue Jay Way.

"Come here!" his mother said, her voice bright and theatrical.

Below the point, in a small cove that had no name, out past the shore-break where the water rose and fell predictably, gently, four or five sea otters rafted among the swirling canopies of giant kelp, on their backs.

"See what they're doing?"

They're beating their chests.

"They swim down under the kelp and find a perfect flat rock and then a clam or an oyster or even an abalone and then they come back up to the surface and roll over and then pound away on their little rock until the shellfish cracks open and they can eat it."

She held his hand, like he was six. "They used to say, until just a few years ago, that what separated Man and the lower animals was that only Man used *tools*. They don't say that anymore, but that's what they taught us in school, probably you, too. But I always knew it was wrong because I knew about this."

Tools. Could this get any more stupid?

She pulled him to her, put their hands behind her back. Her breast was against him. Her perfume had its hands around his throat. He loved her so much and, even now, he felt like she was already gone.

He let go, pulled away from her.

"So what do they say separates us now?" Jimmy said.

"I don't know," she had said.

A cormorant screeched overhead and Jimmy looked over at Jean, a hundred yards away, kneeling next to a rock in her pink canvas shoes.

Jimmy looked back down at the cove. The *selfsame* cove.

Back at the motel, the sign warning guests of the liabilities of the trail down to the beach had said more than, *You proceed at your own risk.* It also said, with an odd stiffness, as if the owners were Swiss or Austrian, *Be advised that the return is more difficult than the descent.*

THEY WENT INTO CARMEL FOR A LATE LUNCH. THERE was more wine. For some reason, Jean was under a cloud and not saying much.

Jimmy didn't really know her but he blamed it on Carmel. He'd never liked the town. It was too relaxed, or relaxed for the wrong reasons. There was too much money here, or too much money too far removed from the labor that produced it. Carmel always seemed to him to have too many retired airline captains and their flight attendant wives, too many personal injury lawyers in their forties who'd had a wonderful tragedy walk into the office one day, the kind that meant more than just another Porsche, that meant *freedom* money. But, as it turned out, here it was only the freedom to fret over the lightness of the pasta or the year of the wine or the elasticity of the skin of the person across the table from you. Most of them didn't even play golf. They just "lived well" and repeated too often that line about revenge.

Jean put her knife and fork across her plate. She ran her fingers through her hair, fluffed it out, like his mother had in his memory, and leaned back, her legs crossed at the ankles under the table. She smiled at him, the way you have to the day after you make love in a motel, if you haven't split already. She had bought clothes at a shop a few doors down from the restaurant, had changed in the dressing room, a silk dress the color of the tarnish on a bell, or the lace lichen they'd just left on Point Lobos. Whether it was the dress or the light filtered through the oaks on the patio, her green eyes looked blue. Blue and sad.

Or maybe she was just hungover.

"Was that where you and your mother were, the memory you told me about when we were talking about perfume?"

"Yes."

"How old were you?"

Of course he couldn't tell her.

"I don't know," he said.

Fifteen or sixteen. Sixteen. It was early in the summer, 1967. The Doors' first album had just come out.

"I looked at *City of Light* the other night," she said.

City of Light was the movie Teresa Miles went off to shoot the week after the day on Point Lobos.

Jimmy wondered again what she knew, how much she knew.

"How many of her movies have you seen?" he said.

"I think they were called *films*."

Jean smiled. Her eyes had gone back to green again.

"All of them," Jean said. "I'm a fan. Now."

A waiter came, asked if they wanted coffee. They didn't. Jimmy ordered a crème brulee.

"We'll share it."

It was another thing you did the day after the night in the motel.

"Most of the books said she had no children," Jean said.

"She tried to keep me out of it," Jimmy said. He was telling her more than he should again.

"One said there was a son. Another that there were *two* boys, one who came along much later in her life. I guess that was—"

"Lies."

"Who was your father?"

"He was a director. Married to someone else."

A bird snapped down onto their table, a finch. It eyed a crust of bread, looked at Jimmy as if waiting for permission. Jimmy kept still. It pecked at the crumb then flew away as quickly as it had come when someone coughed at a table across the way.

"One of the books," Jean began, "one of them said there was a rumor that your mother didn't die, that she was still alive somewhere."

Jimmy looked at her.

"No."

When they finished, Jimmy gave the waiter cash

and Jean crossed the patio into the restaurant to go to the ladies' room. A man paused in his attention to his wife's lines of dialogue to follow Jean with his eyes.

Jimmy stared at him, wanted to yank him out of his chair, shove him until he backed up with his hands in front of him.

He wondered where *that* came from.

They started up the sidewalk. The collectors' car show was on in Monterey. A convoy of restored Corvairs came past in the tunnel of trees, eight or ten of them nose to tail, half of them turquoise. Coming along behind was an enormous old Packard with the spare on the running board and a Klaxon horn that the locals—were they called *Carmelites?*—probably didn't appreciate.

Jean went into a hat store. Jimmy ducked into another shop to buy something for her. When he came out, she was across the street and down in the next short block. She waved happily and called out to him.

She was in front of a tiny redwood chapel, an Episcopal church wedged between the shops and restaurants. Once she knew that he had seen her, she went inside.

Jimmy crossed the street.

He stepped into the dark cave of the chapel. Candles burned in red cups, dozens of them, a decorating touch more California Mission Catholic than Episcopal. Or maybe Jimmy was just in a sour mood. It was warm and pleasant in the tiny sanctuary, smaller than a candle store, and they were alone.

Jean was in the second pew, kneeling on the drop

down pads. She straightened, crossed herself and sat back with her hands in her lap. There was a "good little girl" rigidity to her posture. It was sweet.

Jimmy sat beside her.

She was reading from the Book of Common Prayer.

"It's the *old* book of prayer," she said. "Before the revision. Look. You can tell."

She passed him the book, her finger on a line in what was called The Apostles' Creed. As his eyes crossed the page, she said the line aloud in a soft voice.

"*And sitteth on the right hand of God the Father Almighty; from thence He shall come to judge the quick and the dead—*"

"Now it says, 'the *living* and the dead'," Jean said.

The Quick and The Dead.

Jimmy looked at the altar. All the wood was red. The light of the votives was red, warm, pulsing. It was like being inside a beating heart. He brushed his hair back. He could smell her on his hands. Last night, after they'd made love, when everything was still quiet, before anyone broke the charm, she'd touched his face.

"Tell me your secret," she had said.

CHAPTER 17

"THE KID IS GONE," ANGEL SAID.

Jimmy stripped off his shirt, took a clean shirt from the stack in the closet. Angel had come over to be with Drew at Jimmy's house while he was gone with Jean. When they'd come back, Jimmy had tried to talk her into staying with him for a few days but she'd said no. Angel had sent two of his friends to go home with her, to stand watch over her, to stand between her and *Them*.

"First night you left." Angel waited a beat to deliver the rest of the bad news. "He took the Porsche."

Jimmy buttoned the shirt.

He went into the office, stood over the desk, looking at all the papers and the pictures. The dead, the living. The case. He found the canceled checks from the rafters of the Danko flying school.

Angel came in after him.

"Did you tell him about the moon?"

"I told him the rest," Jimmy said, "but not that."

"Somebody should tell him."

"Somebody probably has."

"What are you going to do about him?"

"Nothing, for as long as I can," Jimmy said.

THERE WAS A SILVERY PATH ACROSS THE WATER TO the fat moon. Jimmy found Kirk, the old Clover Field expert, at the end of the Malibu Pier, a pole over the side, his fishing license in a vellum envelope pinned to his funky hat. Something flapped in a white lard bucket next to the old man's beat-up tacklebox.

Jimmy leaned over for a look in the bucket.

"You don't want to see that," Kirk said. "I don't even know what it is. I'm going to take it back to this science teacher I know."

Jimmy leaned against the rail, turned his back on the moon.

"What do you need?" Kirk said. "You aren't dressed to fish."

He *was* fishing. The checks were for overdue aviation fuel bill payments and rent checks made out to Steadman Industries. They had made him rethink the thing Rosemary Danko had said that he didn't quite hear, when he'd thought she'd said her father's killers were *the pretty people.*

Maybe it was the *airplane people.*

"I found rent checks Bill Danko paid to Steadman Industries."

Kirk nodded. "The old man owned everything at Clover. The airport was the city's but all the buildings belonged to Steadman."

"You ever hear of any run-ins between Danko and him or his people?" Jimmy said.

Kirk shook his head. "Red Steadman wouldn't have anything to do with a small fry like Danko."

"Did you ever meet him, Steadman?"

"Sure, he was there all the time in the war days. He'd pick up a rivet gun, come in over your shoulder, put one in to show you how it was done. He was all right, but he'd definitely tear you a new one if you looked at him wrong."

Jimmy had also come back to the year-end wrap-up:

1977 . . .
A MERGER   A MURDERER   A MONARCH

"When was the merger with Rath Aircraft?"

"I guess seventy-six or -seven. Steadman died Christmas Day, 1973. Three, four years after that. It never could have happened when Red was alive."

"You were still there? After the merger?"

"A year. I finished out my time. It wasn't the same."

"Why?"

"I was out of the old days, when it was 'Steadman and his boys.' The companies may have ended up merging but Red Steadman and Vasek Rath sure as hell never did, never would have. They hated each other. Since we worked for Red we hated Rath, too, even with Red dead and gone. Who'd want to work for that bastard Rath?"

Kirk filled a cup from a thermos. He'd not touched the pole over the side and apparently nothing had touched his bait either.

"I make it sound like I *liked* Red Steadman," he said. "Once he was dead, he got larger than life. You know what I mean?"

Kirk shook his head, shook off the past.

He looked at the moon, startling each time it caught your eye.

"Look at that," he said, "best moon for Pacific seawater fish, fat, almost full."

Jimmy thanked him and started back up the pier. A little boy and his mother came toward him carrying their tackle, a couple of old poles and a battered box. The woman wore a crisp shirt tucked into a long white skirt that caught the light, low heels. Jimmy wondered what their story was. She was too young, too together-looking to have a boy that age, but she did. And it was too late for them to be out here like this, too, but they were.

The boy looked at him the way boys without fathers look at young men, hard and soft at the same time, trying to connect.

Jimmy knew it too well. He pointed a finger at the boy.

"Good luck," he said.

* * *

THE HEADQUARTERS FOR RATH-STEADMAN WAS three identical mirrored boxes with greenbelt all around, standing alone in an industrial park, inland and south almost to Orange County. Jimmy looped the perimeter of the empty parking lot and parked the Mustang in the front row, just as if he belonged there, and settled in to wait out the rest of the night. Dawn came in an hour or two, the orange parking lot lights overcome by a sky flushed an embarrassed pink.

They unlocked the doors at nine. The receptionist was dressed like a pilot, all the way up to her angular cap. Jimmy paused over a glass-tombed model of a passenger jet labeled, "RS-20," Rath-Steadman's latest, and came up to her desk, which was tall and which she stood behind.

"Good morning," she said.

On the wall behind her were portraits of the founders, Vasek Rath and Red Steadman. For two men who hated each other, they looked a lot alike, big-chested, clear-eyed.

"I'd just like an annual report," Jimmy said.

She seemed a little disappointed for some reason.

"Public Relations, Tenth Floor. Your name?"

He told her. *Harry Turner.*

She tapped on a keyboard and a pass popped up out of a slot in the stainless steel.

He was alone in the elevator until it stopped at the third floor and three men in suits got in. Matching suits. As they rode up, the three men traded looks and nodded at each other, wordlessly continuing whatever they'd been in the middle of before. Then, at about the sixth floor, one of them said, darkly, *"Tim,"* and the other two nodded. Nobody said anything else and they got out on nine. They never looked directly at Jimmy.

He had punched the button for the top floor, eighteen.

When the doors parted it was the boardroom and it was empty. The drapes were open. There was a view almost to the ocean, over the planted greenery and then the San Diego freeway and, beyond that, the spires of a refinery with its flaring burn-off stacks. The table was forty feet long, oblong, perfectly smooth, any claw marks buffed out.

There were pictures of the directors in a row across one wall, meat-eaters one and all, including the two women. It was the usual mix of yesterday's politicians and sports statesmen. None of them looked as if they could have stood up to Red Steadman or Vasek Rath in the old days.

Maybe one man.

Jimmy was going through a trashcan when a side door opened and a fruit tray as tall and comic as a Carmen Miranda headpiece came through the door. It was on a cart, wheeled in by a young assistant something or other.

Jimmy excused himself and stepped back into the waiting elevator.

"No problem," the kid said.

Jimmy stopped at Public Relations on the way down.

In the lobby he nodded and smiled at the receptionist on his way to the door and waved his annual report.

She looked disappointed again.

He looked back at her.

"What'd it close at yesterday?"

"Seventy-seven and an eighth," she said. "Up a quarter today, Mr. Turner."

He half expected her to salute.

"Outstanding!" Jimmy said.

He took the corporate report out to the parking lot, sat on the hood of the Mustang and opened it. There were the same pictures of the founders and the directors. Kurt Rath, Vasek Rath's son, had a page of his own as CEO. He was in his thirties, looked like a Luftwaffe pilot. Jimmy ran the math. Rath-the-Younger was just a few years old when Bill Danko and Elaine Kantke died. Vasek Rath had died twenty years ago, five years after the merger, leaving his son enough stock to take control when he came of age.

In the picture, Kurt Rath was trying to manage a bit of a smile but knew not to give away much.

A look that made Jimmy want to buy a hundred shares.

ALONE ON THE PUTTING GREEN AT THE MOST EX-clusive country club on the Westside, Jimmy sank a twenty-footer, clean, straight, no suspense.

"I meant to do that," he said.

He dropped another ball and lined up his shot. Behind him, Kurt Rath, CEO, strode toward him followed by a nervous younger man, the club's starter.

"Is this him?" Rath said.

The starter nodded.

Jimmy turned. *Who me?*

"This idiot jammed us *both* up," Rath said.

Jimmy still stood over his putt.

"Yeah? How'd he do that?"

"I have a standing twelve noon tee-time Thursdays. I've had it for six years. Everybody knows it. And this moke says someone in my office blanked it this morning, which is impossible, and now you've got it."

Rath's partner stepped up. He looked like a nice guy, nice smile, good build, nice tan. He looked like the kind of guy you could beat every Thursday.

"Hey, how's it goin'?" Jimmy said to the beatable man.

The man nodded back. He was already embarrassed by what he knew was coming next from Rath.

"Look," the CEO began again.

"Take it," Jimmy said.

Rath had expected a fight. It took a moment for him to regroup.

"I own a little R-S stock," Jimmy said. "I wouldn't want to be responsible for you having a bad day."

Rath nodded four or five times, started away.

Jimmy dropped his head to concentrate on the long putt.

He sank it. Rath looked back about the time the ball snapped into the cup.

"You want to join us?" Rath said.

Who me?

Jimmy walked after them and caught up and shook Rath's partner's hand.

"Sonny Ball," Rath said.

Jimmy shook Sonny Ball's hand. Rath never offered his.

After the round, they had a drink.

Rath was going back to work so for him it was just a grapefruit juice with a splash of cranberry juice on top, like a dash of blood.

He wasn't talking. And Jimmy hadn't learned anything from Rath on the greens, except that he lifted his head and he was better at long putts than short. Jimmy didn't really know what he was looking for. He'd long ago stopped being restrained by that, by what somebody else would see as a lack of purpose. He just went where it seemed he should go, heard what he heard, saw what he saw.

And thought about it at night instead of sleeping.

Rath drained his drink and spit a cube of ice back into the glass and stood up.

"Enjoyed it," he said. "People never kick my ass, even when they can."

Sonny Ball looked into the Scotch he was having.

"It was only a couple of strokes," Jimmy said.

"Yeah, I remember," Rath said.

Rath patted Ball on the back as he left. When he was ten feet away, he half turned.

"Call my office. We'll get you over for lunch."

He meant Jimmy.

"Outstanding," Jimmy said.

For a while, he chatted with Ball, a retired United pilot with a good long story about Bangkok, but he didn't learn anything about Rath-Steadman there ei-

ther, the old days or the new. Then the rich old men
started filling the place, bright clothes, bright colors
on men you knew had terrorized and ball-busted
"their people" yet had survived it, the company life,
the dictator's life, the acid in the mouth and the unsat-
isfied knot in the gut that usually killed off these guys
long before now.

Jimmy finished his martini, stood to go, leaving the
two fat olives on the spear.

A PAIR OF MOONS HUNG IN A JET BLACK SKY.

Below, a tracked rover the size of a suitcase hustled
over the surface of Mars.

Or at least that's the way it looked.

Behind the glass, Ben, the Jet Propulsion Lab engineer from the Mensa murder mystery night at Joel
Kinser's, wiggled the rover's controls, spun it around
in a circle.

The name "Rath-Steadman" was stenciled on the
side.

Ben offered the controls to Jimmy. Jimmy declined.

"When we were ready to put out the first pictures
from the surface of Mars," Ben said, "I downloaded a
fuzzy image of Elvis and superimposed it over an up-
slope, very dimly, *perfect*. But somebody caught it before it went out."

Ben flicked the stick.

"Watch this."

The multimillion dollar toy popped a wheelie.

In the JPL employee's dining room, Jimmy drank a

bottle of water and watched as Ben attacked his five o'clock "lunch," a can of sardines with a pull-top lid and two slices of dark rye wrapped in wax paper.

"I'm not going to eat that pear," he said.

Jimmy took the pear.

"Rath-Steadman. Past, present or future?" Ben said.

"Whatever you know."

"I know everything," Ben said, a simple statement of fact.

"Start with the past."

"When Rath and Steadman merged in 1977, two rather interesting companies were lost and one rather uninteresting company was born, producing a particularly undistinguished series of spectacularly successful airplanes."

Jimmy took the first bite of the pear. Ben eyed him, as if he now regretted giving it up.

"Presently," Ben said, "R-S is in a becalmed patch of sea, captained by Kurt Rath, who is a real son of a bitch, to use the technical term. As for the future, all eyes are on the sky . . ."

It was a joke. Jimmy didn't get it.

"The war with the birds . . ."

Jimmy still didn't get it.

They took Ben's car, a dust-white twenty-year-old Honda Civic. Ben cut across Pasadena and then up through La Canada/Flintridge. He was a shortcut kind of guy, a surface street guy. He made fifty right and left turns in the twenty-mile trip, maximizing the torque in each gear, sometimes violently downshifting as he yanked the car around a turn, all while *Per-*

sian music squeaked out of the Honda's cheap speakers, snake charmer's music to the untuned ear, and too loud to talk over.

Jimmy held on, his head under the lowered cloud of the torn headliner. They came down Sepulveda from the north, faster than the cars on the adjacent freeway, right and left and right and left down into Van Nuys to an industrial park.

One last turn and they were on the tarmac of Van Nuys Airport.

"You have a plane?" Jimmy said.

Ben threw open the doors of a hangar. There was an experimental plane hardly longer than the Civic with an odd wing configuration, two place, prop aft.

"I built it. In my garage," Ben said as he yanked away the blocks and shoved it toward the doorway.

The light plane had power. There was some chatter on the radio as they came up the runway, fast.

"It's the same model as John Denver's," Ben yelled to Jimmy as he pulled back on the stick and the plane leapt into the sky. "That seems to impress some people."

They crossed the city. What would have taken an hour and a half down below took ten minutes. They flew over the Rath-Steadman headquarters, the parking lot where Jimmy had burned up the last hours of last night. It was late afternoon and the light and the distance and the angle made everything look good, the shining buildings and rolling, green manmade hills around them, even the refinery, Oz in this light.

Ben banked right, a steep turn, and they were fac-

ing the dropping sun. As they approached the coastline, Ben looked down, shouting over the noise.

"See any B-One-RD's?"

"What?"

"B-1-RDs."

"What?"

"Birds."

Jimmy looked over the side.

Below was a grim expanse of what once were wetlands, a broad section that fed, in a few flashing wa-
terways, into the Pacific. It was a landscape dotted
with abandoned tuna boats and decaying pleasure
craft and a few figures too far off to read.

Jimmy's eyes darkened.

"Last wetlands in the South Bay," Ben yelled.
"Rath-Steadman wants to build RS-20s here. Buddy
of mine has been doing a little stealth air-mapping for
them. Immense plant, no more wetlands. Look for the
PR campaign to start soon. '*Birds for Jobs!*' "

Ben pushed the plane into a wild, diving turn.

"I like birds," he shouted, "but I'd bet on Rath-
Steadman . . ."

The little aircraft spiraled down over the cluttered
wetlands for an up-close view.

A man in a peacoat and watch cap looked up, a
gasoline rainbow at his feet.

CHAPTER 18

IT WAS ON WESTERN THE BLOCK ABOVE THIRD, A storefront church with services in Spanish and Korean depending on the night, formerly an adult bookstore, next to a new adult bookstore. Through the open doorway, twenty folding metal chairs, a low stage, a plywood pulpit. A Fender Stratocaster leaned against an amp. It was the end of the day and hot and the Wednesday night services wouldn't begin for another hour but a few people were already in place. A seven-year-old girl in a dress the color of cotton candy played scales on the upright piano.

Jimmy and Angel were out front on the sidewalk.

Jimmy started by telling him about *The Airplane People*.

"Red Steadman owned the building the murdered

boyfriend's business was in, a flight school. I think somehow Danko got mixed up in some Steadman business and they killed him and Elaine Kantke for it."

"I thought it was about disco," Angel said. "What? Mixed up in what?"

"I don't know."

"It's all a long time ago," Angel said. "I don't see how any of it matters now."

Jimmy had an answer for that.

"Rath-Steadman wants to build a new plant down in South Bay," he said. "On some wetlands. That's the link to today."

He waited before he said the next.

"It's down at The Pipe."

Jimmy let it sink in. Angel's eyes darkened the same way his had when he'd looked over the side of the little plane.

A skinny preacher got off a bus and walked toward them up the sidewalk carrying a white-cover Bible the size of a cake box. He rolled his hand across Angel's back as he passed, not wanting to interrupt what might be a witnessing.

"So that's the link with Sailors," Angel said.

"I guess."

"They want it to happen or *don't* want it to?"

"I don't know," Jimmy said.

Angel shook his head. "Are you still seeing them?"

"Not since the chase in the park."

"What about the German woman?"

Jimmy shook his head.

Inside the church, someone played a brash chord

on the guitar. "What about Jean?" Angel said as it blew on down the sidewalk.

"I still haven't seen her."

"Why is that?"

"I stopped calling her, stopped going by."

"Why?"

There was a billboard down the street behind Angel for some movie that had opened and closed a month ago. Now it was peeling in the weather. The stars, man and woman, beamed toothy grins out at Jimmy, in their confidence just about the most pathetic faces on the street.

"I knew your guys were watching out for her."

"Go to her," Angel said. "Tell her her daddy didn't do it and whoever did is probably long since dead. Whoever did it and for whatever reason."

Jimmy nodded.

"Get her in the *now*," Angel said.

"I'm trying."

"Get *yourself* in the now."

Jimmy smiled. "I've never had much luck at that."

"Then you can maybe see what there could be with her. You could use some *love* in your life."

"I already got you," Jimmy said.

The music inside started, drums, piano and guitar.

"You wanna come in?" Angel said.

Jimmy shook his head.

Angel pulled him close for an embrace, then pushed him away.

"Con dios."

Jimmy started toward the Mustang down the street.

"'*Someday this wall shall crumble, tumble and fall . . .* '" Angel called after him.

Jimmy turned. "What book of the Bible is that from?"

"Los Lobos," Angel said.

IKE'S WAS DEAD AND SCOTT WASN'T BEHIND THE bar.

Jimmy drank a beer. The handful of people who were there all had the same guilty look, embarrassed that they'd not known what everyone else apparently had known, that tonight you didn't go to Ike's.

The cop Connor came in. He was out of uniform, wearing his out-of-uniform uniform, a starched Brooks Brothers button-down shirt with the tail out over ironed, creased jeans.

"Nobody's seen him," Connor said. "His neighbor said he didn't come back last night, after his shift."

They were talking about Scott.

Jimmy turned around on the stool to face the bar, but avoided the image of himself in the mirror that was waiting there.

"What the hell is going on?"

"It's getting close," Connor said. "People are getting stressed. Let's go look for him."

Jimmy put some money on the bar and got up.

Then Jean came in. Angel and two of his men were behind her. The bodyguards were Hispanic. Big arms. Angel saw Jimmy and Connor, tipped his chin up to

say hello. He and his men took a table out of the way
as Jean came to the bar.

Connor stepped away to leave them alone. He went
over to the jukebox. After a minute a saxophone piece
started, so sentimental and blue the few people in the
place turned to look, wondering if it was meant to be
a joke.

"I was thinking about you all day," Jimmy said to
Jean. The way he said it didn't have all that much ro-
mance in it.

She nodded in a way that meant she'd been thinking about him, too, and maybe the other way.

"I called," she said. "Then I thought you might be
here."

"I came by a few times," Jimmy said. He came by
once.

"I've been staying in a hotel. I found myself leaving all the lights on at home," she said.

"Come stay with me."

He didn't say anything else.

She nodded.

He was still standing. He looked over at Connor.

"We have to go see about a friend of ours," Jimmy
said. "We'll come back for you here."

"Can I come with you?"

Maybe it was time.

They left Angel's truck and Connor's red Corvette
in the lot behind Ike's and the four of them took the
Mustang, Jean and Connor in the tight backseat. The
traffic was light, even down the Strip. Angel's friends

followed closely in a low-slung Chevy for a block or two then flashed their lights and peeled off.

Scott's apartment was on Doheny Drive at the corner of Elevado three or four short blocks up from Santa Monica Boulevard in West Hollywood, a cool white tower ten stories tall, lights in the landscaping shining on its face.

Jimmy stayed behind the wheel while Angel and Connor got out. Connor rang the bell downstairs and waited. Angel looked over at Jimmy, then got out a ring of keys and unlocked the outer door and went in. They all had each other's keys.

Jean took this in, put it with the other things she'd learned that deepened the mystery.

"Scott is the bartender at Ike's. He didn't come in today." Jimmy didn't turn around when he spoke to her, didn't even look at her in the mirror. "Nobody's seen him since he left work last night. A neighbor said he'd looked a little shaky the last few days."

Jean just looked at the back of Jimmy's head.

Angel and Connor came out. Connor stepped into the backseat again, Angel got in front.

Angel shook his head.

"Maybe we'd better—"

"Yeah, I know," Jimmy said and put it in gear.

He made a U-turn on Doheny and then a left on Santa Monica Boulevard, drove past The Troubadour, then across West Hollywood into Hollywood.

To the foot of the Roosevelt Hotel.

And the *Walkers*.

This time there were dozens of them in clusters in the alleyways in the three blocks around the hotel, the men (and a few women) Boney M had wanted Jimmy to be reminded of from that perch up on the roof.

They never stopped moving, Sailors ashore forever. They wore whatever they wanted, whatever they had. They lived on the street or in a few hotels the other Sailors kept open in an act of kindness. And *fear,* fear that any Sailor could end up with the same dead look in his eyes, the same lack of purpose—either for good or for bad—that was in their shuffling movements. This was the worst the worst Sailors could wish on you, what they could threaten you with, what they could hold you out over a precipice and make you see, what they could drive you toward, what they could hand you instead of death. It was a mystery how it happened but some Sailors saw something that made them fold, made them shuffle like this, made them *walk.* Death would be a step up.

Jimmy drove slowly past one knot of men.

"Did the kid come back?" Angel said to Jimmy.

"No," Jimmy said, knowing Angel was thinking maybe Drew was down here, too.

"Stop," Connor said. "*There.*"

"Scott's not here," Jimmy said.

There was a man apart from the others who was probably Scott's age, who at least looked up at the Mustang. He was dark with filth. He didn't look like anybody anyone could recognize anymore.

"That's not him," Jimmy said.

"Let me check," Connor said.

Jimmy stopped and they let him out and the cop walked over to the blackened man.

"He couldn't have fallen that far in a day," Jimmy said.

Then he remembered Jean in the backseat.

Jimmy turned to look her in the face. She had that *world-hurt* face again, but brave, taking her medicine. He felt ashamed of himself for not having the courage to tell her a better, *easier* version of the truth of who he was.

Connor came back. He got into the backseat beside Jean. She could smell the men on him.

Connor shook his head.

"He's not with them," Angel said.

"I believe I just said that," Jimmy said.

He sped away from the men, faster than he meant to.

"What about his old place?" Connor said.

Jimmy nodded.

WHEN YOU WERE ONE OF THEM, YOU KNEW EVERY-
one's story, how *It* had happened. Five years before this night, Scott had put a bullet in his head. His boyfriend had died exactly a year earlier.

And now here was the apartment building where they'd lived together. It was a twenty-unit four-story box of a design duplicated all over L.A., screaming *seventies!* The front was all glass, the foyer two stories tall. A long light fixture hung from the ceiling looking like an protoplasmic explosion. It was on a street called North Rossmore, a *transitional* street, also duplicated all over L.A. A block north was a golf course edged with million-dollar houses, a block south the last funky half mile of Hollywood.

Jimmy tried a key in the glass door of the entryway. They'd changed the locks. Angel came around from the side of the building. "Over here, door into the garage."

Jean came with them this time. They all went down some steps and in through the garage. They came out into the entryway where the mailboxes were and the elevator.

Angel hit the button. They rode up, not talking.

Jimmy knocked on the door to the apartment. There wasn't any sound from inside. A stereo thumped somewhere down the hall, or maybe it was just someone thudding a fist against the common wall.

Jimmy was about to try his key when the door in front of him was yanked open.

A man with bugged out eyes.

"Just *leave* it!" He was what they used to call a *hype.* "Just *leave* it, man!"

Jimmy asked the wired man if anyone out of the past had been by the apartment that night. He got the door slammed in his face. The pounding down the hall stopped, took a breath or two, started again.

Angel was ready to go but Connor, who had cop instincts, who remembered things other people didn't, looked at Jimmy and shot his eyes up toward the ceiling, the roof. They were on the fourth floor. There were stairs up.

The door at the top was jammed. Angel put a shoulder against it and it opened and the four of them came out onto the roof.

The building wasn't deluxe enough for any decking or patio furniture or umbrellas, or tall enough to offer much of a view.

While Angel and Connor stepped off in different directions, Jimmy went over to the edge and looked down at the traffic on Melrose. There was a car double-parked in front of a restaurant, five cars behind it, honking, nobody willing to give in and pull around it in the open inside lane. Across Rossmore and down a ways was the Ravenswood with its neon rooftop sign, where Mae West had lived out her life. Next to that, the El Royale, where George Raft had kept a bachelor's pad.

Jean came up behind Jimmy, put her arms around him.

He didn't expect it. Later, when he thought about it, maybe when he thought about it too much, he remembered it feeling in the moment like she was holding someone else.

"Jimmy," Connor said.

Angel had found Scott at the other edge of the roof, sitting cross-legged, his back against a TV antenna.

Jimmy left Jean and went to him. She stayed where she was.

The three men stood over their friend a moment and Jimmy said something and Scott nodded. Angel squatted beside him. Jimmy crouched down and offered his hand. Scott took it and they held hands that way a moment. Connor seemed to stand guard, though against *what* wasn't clear.

Jimmy pulled Scott to him and said things into his ear in a voice so low Jean couldn't hear any of it, just as it had been with the kid Drew standing in the middle of the canyon road, trying to put it together, eyes on the moon.

More questions than answers.

There was a fuzz around the green letters on the El Royale sign and, up Vine, the Hollywood Hills were wrapped in something. Maybe it was going to rain overnight. But the weather had gone a little haywire. No one was predicting anything with much confidence.

What was going on?

Even she felt it, that everything was lurching toward something, not out of control exactly, just out of *our* control, in the control of something very very basic, like a car coming down out of the hills on a rain-slicked street.

CHAPTER 19

IT WAS MORNING AND RAINING. JEAN BROUGHT A cup of coffee into the living room in Jimmy's house. She looked out the tall window. Two more of the weight lifters from Angel's backyard stood guard under the dripping overhang of the four-bay garage. The garage doors were up. There was the Mustang and empty spaces for the wrecked Dodge Challenger and the Porsche Drew had taken. In the last bay was the tarp-covered car with the high fins. Jean watched as one of the iron men lifted the corner of the cover for a look.

The rain helped, made her feel safer. She'd lived years in Northern California and so she liked the rain. Here, when it rained everything fell apart. The weathermen apologized, the freeways clogged with spun-out cars, mudslides slopped across the curvy foothill roads. Everybody either drove too fast or too slow and everyone bitched. People walking their dogs looked out from under their umbrellas and rolled their eyes instead of saying *Good morning,* if they looked at you at all.

Jean cranked open a window an inch or two so she could hear it and smell it. It reminded her of San Francisco, of Tiberon, of Atherton, of the hills above Stanford, brown today and green tomorrow, as the drops ticked into the gravel under the eaves. In California, the rain was usually like this, flat, steady, without drama.

Maybe that was what the locals hated about it.

It was a huge room. A child could stand in the fireplace. Everyone knew the history of the house. It had been built by one of Los Angeles's first oil barons in the twenties. A movie star had owned it in the forties, put in the pool in back, the motor court and the garage. The star had sold off a half acre in the fifties but there were four and a half acres left. It became a museum in the sixties, restored more or less to the look of the oil baron's home, paid for by the family out of their great wealth. Out of vanity. No one ever toured it except elementary school kids coming in buses for field trips. The grounds were good for picnics.

Then Jimmy had bought it.

But his name wasn't on the deed. Jean had checked. It was owned by a trust. *Blue Moon.* She wondered what the name meant.

There was a grand piano, the wood as black as the

black keys and so shiny you didn't want to touch it. Next to it was a tall glass case with a beautiful white dress in it. And a picture of Teresa Miles, in her prime, in the fifties, wearing the same dress in a scene from a movie. *Morning at the Window*. Jean opened the case and felt the fabric. She lifted her fingertips to her nose and breathed in the scent on the cloth.

They'd made love again last night. After that first night in Big Sur, they'd slept in the same bed two more nights in a small hotel in Pacific Grove with a view across Monterey Bay, but had not made love again. It was a comfortable avoidance. Neither of them thought it meant anything worrisome, only that what had happened the first night could stand on its own.

And she had not asked again what his secret was.

He wasn't in bed when she awoke at seven that morning. He'd stayed beside her all night, curled against her. She awoke several times, pulled out of sleep by the strangeness of the bed and the room, needing a moment to realize where she was. Then she would close her eyes again as she felt him against her. She knew he was awake. (She'd not yet seen him asleep.) She thought of him as a restless man, an unsettled man, but he wasn't restless in the middle in the night, with her. He was the kind of man who held you while you slept.

Jean closed the glass cabinet.

She went into Jimmy's study. The bank of security monitors was lit, color images, cameras panning automatically across a half dozen sections of the brick and iron wall that surrounded the property. Another of An-

gel's men stood in the rain just inside the gate below
the house down a slow hill. And another patrolled a
back gate.

*Was this really now that dangerous? What had
changed?*

On the desk, spread out, was the case. Jean stood
before it, picked up the old *Time* magazine. She
looked at the pictures, at a photocopy of a one-inch
story about Bill Danko's arrest for "drunken flying"
she'd never seen before. It mentioned "a female
companion." She'd thought her father had managed
to keep all of it out of the papers. She looked through
the cancelled checks.

There was a clip from the business section of *The
Times*:

> The aviation industry was stunned in early
> June when directors of Steadman Aircraft
> and The Rath Corp., former bitter rivals,
> announced the two companies had agreed to
> merge.

And there was the year-end wrap-up.

1977 . . .
A MERGER   A MURDERER   A MONARCH

Cut into the copy was a picture of her father being
led into the courthouse in handcuffs, Jack Kantke in a
gray suit, three-button, buttoned up, a narrow black
tie. Jean had seen the picture before but this time she

noticed what a bright day it had been, everything almost washed out, and the pathetic smile on her father's face.

She looked into his eyes and felt embarrassed for him.

What had changed?

She'd never felt embarrassed for him before. She wondered what of him was carried on in her. It was every child's question if you waited long enough or if circumstances exploded in your face.

At least the picture of the *Queen Mary* was simple enough. *The Monarch.* Nineteen seventy-seven had seen the "gala" tenth anniversary of the arrival of the ship to Long Beach Harbor as a tourist attraction.

Scott stepped into the doorway.

"Sorry," he said when she jumped.

They considered each other a moment.

"I was looking for Jimmy," he said.

It was awkward. Jean had the thought that it was as if the bartender and Jimmy were lovers, which wasn't true and made no sense, like they were both Jimmy's lover.

It's just that they share such a secret, she thought.

"I don't know where he is," Jean said.

"He just went for a walk in the rain," Scott said. "We spoke. I thought maybe he had come back."

It stayed awkward. He looked at the bank of monitors, points of view like eyes moving from side to side, like heads saying *no* very slowly. He looked at her again and then looked away. He felt ashamed about what she'd seen on the roof the night before.

"I made some coffee," Jean said. She held up her coffee mug. "In the kitchen."

She sat down behind the desk to make it seem as if she belonged there, that she wasn't snooping, that she had permission. Or, maybe *that she knew*.

Scott looked at the clippings, upside down.

"This is about you?"

She nodded. "My father. And mother. It started out simpler."

"Yeah, things get complicated."

There was another silence.

"How long have you known Jimmy?" she said.

"Years."

Jean realized she couldn't tell how old he was. A week ago, behind the bar, he looked liked he was in his twenties. Now, here, before her, he looked fifty.

"Can I ask you something?"

She saw him flinch slightly. He waited to hear what it was.

"Why does he order a second drink when he comes in Ike's and then just leaves it on the bar?" she said.

"A manhattan."

She waited.

"It was what his mother drank."

"What do you do with it when he leaves?"

Scott smiled. "Give it to someone who looks like they need it. Tell them it's from a secret admirer."

Jimmy came in, drying his hair with a towel. He'd heard the last of what Scott said.

"Do they believe it?" Jimmy said.

Scott turned. "Every time." He left them alone. Jimmy patted his back as he went past.

Jean was still behind the desk, the case in front of her.

Jimmy tried to read what was on her face.

"Now you know everything," he said.

Jean stood. "Sorry."

"It's all right, stay there."

Jimmy smiled. "You put everything in piles."

Jean looked down at the neatened desk. She'd hadn't remembered doing it.

"That's a little embarrassing," she said.

He put a different look on his face. "What do you want to know?"

"Nothing," she said.

"My turn to talk you into it," he said.

"No."

He stood in the same place, across the desk from her, with all of *It* between them. She knew he was going to wait for her to say something.

"Who's this?" She took a photo from the desk, Harry Turner.

He told her his name. "A lawyer. Or at least he started out as one. He was behind the scenes in your father's defense. He runs things. That's what he does. Who he is."

She dropped the picture, careful *not* to put it atop one of her piles.

Jimmy wasn't finished.

"And he's on the board of directors of Rath-Steadman."

Harry Turner's was the face Jimmy had recognized from the wall in the boardroom on the top floor of Rath-Steadman as maybe the one man who could have stood up to the old men, to Vasek Rath and Red Steadman.

"The merger in 1977 is connected to the murders?"

He nodded. "Rath-Steadman is ready to build a new assembly plant down in Long Beach. Somehow that's connected to this."

Jean came around the desk to him. She thought she was going to go into his arms but he didn't want that. Without pushing her away, he pushed her away. Maybe *he'd* decided something. There was an anger in him this morning she didn't understand.

"Are you going to stop now?"

"No."

"I told you I don't care about this anymore," she said.

"It's taken on its own life."

"Why are you doing this?" she said. "Pushing my face into it?"

"I want you to know everything I know."

"I don't care about Rath-Steadman. I'm at peace with the idea of my father, what he did or didn't do. I don't *want* to know everything. Not anymore. I want . . ."

And she waited before she said it.

"You."

"Your brother Carey is on the board, too," Jimmy said.

Something broke inside her, like a support, something that held up part of the façade. He saw her crumble.

He heard himself, the way he'd said it, wondered if some part of him meant to break her. Or even drive her away.

"He doesn't have any hand in the day-to-day operation of the company," Jimmy said. "He's just on the board."

She sat in the chair.

He waited. "And he has three million dollars' worth of R-S stock."

"Where does he live?" she said, suddenly smaller.

"He has a house in Palos Verdes. And a penthouse in a high-rise on the harbor in Long Beach."

He could see her pulling herself together again.

"Have you talked to him?" she said.

"No. Have *you?*"

She didn't understand the accusation in it. She said, "Carey called me on some anniversary of the execution. I was at Stanford. That was the last time I talked to him. I heard seven or eight years ago that he was a lawyer, that he was living in Arizona."

"He practiced four years," Jimmy said, "private practice, then filed for bankruptcy. He's had inactive status with the Arizona Bar ever since."

She wanted out of there.

"Was there bad blood between the two of you?"

"No," Jean said. "There wasn't anything. There *isn't* anything."

"Where did he go to live after the murders?"

"He was eight. A boarding school in Scottsdale."

"Why didn't he live with you and your grand-mother?"

"I don't know," she said. She got out of the chair.

"You never asked?"

"Why are you being this way?" she said.

He didn't tell her, he didn't know.

"I'm sorry," he said.

She knew he'd hold her now but now she didn't want it.

THERE WAS A FULL DAYLIGHT MOON OVER THE high-rise Deco apartment building on Long Beach Harbor. It was a pretty building, twenty stories high with ornate bas-relief detail over the black frames of the windows. It was from the twenties, recently refurbished, reconfigured into condominiums for young professionals and widows with a sense of style. The rain had ended at noon and left behind the brightest kind of sky, a few round white clouds and a view all the way to Catalina.

The gate on the subterranean parking lifted. After a moment, a white Porsche Cabriolet came out. It stopped. The top folded back.

It was Carey Kantke.

He looked like his father, wore his hair in the same crew cut though there was probably a different name for it now. He was in his late thirties, the same age as his father at the time of the murders, the trial. He ran his hand through his short hair, checked it in the mirror and pulled out of the parking garage and onto West Shoreline Drive, turning right.

Jimmy waited and then fell in behind.

Jean had gone in to her office after they'd talked in the study. Jimmy had told her to stay there at the house behind its high walls, that things were getting weird, but she'd had other ideas. Angel's men went with her. Jimmy thought that if they could get through these next days, with all they would hold, he and Jean might be together for a while, might have a chance. But he didn't tell her that.

There was a stop for lunch, a sidewalk café on East Second Street, a street of gentrified shops and galleries with only a few taco stands and tiki bars left over from the old days. Carey Kantke ate alone, got up once to collapse the green umbrella that shaded his table. Jimmy watched from across the street on a stool at a sidewalk Mexican juice bar splashed with orange and yellow paint. Carey had a coffee and a refill and then paid for his lunch with cash, standing beside the table, talking with the young waitress, all the time in the world.

The valet pulled up with the white Porsche. Jimmy drank the rest of his milky, too sweet *horchada,* left two bucks for the man behind the counter. Carey never saw him, never looked around as he dropped behind the wheel. This wasn't a wary man.

The white Porsche humped up and over the concrete bridge on East Street, into Naples, then right onto the perimeter loop called The Toledo.

And then right again, onto Rivo Alto Canal.

Maybe Carey Kantke had his own version of *returning*.

Jimmy dropped back and parked the Mustang and jumped out and followed the Porsche on foot. The lanes behind the houses were narrow and the pace was slow, slower even than the three-mile-per-hour speed limit posted on funny hand-painted signs.

Carey drove past the house at One-Ten, the murder house, and parked behind the garage of the two-story house two doors down. He got out and went up the walkway between the houses leading to the front, to the canal and the waterfront sidewalk.

It was the house where Jimmy had heard Abba's "Dancing Queen" drifting out of the upstairs window.

JIMMY WATCHED THE HOUSE FROM A RENTAL BOAT, cruising in the canal. Carey Kantke had been inside forty-five minutes. Jimmy cut the engine and let it coast until it thunked into an empty dock. He took the housing off the little outboard and pretended to adjust the carb while he kept his eyes on the house.

In time, Carey came out onto the porch with a Coke. He unbuttoned his shirt and dropped into a pink Adirondack chair, lifting his face into the sun.

Right at home. *Why?* What was Carey Kantke doing there, two doors down from the house where his young life and his sister's had been blown apart with a pair of gunshots in the middle of a summer night?

Then the answer, at least part of it, came out the

front door. A young woman. She was in her early twenties but with this kind of good looks it was hard to tell. She could have been sixteen. Or thirty. She wore white shorts and a short top that tied up high enough to show her stomach. She handed Carey a portable phone with someone on the line. Carey said hello, listened, said a few words and handed it back to her. She sat in a second matching Adirondack chair, a long tan leg over the armrest. There was something very familiar about her.

Then the next part of the answer came out.

Vivian Goreck.

The real estate lady Jimmy had talked with at the empty Palos Verdes house. Former Jolly Girl.

She was the young woman's mother. It was obvious when they were next to each other. Vivian stood over her daughter and brushed her fingers through her blond hair until the young woman pushed her mother's hand away.

Jimmy would learn that her name was Lynne.

Vivian sat on the low wall that edged the porch and joined in the conversation between the young people. No one was in much of a hurry. A seagull landed on the neighbor's fountain, atop a *cement* seagull, balancing on the other gull's back. They all watched it, enjoying the joke. It drank. It flew.

After a few more minutes the young woman and Carey got up. He kissed Vivian Goreck on her cheek and they left. The Jolly Girl stayed seated on the low wall. She looked down, pulled out a dandelion growing from a crack in the concrete.

Jimmy got the boat to a dock and then ran between the two closest houses.

He came out onto the alleyway just as Lynne and Carey got into the white Porsche and drove off.

The garage was open. There was Vivian's Rolls, with its BUY BUY license plates.

ON A BLUFF ABOVE THE OCEAN AT PALOS VERDES was a glass and steel house with an angular face like the prow of a ship. Jimmy was above it on the adjacent point, an empty lot muddied from the overnight rain. He scanned the scene with binoculars. The white Porsche was in the driveway.

This was Carey's other address.

He stepped into view in the glass living room. He went to the tall window, looked out at the expanse of ocean with his hands behind his back like a captain of a ship.

But wait.

Was it Carey?

Lynne Goreck came into the room. She went to him at the window, went into his arms. They kissed. She stepped away. He turned again to look out at the Pacific, then followed her, moving out of view.

A minute passed. Jimmy heard an engine start. The white Porsche curled around the circle drive and sped away up to the coast road, Carey behind the wheel, alone now.

Jimmy looked back at the living room. The room was empty.

But then they were back, the man and Lynne Goreck.

The phone in Jimmy's pocket rang.

It was Jean.

He listened for a long time.

"I'll meet you there," he said.

CHAPTER 20

THE BACK OF THE HOUSE AT ONE-TEN RIVO ALTO
Canal was blackened but not burned out. A fireman
kneeled just inside the backdoor, beside the water
heater.

"What was it?" Jimmy said.

The fireman looked the two of them over.

"I own the house," Jean said.

"Oily rags under the water heater," the fireman
said.

"Was anybody—"

Jimmy pushed past him and headed upstairs.

"No. They got out," the fireman told Jean.

Jean followed Jimmy. She slowed as she moved
through the living room. It hadn't been burned but the
smoke had crawled across the ceiling and stained it.

Her eyes went over the pictures on the walls, the coffee table, the divan. She'd never been back.

Jimmy was already at the door of the back bedroom upstairs. The doorframe was blackened and some of the dirty carpet had been burned over to the doorway.

Jean came up behind him.

"They said she got out."

They stepped into the room together. The fire had burned the shades off the windows so there was light. The TV was melted, the recliner singed and blackened and its plastic melted, too.

A voice startled them. "You the owners?"

A fire marshal, a handsome man in a perfectly white shirt with a badge on the pocket, stepped out of the second bathroom. He wore rubber gloves.

"I am," Jean said.

"Who was she?"

Jean said, "No one. No one was supposed to be living here."

"It was a woman. I guess a transient," the fire marshal said. "Living here." He looked around the room. "And six or seven cats. So far."

Jean turned and walked out.

"It burned itself out up here," the fire marshal said to Jimmy. "There's not much structural damage. It came straight up from the water heater below, rode up the stack."

"Was the backdoor locked when you got here?" Jimmy asked.

"Yeah, it was. Pulled tight."

Jimmy looked into the bathroom. It was smoke-damaged but not burned. A yellowed shower curtain with flamingos on it still hung on its rings. The mirror above the sink over the years had lost most of its silvering. There was a splotchy black hole in its center where your face would be.

The fire marshal squatted next to the carcasses of two cats at the base of the bay window, trying to decide what to do with them.

"Her name was Rosemary Danko," Jimmy said.

The fire marshal stood.

"You knew her?"

"I talked to her once."

"You want to tell me why?"

Jimmy told him. Some of it.

Jean was in the car when he came down. He got in without saying anything, started the engine and pulled away.

He looked in the mirror. Vivian Goreck was standing with the other neighbors in the middle of the lane.

"Where are we going?" Jean said.

"She had another place," Jimmy said.

AND ANOTHER FIRE.

A red L.A.F.D. Suburban was parked in front of the apartment building in Garden Grove Jimmy had followed her to, crossing town on a hot bus.

Jean stayed in the car.

Jimmy walked around the side of the building. On

the service porch of the corner ground-floor unit another fire marshal stood beside another water heater.

"Who are you?"

"I knew the woman who lived here."

"Where is she? We thought it was vacant."

Every time Jimmy heard that word *vacant*, he thought of the look in Rosemary's eyes.

He came in off of the service porch through the kitchen and into the living room. It was gutted, burned to the studs, and the cabinet that had been full of pictures was now a collapsed, empty box.

It would have been neater if there was a body in one of the two places—*If I just could be sure*—but whatever threat in her madness Rosemary Danko had been to them, it was gone, as gone as she was. They'd cut her out of the story. And the traces of her mother with her.

Five-foot-one.

Jimmy stood in the warm sun out front for a moment. It was good to breathe the open air.

He got in the Mustang. Jean looked at him and he shook his head, though it wasn't clear what he meant by that.

It just meant *no*.

NINE O'CLOCK AT NIGHT AND THE TRAFFIC ON THE 405 north was still clogged. It should have opened up hours ago. They were stopped cold in the fast lane at the top of Sepulveda Pass, up where Mulholland crossed overhead with a high bridge. The line of cars ahead of them stretched for two miles down across the San Fernando Valley, the spaces between the sets of red taillights never expanding beyond a car length.

Jean had a beach house north of Malibu at Point Dume. Jimmy was taking her there the back way over Kanan Dume Road, *the fast way* he had thought, until a half hour ago. This time she hadn't said no when he told her what to do, when he told her she had to leave town because they'd kill her, too, if they thought she knew something, if they thought she was in their way, cut *her* out of the story, too. He had said she should go to San Francisco, had said something that made no sense to her—*They won't follow you out of the city*—but she told him about her house at the beach.

Both of them could still smell the smoke on their clothes.

"That was my room," Jean said.

There was nothing to say to that.

"How old was she?" Jean asked.

"In her forties."

"What was she like?"

"Crazy."

It wasn't enough for Jean. She looked at him.

"Lost," he said. "Haunted."

He had plenty more words where those came from. His life had been filled with Rosemary Dankos.

"What was the other place?"

"It was her mother's."

"I'd like to think she lived there most of the time. At her mother's."

"She probably did," Jimmy said.

"Are you sure she's dead?"

"No. Not sure. But I don't know where she'd be if she wasn't, where they would have taken her, why."

"So she's dead."

"I would guess she is."

"What do you think caused her to come to my house?"

"I don't know. Maybe it was when her mother died. She had nowhere else to go for family. Her father had 'lived' there in a way, had history there. She sat around thinking about it. Sometimes you have an idea in your head about something like that—and then it just starts growing, like a potato under the sink."

A car edged up beside them. The man looked over at them, at Jean, liked her looks, kept his eyes on her as if they were in a bar.

"So you think they killed her?"

"I don't know."

"Is my brother involved in this?"

"Rath-Steadman is," Jimmy said. "I don't know."

"Yes, you do. Tell me."

They had inched up over the crest of the mountain to where they could look down on the scene ahead, the shimmering valley lights and the traffic stilled in both directions, red taillights down, white headlights up in the opposite lane.

Now they could see what it was. A mile down the steep run of the freeway where the 405 met the 101 there were clustered spinning lights, red and blue, an accident.

Her hand was on the seat beside her. He took it.

"You'll be all right at the beach," he said. That was all he would tell her. For now.

"This could all be over in a few days," he said.

She wondered what difference a day or two made now but she didn't ask and the two of them said nothing for a long time, watching the dead traffic in front of them, the accident far below, the TV news helicopters that floated, turning, high above the scene, red lights blinking, like sparks above a fire.

CHAPTER 21

HE FELT LIKE RUNNING, AS IF THIS WAS SOME-
thing he could outrun. After he left Jean at her Malibu
house, Jimmy drove *north,* not south, up California 1,
then back inland through the mountains to Thousand
Oaks and the 101 East, a great loop onto the 210 to
cross the base of the Angeles Forest and the mountains above Glendale.

Now it was way after midnight.

When he turned back down into it, when he was
riding down out of the foothills, it was like L.A. was
on the bottom of a dark ocean, the spikes of downtown still a half mile below the surface, the green cop-
per dome of Griffith Observatory a decorative toy on
the floor of a midnight aquarium. And the air was bad,
even in the middle of the night. The air was heavy. He

felt *compressed*. The feeling was so real it was hard to breathe. He had to fight the panic, the urge to jump from the car and swim frantically for the surface.

He tried to drive it out. He cruised the streets of Hollywood until the whores were gone, down through the canyon of billboards on the Strip, past the all night newsstand.

He didn't go home.

He drove all the way out through the winding turns of Sunset Boulevard, all the way back out to Malibu, to the beach at Point Dume, almost where he'd started. He parked on the access road. He found at the edge of the dial a drifting Mexican pirate rock station with old music. When morning came, an offshore wind came with it and stood the waves up straight and tall. Jimmy watched at the water's edge. The wind came up stronger until there was a wave that rose and rose and rose and wouldn't break.

CHAPTER 22

THERE WAS ONE LAST SET OF CHECKS.

In the study, standing at his desk, Jimmy shuffled the deck until he came to one made out to somebody named Roy Pool with the notation "Payroll." He turned it over. On the back was an endorsement by Mr. Pool, notably florid, and a deposit stamp that said, "Ringside Liquor."

It was still there. It was in Hawaiian Gardens, south and inland, straight in from Long Beach. Everyone said there was no *heritage* in L.A., but some things survived the perpetual reinvention, like red sauce Italian restaurants and old-style Mexican places with dusty sombreros on the walls. And corner liquor stores. Most of them had come right after the war with

names that meant more then than now, names like Full
House, Victory Liquor and Ringside.

The clerk was in his sixties. He came out the front
door with Jimmy and squinted in the sun on the sidewalk and pointed down the block and then over.

Jimmy set out walking, drinking the bottle of water
he'd felt obliged to buy. The heat wave had broken,
but it was still hot. Hawaiian Gardens didn't have
much to do with either Hawaii or gardens, block after
block of apartment buildings and strip malls, a few
dead cars on every block painted with dirt and plas-
tered with Day-Glo *Notice to Remove* stickers. A bus
smoked past, covered top to bottom and front to back
with an ad for a movie, a grinning black man with a .9
millimeter that stretched ten feet.

The clerk at Ringside Liquors had given Jimmy a
number from his files, three-by-five cards in a green
shoebox, but Roy Pool's house was gone. Now a big
ugly apartment building covered the space of four
numbers.

But there was a neighbor, a sole survivor in a Spanish bungalow—they liked to call it *Mediterranean*—
with peeling pink paint and a few yard-birds in even
greater need of a touch-up. Jimmy knocked on the steel
security door that ruined the look of the little house.

It took a long time, then an old lady answered. She
never opened the steel mesh door, even after she saw
that he was a nice young man, but she told him where
to find Roy Pool, that he was "still kicking" as she
said, though his house was long gone.

Capri Retirement Villa wasn't as grim as it could have been. The sidewalk out front was clean, the paint was fresh, and a pair of fluffy Boston ferns hung from hooks in the overhang out front. Somebody cared. Jimmy stopped by the desk, then came down the corridor and found the room.

At least he was awake. Everyone else was sleeping.

Roy Pool, who looked to be in his sixties but was probably older, sat in a wheelchair looking out the sliding glass door at the concrete "garden" in the middle of the four-sided nursing home. He wore silk pajamas with a scarf at the neck. The vintage bodybuilder magazine hidden under the desk at the Danko flight school was his.

"Hi."

He turned. "Hello."

"I'm Jimmy Miles. You're Mr. Pool?"

"Yes, I am."

"I'm an investigator. Can I ask you about Bill Danko?"

"What kind of investigator?"

"Private."

"My," Pool said.

He wheeled around to face his guest and looked him over, his eyes lingering on Jimmy's shoes, black suede loafers with silver diamond shapes across the top.

"This isn't for one of those television shows, is it? I detest television."

"I'll watch a ballgame every once in awhile," Jimmy said. "That's about it."

There were three or four old movie star pictures on the walls and a one-sheet for *Now, Voyager*. A magnolia blossom floated in fresh water in a globe that used to be a fishbowl. On the desk in a plain black frame was an eight-by-ten of a much younger Roy Pool, a dramatic, side-lit pose.

Pool saw Jimmy looking at it. "The older I get, the better-looking I was," he said.

At Pool's feet was a small oxygen bottle. He lifted the pale green mask to his mouth and inhaled, held it delicately with two fingers like the cigarettes he once smoked, which made this necessary now.

He took the mask away and exhaled. "So, who's your patron?"

"Elaine Kantke's daughter."

"Who apparently has never been told that The Past doesn't care what we think about it."

"What about the future?" Jimmy said.

"Cares even less," Pool said.

Jimmy straightened the photo on the desk. "You were Bill Danko's—"

"*Secretary.* There's nothing wrong with the word."

"I want to know if there was some connection to Rath-Steadman."

Roy Pool looked at Jimmy levelly for a long moment, then got out of the wheelchair and stepped over and closed the door.

"Not that anyone in this place can *hear* . . ."

He moved gracefully. Jimmy thought the word *queen* wasn't really such a pejorative. Pool dropped into the chair by the desk and crossed his legs at the knees and then lifted his face into the light angling in from the patio, as if he wanted Jimmy to remember exactly how he had looked when he told him what he was about to tell him.

"So, there was a connection between—"

Pool held up his hand.

Jimmy gave him his moment.

"One week before he was murdered, Mr. Danko—I always called him that although he would repeatedly ask me to call him 'Bill'—Mr. Danko took several important persons up one night to fly over the proposed site for an industrial park in the Inland Empire."

"At night?"

"There was a full moon." He gave Jimmy a look meant to squelch any further interruptions. "Among those passengers was Vasek Rath of Rath Aircraft and . . ."

He allowed a ridiculously long pause.

"*Red Steadman* of Steadman Industries . . ."

Pool let his wild revelation hang in the air a moment. He'd waited years to give this speech.

"Though, of course, Red Steadman had died some four years *previous* to that time, so how could that be?"

He looked Jimmy in the eye, ready for a challenge.

He wasn't going to get it.

"Mr. Steadman was wearing a disguise, but not a very good disguise," Pool concluded. "My point being that Mr. Danko that night saw something or realized something that he was not meant to, namely that the two companies were about to merge—and that Mr. Red Steadman had apparently *faked* his own death some years earlier."

He took another drag of bottled oxygen.

"Did *you* actually see them?" Jimmy asked.

"They left at midnight. Mr. Danko told me about it in great detail the next morning." Pool picked at something on the knee of his pajamas. "I should have bought some stock."

"Who else do you think he told?"

"The events that followed would suggest Mrs. Kantke." There was another theatrical pause. "And perhaps Michelle."

Pool waited to see if Jimmy knew the name.

"Espinosa," Jimmy said.

"Yes, eventually that would be her last name."

"They were still in touch? Michelle and Danko. Or was there something more?"

"Mr. Danko had a weakness for her."

"There was some evidence the actual killer was short," Jimmy said, just to see what would happen.

"Michelle *was* short."

"And so was Estella Danko."

Pool went a bit sad and sentimental. "And neither of them wanted anything other than Bill alive and loving them."

He corrected himself. "*Mr. Danko.*"

"You never testified?"

"No."

"Why?"

"No one asked. And, for a long time, I was quite peeved at that."

Here was another soul who wanted Jimmy to stay a little longer. Pool took a thick manila envelope from his bedside table, unwound the string closure and handed it over. Jimmy knew everything he needed to know, enough to pull him down further, make him feel that weight, that *compression* again, but he took the folder.

It was a file of clippings and pictures, like Jean's, which now had become his. There was a two-inch article about the drowning at Mothers' Beach in Marina del Ray. There was no clip about Tone Espinosa shot dead. The newspaper picture of Red Steadman in his prime was almost brown but time hadn't taken the hardness out of the boss's eye, that look the old man on the pier had remembered. That same look, softened only a little, had been in the eyes in the wax figure presiding over the boardroom at the Museum of Flight. Red Steadman.

And somewhere else. *In the now.*

JEAN WAS OUT PAST THE SHORE BREAK. IT WAS afternoon. She pulled hard on a concluding stroke and rolled onto her back with the last of the energy, gliding like a seal.

She watched her hands describing figure eights as she treaded water. The waves, from this far out, seen from behind, looked like hands pushing something away.

She looked skyward. There was a daylight moon, just risen.

White.

A perfect circle.

A communion wafer.

Where did that come from? She hadn't taken communion in ten years. She thought of the little church in Carmel, that afternoon, the way the candles weighted the air. *The Quick and The Dead*. That memory led her to another from long ago, a little girl—*four?*—with her mother in an Episcopal church in Long Beach in a straight wool coat, pink with pink buttons in a style like the one John John Kennedy had worn in the famous picture, and the hat, too, which she held in her hands because her mother was kneeling beside her. Suddenly there was a bird, a brown wren probably, something small and common, flying around the airy vault above the altar. There were a few other children and they began to laugh and Jean began to laugh with them until the adults got up from their knees.

Jean didn't remember what happened next. How odd that she wouldn't remember the ending.

A swell lifted her and she saw Jimmy on the beach.

She washed the salt out of her hair over the kitchen sink with a round striped pitcher.

"Have you been all right up here?" Jimmy said.

"I'm fine," she said.

She squeezed the water out of her hair with a kitchen towel and stepped closer to him.

She kissed him.

He wondered if she could feel the change in him.

He found a blue bottle of vodka in the freezer and poured an inch of it into a green glass and walked with it to the windows that tried to frame the ocean. He stood with his back to her. Far away, almost at the horizon, a sloop was passing, so far out it was flying a spinnaker. He waited. He felt himself going back to his life, back to *before,* back into himself, from wherever he had been with her. It felt like falling backwards. It felt like a plug being pulled. It hurt and was sad. If he wasn't a man, he would have howled like a dog.

There was a TV on the countertop, the first of the afternoon news shows, a brushfire somewhere, tanker helos dropping showers of red water. Jean watched it. The sound was low.

Jimmy still was looking out at the sea.

"One of The Jolly Girls, Vivian Goreck, still lives two doors down from your house," he said. "With her daughter, Lynne."

Jean remembered the picture, the four of them at the Yacht Club bar, starched white blouses and round pearlesque earrings the size of quarters.

"I remember her."

Something had changed in Jean, too, and he felt it. She had decided something. He didn't know what it was.

"She was pretty."

"Vivian Goreck bought ten thousand dollars' worth of Steadman stock in July of 1977, three weeks before the merger of Rath and Steadman. It was worth a hundred grand six months later. Today, it's two or three million."

"She's the one who ties this to the past?"

"One of the ones. Also her daughter. She's seeing your brother."

Jean nodded. She accepted it.

He was surprised that she *wasn't* surprised.

"My mother was killed because of stock?"

Jimmy told her about Roy Pool and the midnight flight of Vasek Rath and Red Steadman. He told it just the way Pool had told it, Bill Danko and some big shots, a man thought to be dead wearing a disguise, a famous man who'd apparently faked his own death for some reason.

"They needed a pilot too dumb to know what it meant. But Danko wasn't *that* dumb, or your mother wasn't. Danko probably told your mother. I don't know who she told. After the drunk flying thing, I guess Rath and Steadman knew Danko was a problem."

"Maybe Vivian and my father were having a thing."

"Maybe." It was something he'd thought of, too, something cued by one of Vivian Goreck's smiles. "Maybe *she's* the one who put that half smile on his face," Jimmy said.

"So who killed my mother and Bill Danko?" Jean said, too coolly.

"Nobody. Somebody in the shadows. Somebody who's probably dead now, too. Somebody short."

He kept his eyes on the water.

"So there it is. It's over. That's everything there is to know."

She nodded, whether she believed that lie or not.

"My father had a stroke, a small one," Jean said. "Half of his face was slightly paralyzed. Carey told me that, when I was at Stanford. I never knew. The jury thought he was smirking at them, too."

There was always something else to learn.

He still wasn't looking at her.

"Where is Carey's house?" she said. "You said he had a house and an apartment."

"Out on the point. Crown Road. It looks like a ship."

She went to him. She put her head against his back as he stood at the window.

"I have to go," he said.

"Why? Where are you going? Stay here."

Jimmy turned to face her. "I can't. But you should still stay here," he said.

She remembered his line, *this could all be over soon.*

"When are you coming back?" she said.

He told her he'd call her in the morning. She pulled him to her but he was somewhere else already.

"I'll call you," he said.

As he walked away, she looked at the television. A shimmering live shot of the daylight moon filled the frame, icy. The newscaster was saying, "Tonight Southlanders will witness a rare conjunction of folklore and science, a real live 'blue moon.'"

She heard Jimmy's voice out front, speaking to the guards, Angel's men.

"A blue moon—I'll bet you didn't know this Trish—a blue moon is two full moons in one month," the voice-over said. "It only happens once every eight or ten years. It looks like any other moon but this one seems to be bringing with it unusually high tides along our coastline."

She heard the Mustang start.

"Once in a blue moon . . ." the newscaster said.

C H A P T E R   2 3

ANGEL WAS STANDING IN THE DRIVEWAY IN FRONT
of the garages when Jimmy came back from Malibu.
It was dark already, the moon through the trees.

"Your Porsche is downtown," he said before Jimmy
got out.

They both knew what all it meant.

Jimmy went in and took a long shower, changed
clothes. He sat in the dining room and drank a glass of
water. He'd looked at the blue revolver in the desk
drawer in the office but closed it without taking it.
Who was he going to shoot?

They drove out Sunset in Angel's pickup. It was a
Thursday night but there was traffic, a rattle and hum
in the air, people either driving fast or way too slow,
sudden screeching U-turns in front of you, cars

double-parked, as if everyone was off on his own trip.

Angel went south on Highland.

"Where'd you spend last night?"

Jimmy just shook his head.

"I called, came by," Angel said.

"I just rode around."

"Rode around."

"I ended up out at the beach."

"A sailor watching the sea."

"I'm all right," Jimmy said.

"Good," Angel said. "We'll see about *tomorrow*."

They came south six more blocks.

The wave was breaking.

Returning . . .

Jimmy looked over as they passed the recording studio. *Clover.* The past was knocking him on his ass, had been for days now, since Big Sur. Old music kept going through his head. On every other street corner he saw a memory in bright relief, a piece of a scene, in daylight or dark, played at double speed, or half.

There was the razor wire around the roof. They used to go up there, on the roof, smoke and look out over low Hollywood.

He was on the roof with _____ one night at the end of a session and the singer said he'd give Jimmy a ride back to the Chateau Marmont. Jimmy didn't have a car but in those days you didn't need one if you looked right, if you were in on the joke, in on the big idea they'd all just that summer discovered. 1969. You stood by the side of the road looking the way you looked and someone would stop and you'd get where you wanted to go, particularly if you didn't much care where you went.

This night it was _____.

But they hadn't gone back to the Chateau Marmont but to three or four houses instead, up in Laurel Canyon and, even though it was four in the morning by then, all the way out to Topanga. There was downstairs cocaine for everybody who came by and upstairs coke for the famous people and their friends, even their new friends. His mother was gone, off on location again. No one was waiting up for him.

The singer came through the room, said some of them were leaving for the desert, to ride horses. And peyote.

Jimmy told him he'd see him tomorrow night at Clover.

He had talked for hours with a girl who'd been to Morocco but he was alone on the deck when the new sun broke over the ridgeline and lit up the head of a royal palm across the canyon, as suddenly as if fire was involved.

Angel drove, low in the seat, his arm on the armrest between them. Now they were down in South Central. Angel wasn't afraid of any part of L.A. so they were on surface streets. Black men sat on the fenders of cars parked in front of houses with barred windows but nice little yards, one of those TV news neighborhoods where the mothers put their children to bed in the bathtubs some nights in fear of gunfire.

Jimmy dropped his window. Angel reached over and turned off the A.C.

"I used to live down here, block west of Normandie," Angel said.

There was vague music from multiple sources. Angel drove slowly, out of respect for the people who lived there. The streets were concrete with a bead of black tar in the expansion joints. The truck's tires thumped rhythmically, like a heartbeat, another kind of music. They slipped past one bungalow, all blue-lit inside, just as the front door came open, letting out an explosion of television laughter. A woman stepped onto the porch and called out something to the men. Two of them had a pit bull spread-legged on the hood of a Buick Regal, slapping it in the face every time it thought to move.

"Her father is a Sailor," Jimmy said.

He hadn't said anything since Highland, since Angel had asked him where he spent the night.

"I thought maybe it was headed that way," Angel said. "How did you find out?"

"I saw him. Palos Verdes. A house his son owns. I saw him kiss a young woman, the daughter of one of The Jolly Girls. She looks just like the mother did then."

Angel nodded.

It was a Sailor thing, you drove the car you drove then or would like to have driven. You lived in the house you lived in then, if you could. And you tried to find a new version of the girl you loved then.

"How much are you going to tell her?" Angel said.

"Not much. There's not much I can tell her without telling her everything."

"Maybe she already knows."

Jimmy shook his head.

"I don't think so."

"He was living here all along, ten miles away? And you think she didn't know? She just happened to find an investigator who was a Sailor, too?"

Jimmy didn't answer it. He'd asked himself the question enough. None of it was important to him anymore. None of it would make any difference.

He would just let the wave break.

"How much longer did you think you could wait before you told her what was up with you?"

"Longer," Jimmy said.

They rode another block. An ice truck came past. *Hollywood Ice.* Angel turned left on Exposition to head downtown. His rough leather-bound Bible on the dash started to slide sideways.

Angel put a hand on it to stop it.

"I wish I had what you have," Jimmy said.

"What's that?"

"Believing that everything is part of the plan."

"Me or you believing it isn't what makes it true," Angel said.

They drove under the Harbor Freeway toward downtown and something else came to Jimmy, something else he should have seen before. That he was the same age as the kid Drew that daybreak in Topanga Canyon, the morning of the last day of his life.

*   *   *

THE ALLEY WAS A DEAD-END. JIMMY'S BLACK
Porsche sat, top down, dead center in the circle of
light an old-fashioned incandescent streetlight threw.

It looked like what it was, bait in a trap.

They got out of the truck. The key was in the igni-
tion. The Porsche was clean. There weren't even any
fingerprints on the glass. It was as if someone had
wiped it down just minutes before they arrived.

It was almost eleven o'clock. There were a few
homeless people but no Sailors. And this wasn't
where the Walkers lived. Downtown was *real* Sailor
territory, too hardcore for anybody but the strong
ones.

Drew had come right down into the middle of the
darkest version of the Sailor world.

Or been *brought* to it.

There was shuffling in the shadows. A man in a peacoat and watch cap. He said nothing and barely
looked at Jimmy. He finished his cigarette and
dropped it at his feet and stepped back into the deeper
darkness without lifting his eyes again.

Jimmy turned to look at Angel, who stood beside
his truck.

"Why not?" Jimmy said.

CHAPTER 24

"HELLO, SWEETHEART," JACK KANTKE SAID.

The wind off the water stirred the flame-vine over the door. The night air was cool. He stood in the doorway in a white short-sleeve shirt over black beltless slacks and black oxfords. There was a cigarette in his hand. The smoke curled up his arm.

He had aged. But not enough.

"Hello," Jean said.

"Come in."

The view through the floor-to-ceiling windows in the living room was of the ocean crossed by the light of the full moon. The large room was sparsely furnished with a nautical theme. There was a loud ticking from an unseen clock.

And a real live Jolly Girl stood in the middle of the

room. Or so it seemed. The hair, the eyes, the heels, the sawed off pants they used to call *Capri*. Lynn Goreck smiled politely at Jean, her hands clasped in front of her.

Jean sat in a chair.

Her father sat across from her.

Lynne leaned on the arm of Jack Kantke's chair, her hand on his shoulder, a possessive.

"Would you like anything?" he said.

Jean shook her head.

"Could you get me some water," he said to Lynne.

The girl gave him a flip look and stepped away.

Jean couldn't stop staring at her father.

"You saw me someplace, didn't you?" he said.

She realized for the first time that he was very moved at seeing her. He looked as if he was about to cry.

"A year ago," Jean said. "I was down at Balboa Island. I saw Carey. I thought he was still living in Arizona. I followed him. I was about to go up to him—"

"And you saw me."

Lynne came back with a glass of water, no ice. She set it down on the arm of his chair. Kantke looked at her, a look meant to send her away. She turned and left the room.

"She's Vivian's daughter?" Jean said when she was gone.

Kantke nodded.

"I've been waiting for you to come see me," he said.

"So Vivian knows? About you?"

He shook his head. "She wouldn't understand," he

said. "She thinks Lynne is involved with your brother. Vivian's never seen me." Kantke looked over at the doorway Lynne had stepped through. "I've found people of your generation more accepting of something like this," he said.

He smiled that half smile.

"Or maybe she just thinks I'm insane."

The ticking continued. Kantke looked at the source, a large ship's clock on the wall, then back at Jean.

"I didn't kill your mother," he said.

They both listened to the clock. Jean didn't let him off, offered nothing to help him.

"You look so much like her," he said and it caught in his throat. "It's not easy, seeing you."

She said nothing.

He stood, stood over her for a moment. He seemed as tall, for a moment, as a father seems to a child.

"I don't know what your investigator has told you . . ."

She waited.

He stepped over to the windows, walked toward his reflection, considering it from head to toe. It would not have surprised Jean if he had walked through the glass into the night, leaving the reflection to come forward to speak to her.

He stopped at the glass.

"How'd you find a detective who was a Sailor?"

"What does that mean?"

"It's what we call ourselves."

"How long have you known I had someone looking into this?"

The way he smiled—she could see his face in the glass—made her wonder what powers he might have, how much he knew, what he could do, what *they* could do.

"I saw him on the bluff, yesterday, watching the house," he said.

"How did you know that he was—"

"We can spot each other. What has he told you?"

"Not very much. Nothing about *this*."

"How could he, once he was in love with you?"

He still looked out at the water, like Jimmy in Malibu.

"Maybe you should explain it to me."

He took a cigarette from one pocket and a gold lighter from the other and lit it.

"Death," he said, with the tone of voice fathers use to explain things to their children, "doesn't end everything. Not always. Sometimes something is unfinished in a life and this happens. Someone is left behind until the unfinished thing is finished."

He turned to look at her.

"I was executed. They buried my body. A few days later, I was walking the streets again."

She could walk out the door, but she didn't. She met him where he was, continued in the scene as if he'd just said he'd been sick, been treated, rose up off his sickbed, healed. In that way she surprised herself more than he'd surprised her. She felt very strong. *So this was the kind of knowledge that made you stronger.*

"Is that what's been left unfinished," Jean asked, "this business about Mother?"

"I don't know," he said. "We never know what it is."

He blew out smoke. "It's not like we hear voices from the clouds, telling us what to do. There are rules. We just don't know what they are."

He smiled. But then it was gone. He walked back to his chair and picked up the glass and drank the water, all of it. He looked at the big clock again, seemed as if he had things to do, places to go. He put down the glass and stepped closer and stood over her again, casting a shadow over her, as he meant.

"You've inadvertently threatened some powerful people," he said. "I'm worried about you."

"They were responsible for Mother's murder."

"It was a long time ago. It doesn't matter anymore."

"But it's true, isn't it?"

"It was a long time ago, Jeanie."

"They killed a woman who was living in the house," Jean said. "Bill Danko's daughter. They're killing people *now*."

Kantke lifted a hand to stop her.

"There are killings every day, every week, every year for a thousand years in all directions. You have to stop this, sweetheart."

He looked at the clock again. "You should go. Go back to the house at Point Dume. You'll be safe there. They won't follow you out of the city. This all will be over soon."

Jean stood, but not to leave.

"Why? What do you mean? What happens now?"

He held out his hand to her, pulled her close to him. With his touch, the *reality* of it hit her, unreal as it was. She felt as if someone had pulled the plug on her power source. She was in free fall. Maybe now the floor beneath her would open up and she'd fall through to some other unthinkable *other* world. Long seconds passed to the ticking of the ship's clock.

"I remember your aftershave," she said in his arms.

"Aqua Velva," he said. "You mother always hated it."

Kantke held her tightly, as if he would never see her again, breathing in her scent, his eyes on the round moon out the window, which looked like the head of a hammer.

Now *she* had a secret.

CHAPTER 25

THE SHADOWS WHERE THE MAN IN THE PEACOAT and watch cap had been led to a canyon between buildings, a grid of alleyways, unpeopled. Jimmy and Angel walked straight ahead, not following the man, who was out of sight, but just going the only way there was to go. As they stepped past one intersecting alley suddenly there was light from above, like a spotlight, the full moon in a wedge of sky.

Ahead was an abandoned building, an old factory from the looks of it with a loading dock ramp and painted-out windows. A sliding iron door stood open.

"I guess all this is part of the plan," Jimmy said. "*Somebody's* plan."

Inside the shell of the factory, five Sailors stood in a rhombus of moonlight cast onto the floor from a skylight, all of them pulsing blue, more strongly than before.

They parted.

There was Drew in his blue snowboarder's cap, sitting on the floor. The Sailors seemed to enjoy the drama of the reveal. Others of them appeared behind Jimmy and Angel to block their exit.

It wasn't necessary, Jimmy and Angel were already resigned to what would come next. The Sailors surrounded them and Drew, took them by the upper arms and they set out.

They went down ten steps into an underground passageway, a corridor lined on three sides with asbestos-covered pipes. As they walked—it could have been a half mile—the passageway shuddered sometimes, probably trucks passing overhead. You would have expected to see rats but there weren't any. They would have been welcome.

"I gotta say, man," Drew said to Jimmy as they were hustled along, "I thought you and your people were messed up, but these people are *really* messed up."

One of the Sailors shoved him forward.

Drew yanked his arm away. "Back off! We're going!"

He looked at Jimmy. "*Where* are we going?"

Jimmy knew but there was no reason to tell him.

They came to an elevator. Old, brass. They rode up, eight of them crammed into the space.

Drew said, "Everybody's getting real jumpy. Something's about to happen, right?"

Jimmy just watched the numbers.

"Yes, but not here," he said. "This is something else."

The elevator doors opened onto a landing. They were pushed through a pair of heavy doors.

It was a courtroom.

Jimmy and Angel had never been here but they knew about it. They were on the top floor of the old Hall of Justice, a Gothic granite block on Spring Street across West First from the modern Criminal Justice Building that replaced it. Everywhere across L.A. Sailors were in control of abandoned places, of spaces like this, for whatever purposes. A part of the night was theirs and there were enough of them to assure its continuance.

The courtroom echoed with the sound of a dog barking incessantly, sharp, regular. Clocks covered the tall paneled walls, clocks of all sizes and shapes, *named* clocks from banks and long-closed businesses: square, round, octagonal, all running at different speeds, some backwards, some very slow, like clocks in hell, and some too fast to watch, hands spinning like knives.

Drew was scared, or just creeped out.

"Anybody know what time it is?"

Jimmy seized him by the front of his shirt. "They can't do anything to us," he said. "Nothing that really matters. Remember that."

He let the kid go.

"Whoa," Drew said.

The barking continued, unbroken, like a metronome. Drew narrowed his eyes to look into the shadows. The hanging lights high above them were dim, half of the bulbs burned out. Shutters covered the tall windows on the west wall, keeping the light in. The wooden seats had been ripped out, stacked in the back, but the high bench remained at the front of the courtroom.

A collection of Sailors, twenty or thirty of them, milled about the room or leaned against the walls. Here there were some women, too, though they wore the same clothes as the men and most of their sex had been taken from them, or let go. Their eyes bore the same open yet dead look as the men, a look that might come to the rest of us from staring at great distances for long hours.

They all pulsed blue, as blue as blue could be.

"Somebody oughta do something about that dog," Drew said.

"It ain't a dog," Angel told him.

Jimmy's eyes were on something else, *someone*. A woman, the only woman in the room in a dress, though it was a shabby one with faded roses.

Rosemary Danko. Alive.

She stood before the high bench, looking up at it.

Jimmy started off across the room toward her.

"Who is she?" Drew said.

Angel said, "I think somebody from one of Jimmy's cases. But she was supposed to be dead, killed a few days ago."

"She's one of us?"

"No. Look at her." She *wasn't* wrapped in the blue. Rosemary was still staring at the judge's bench, a smile on her face, when Jimmy touched her on the shoulder.

She turned to look at him. "I knew you'd be in on this, sooner or later," she said. She turned her attention back to the bench and the big clock behind it, the only one in the room that showed the real time.

It was a quarter to midnight.

"Tell me what happened," Jimmy said.

"I looked up and they were there, just like you," she said, "a short one and a tall one. They had a lot of questions, just like you, and then they took me out of there. The tall one with red hair started that fire on our way out. We rode in a car over to Garden Grove. It was dark, after the news."

She was still looking at the high bench. It was the old style of courtroom, the kind that still ends up in movies, though the justice system has moved on to blond Formica and low tables and "theater seating."

There was a wooden chair beside the bench. Maybe there'd be a last-minute witness in the case, a quick wrap-up, surprising, yet the only thing that could have happened.

"What did they do to you?" Jimmy said.

"They could have killed me quick but they just kept asking questions."

The big hand on the big clock jumped, a minute.

"I guess *now* is when they're going to kill me," Rosemary said.

"Nobody's going to kill you," Jimmy said. But he wasn't so sure.

She stepped up and sat in the witness chair. She

leaned over to look at her feet on the footrest, ran her hands over the dark worn wood of the arms.

She raised her right hand.

The barking stopped.

Rosemary laughed, thinking she'd caused it.

There was silence in the room now, only the whirring of the clocks. The peacoats as one had turned toward her but it was not because of her.

A door had opened behind her, the door beneath the biggest clock, the only one that told the right time.

Angel and Drew came up to stand behind Jimmy.

Los Angeles still existed, the *regular* world, wrapped in its regularity and regulations, laws and principalities. It was just outside, down at street level. A cab on Alameda, street people in doorways, Salvadorans a block over getting off a Greyhound, Japanese tourists lifting food to their mouths in the glass restaurant atop the Otani five blocks away, laughter in The Jonathan Club, Dodger Stadium a half mile away.

The regular world was still out there, *alive*.

But this, starting *now*, starting here, was something else.

The first through the door was Boney M, tall, red hair.

Next was a very short man built like a boxer, a prison boxer, a man in his fifties, gang-tattooed, Mexican.

Angel looked at Jimmy.

"You know him?" Jimmy said.

"*Perversito*," was the answer. Little Evil.

There was a moment when the doorway was empty

and then Red Steadman stepped in. He wore a brown suit, white shirt, tie, very chairman of the board. He was a huge man, six-five, barrel-chested and heavy in that way men used to be.

Here was the familiar big man in the back of the Lincoln at the end of the chase in Griffith Park.

He stepped to the front so they could all see him.

He filled his bull chest with air. His blue aura was faded, old, but intense in its own way.

He seemed, in this moment, their king.

Rosemary Danko, still in the witness chair, the only wholly live person in the room, trembled pitifully at the sight of Red Steadman and the others. She knew who they were. Here were her *airplane people,* in the flesh. Or some version of it.

She stepped down off the stand.

She got as far away from them as she could in the room.

Steadman fixed his eyes on Jimmy. Jimmy remembered old man Kirk's line about his former boss: *He'd definitely tear you a new one if you looked at him wrong.* What unfinished business had cast *him* here? He was such a ruler it was hard to imagine him in a personal way, to picture his family, a naked moment, a love in his life beyond the things he built.

He stared at Jimmy. It was hard not to shake.

"There's a price for defiance," Steadman said.

There was an ugly sound from the Sailors.

"Tie their legs," Steadman ordered.

The closest peacoats seized Jimmy and Angel and Drew.

"Not him," Steadman said. He meant Drew.

"He's with us," Jimmy said. The men were already wrapping duct tape around his ankles, around Angel's ankles.

"We'll see," Steadman said.

It was called *Clocking*. Ropes came out from somewhere and the peacoats threw them over the light fixtures and knotted them and took the ends and threaded them through Jimmy's and Angel's ankles.

"Tight, so they won't get loose," Steadman said. "Let them spend the night *here*." It sounded like the worst kind of threat.

They strung them up upside down.

The ghouls now started shoving Jimmy and Angel, hanging that way, until they were swinging from one end of the courtroom to the other, in separate arcs, hung from separate light fixtures.

Drew watched.

Rosemary cowered in the farthest corner.

Jimmy and Angel bent at the waist to keep their heads from dragging on the floor. The peacoats would shove hard each time a man came by until Jimmy and Angel were crashing into the walls.

Jimmy slammed into the big clock over the bench. It fell, shattered, but the scattered pieces kept spinning.

Then the clocks stopped.

All of them.

As Jimmy and Angel still swung back and forth, the peacoats all turned to watch the dozens of clock faces on the walls as now, slowly, they synchronized, zeroing, going to midnight.

Out the open window, the moon had just turned full, a specific moment none of us could see or sense, but they could.

The room began to empty.

"Take the boy," Steadman shouted.

Sailors surrounded Drew and dragged him away toward the elevator.

Steadman exited through the door behind the bench with his men and then they were alone in the hollow room, Jimmy and Angel, the pendulums centering.

No one had touched Rosemary. They were going to let her live. When she realized that, she made her own way toward an exit.

As Jimmy and Angel pulled themselves up, grasping at their ropes . . .

Tick.

The clocks as one recorded a minute lost, a minute after midnight, the beginning of what was called *The Day.*

The last day for some of them.

CHAPTER 26

A CRAB, JUST A PAIR OF RAGGED CLAWS, SCUTTLED across the surface of the moon reflected in an oily pool.

Rats scurried over broken glass. The air stank.

You came in this way: There was a pipe, on its side, an immense section of pipe tall enough to walk through standing up—and three peacoats now walked through it—a gateway through the sawgrass that rimmed the last remaining acres of wetlands of Long Beach.

It was after one.

"I hate these last hours," Jimmy said.

Angel, in spite of himself, felt his own spirit dropping. It was all converging, and it was all about death.

He spoke a prayer in his head, the words echoing there as if he'd said them aloud: *Lord, just let me see Your face.* He wanted to be strong. Clear. Sure. The one the others depended upon. They all hated this time, when it came round again, *the blue moon,* for all the pressure, the insecurity it brought, the questions it threw at them. They even hated it for what was at its core, the promise or the *threat* of resolution.

The tide was coming in. Before them was a wasteland of flotsam and jetsam, of abandoned boats, of bleached logs, of weather-battered and sea-battered squares of plywood, of hundreds of big and little chunks of Styrofoam reflecting white in the light of all that moon, looking like bones strewn across a cemetery after a flood.

"There's a fire up there," Angel said.

They were closing in on the hull of a rusted tuna boat, big as a gas station, at a wrong angle, listing in a sea of mud and grass. Fire flickered in the broken out windows.

They were looking for Drew.

"I don't get this," Angel said. "Why'd they do this?"

"They just want to mess with us."

As they slogged forward, they came upon a body floating face down, a peacoat, arms outstretched, the dead man float. Angel lifted him by the collar. He was alive. Angel yanked him out of the muck, holding him by the collar like something foul.

The man coughed his thanks.

"I know you, Brother," he said, like a punch line.

Angel deposited him in a derelict turquoise speed-
boat. The man sputtered and then grasped the wheel,
as if heading out for a day on the lake.

"*Get me out of here,*" Jimmy said.

A few faces appeared. Fifty or more of them lived
down here, who feared the downtown, not Walkers,
but who didn't have it together enough to be of use to
the powerful Sailors. Or maybe they were just waiting
like everybody else and liked the water, even this
brackish swamp. They lived in houses made of boat
wreckage, cabins from cruisers stripped of their hulls
or shacks of plywood built in where the grass was
tallest, to hide them. Some had put a few boats sea-
worthy enough to cruise out to fish in the dark. Some
of them now stood in front of their shacks, watching
without much feeling as Jimmy and Angel passed.

They reached the stern of the tuna boat where the
fire burned. There were crude steps made out of oil
drums stuck into the mud. Jimmy and Angel stepped
up them, though the bow of the boat was almost afloat
with the rising tide, shifting, moving underfoot.

They crossed the canted deck and went down into
the hold. Below, the fire burned in another oil drum,
black smoke rising through a rusted out gap in the
overhead. The space was empty but there were rough
sounds, men's voices, from the next chamber.

The boat shifted. The oil drum fire slid sideways.
Angel danced out of its way.

In that next chamber they found three men beating
a kid. Jimmy saw a flash of blue, Drew's snowboarder's cap. He pulled away one of the men as An-

gel slammed another against the bulkhead. The third man struck the kid two more times and then stood up.

The kid said, "OK. All right."

It was some other kid.

Jimmy yanked him to his feet.

"Where did you get the cap? Where is he?"

"I don't know, man," the kid said. "What difference does it make? He was here. Now he's gone. Who are you?"

Jimmy snatched the snowboarder's cap off the kid's head. The boat shifted again. Angel fell against the steel wall. Something crashed down behind them.

"Let's get out of here," Angel said.

The tuna boat was fully afloat though still heeled over onto its side when they came back out onto the deck into the stinking air.

"Maybe they already took him on board," Jimmy said.

There were people all around the tuna boat now, wading up to their chests some of them, others trying to make use of the wrecked boats that still floated. A pregnant woman, full and round in her rags, sat in a Zodiac as a man waded beside her, hand on the gunwale, hauling the boat tenderly, as if she were Mary on the donkey.

They all moved in the same direction across the wetlands.

"What time is it?" Jimmy said.

"*There,*" Angel said. "Your guys."

Across the watery grasslands, the bad-joke Sailors

Lon and Vince slogged through, dragging Drew with them.

They were in water up to their knees and easy to catch.

Jimmy pulled Drew away from Vince, the shorter one, and knocked down Lon, the tall one.

Drew wore a peacoat and watch cap now. Jimmy yanked at the lapel of Drew's coat.

"They put this on you?"

"We didn't do nothing," Vince said.

"He did it," Lon said.

"They said if I was with them I could go home," Drew said.

Jimmy dragged him away.

"They lied," he said.

Lon came back after him. Jimmy grabbed him by the back of the neck and shoved him face down into the tide and held him there until his legs stopped kicking.

Angel pulled Jimmy's hand away.

Lon surfaced, sucking in air again.

Vince half thought of coming after Angel. Angel hit him in the face for it, three quick blows, dropping him backwards into the water beside Lon.

"So this is where—" Drew began. It was like he was stoned.

"No," Jimmy said.

"Come on," Angel said.

And so Jimmy and Angel and Drew fell in with the others, moving like an arrow, all of them, in the landscape of refuse and nature, men and women, the moon reflected a hundred times in scattered shards of water. A wider, higher view would show their destination five-miles distant across the wetlands and then across the sculpted landscaping and empty parking lots of the Long Beach harbor.

There, lit like a cathedral, *The Queen Mary.*

CHAPTER 27

ANGEL LOOKED AT THE SKY AS THEY MOVED UP THE gangway. There was a little breeze. It was cool in that off-the-water way. A few clouds were crossing the moon.

Tonight it almost was blue.

"Beautiful night," Angel said. He looked at Jimmy. "And it'll be a good day tomorrow, whatever comes."

Jimmy nodded, but didn't look like a believer.

Not everything in the Sailor world had a name but this was called *The Hour.* It came—it was not an hour but a *moment,* a click of the clock—when the blue moon was at its zenith.

It would come tonight at forty-seven minutes after three.

The Hour had a certain formality to it, a ceremo-

nial air, nothing handed down from on high but a
man-designed affair which had become this over time.
Or so the older Sailors said. They could have been lying or simply had it wrong. Theirs was not a *holy* order. A few Sailors were on the decks, leaning over the
railing as people will do, smoking, watching the others. Some strolled the promenade deck, arm in arm.
Others were just arriving. Everyone knew not to come
too early so they all tended to appear at once, when
the hour changed, when the last hour came.

The long iron gangway that during the day carried
tourists onto the haunted black and white ship now
carried the wetlands people, the people from The
Pipe, the moody Sailors from downtown, regular citi-
zens, the powerful from on high and the weakest of
the weak.

All but the Walkers, who no longer knew to come,
to hope.

As they stepped onto the gangway, some removed
their peacoats and watch caps, threw them in a pile as
if they'd never need them again. Underneath, some
wore period clothes, clothes from their specific time,
polyester from the seventies, denim from the sixties, a
few ancient Sailors in wool suits who at least looked
like they belonged on the *Queen Mary*. Some, like the
people from the wetlands, walked in in that stunned,
doomed way, but others were treating it like a holiday.
Inside there would even be Sailors in festive costume
as if putting on some other guise would better prepare
them for what was to come.

At the end of the gangway, an officer greeted them,

or at least a man in an officer's uniform. He nodded to each man or woman as they stepped aboard and checked his watch from time to time, a large gold pocket watch.

The pregnant woman from The Pipe stepped forward on the arm of her man. A gentleman in a cutaway tuxedo, vest and striped trousers, certainly the oldest among them all, tipped his hat and gave a little bow. The woman blushed at the attention. The night had already become unreal and otherworldly, even for them.

The welcoming officer stopped the pregnant woman.

She wasn't a Sailor.

The man with her protested but without much conviction because he knew the rules. She waited where she was and her "husband" went aboard without her, looking back once. She picked up his watch cap where he had dropped it.

More cars were pulling into the parking lot. Some were big, expensive. The custom was to leave the keys in the ignitions, the doors unlocked. Whoever was left when it was over could take what they wanted.

A security car arrived. An excited guard jumped out almost before the car stopped rolling. He pushed his way into the middle of the Sailors, wide-eyed at the improbability of it all.

"Who are you? What is this?"

What did he expect to hear? A *prom?*

A hand touched the excited guard's shoulder.

It was Connor. In uniform.

"It's a private party," the cop said.

The security guard started to protest.

"It's all right," Connor said calmly. "We're here."

The guard went away.

Jimmy and Angel were about to board when Jimmy saw Jean.

She was at the mouth of the gangway. Waiting, watching.

Jimmy went down the ramp to her, against the stream of Sailors boarding.

"You have to go," he said.

"What is this?"

The clouds passed off the moon. The light brightened.

"I can't explain it," Jimmy said. "And you can't see it."

He started away.

"Is my father here?" Jean said.

He stopped. He was ten steps past her. He looked at her.

"I talked to him," she said. "Tonight."

"What did he tell you?"

Jimmy didn't want to know, but it was the next thing to say.

"That he didn't kill my mother." She waited a moment. "And *what this is*."

He felt as if she was suddenly across the widest ocean.

"Go back to the beach house," he said.

"I'm coming aboard."

"No."

Angel stepped up. "It's time," he said.

"You can't be here," Jimmy said to Jean.

"*Tell her*," he said to Angel and walked away from her.

"Go home," Angel said. "He doesn't want you hurt."

Angel went after Jimmy.

She followed after them.

"I'm coming aboard," she said. She caught up. "I'm coming aboard," she said again.

The officer on deck put out a hand to stop Jean.

"You know she can't come aboard," he said.

Jimmy shoved him back out of the way. *Let her see it.*

THE THREE OF THEM ENTERED THE GRAND BALL-room, a tall Deco space with funereal elegance. There were multiple levels where once there had been cock-tail tables or roulette wheels. An enormous crystal chandelier hung over their heads.

The room was filled with Sailors. They stood in clusters, among friends, waiting. Scott the bartender was there, Krisha, the woman doctor who treated Drew, one of Angel's bodybuilder friends, Connor.

And Perversito.

And Boney M.

And Lon and Vince.

The old man in the tuxedo played an out of tune grand piano, the bad notes giving the scene the feel of a cheap dance hall somewhere or a wake.

The room was ablaze in blue light.

Jimmy held Jean's arm. She pulled away from him and set off on her own to find her father.

Jimmy just watched her go.

"Three minutes," Angel said.

There was an ornate clock. *Very English.* It ticked loudly enough to be heard over the voices and the music.

"Just stay with us," Jimmy said to Drew as they moved back through the crowd. "Just do what we do and watch." He remembered the first blue moon, when *he* was a kid and went from knowing everything to knowing nothing.

Drew did as he was told, fell in behind Jimmy and Angel as they moved through the clusters of Sailors. The room was almost howling now in anticipation, pulsing like a blue cloud somehow captured in a room, like a storm in a box. The tuxedo man played louder and louder to be heard over the growing din, lifting his curled fingers in great dramatic gestures with each chord.

"Does this just keep getting weirder and weirder?" Drew said as they moved through it.

Jimmy looked at him. "It's beautiful."

Jimmy kept going.

Angel put an arm around the boy. "It's a *little* weird," he said.

Jimmy saw Jean with her father, talking, close. So there he was, just like the picture from the *Press Telegram,* the narrow black tie, the white shirt, the gray suit. *The half smile.*

Before he thought about what he was doing, Jimmy charged up to them and threw Jack Kantke against the wall. Jimmy's anger wasn't at Kantke and Kantke's anger wasn't at him but neither man cared in the moment, they both just wanted to tear something apart.

Kantke threw a punch. Jimmy avoided it and shoved him back into a glass cabinet, shattering it. Kantke recovered and came after him and Jimmy knocked him down onto the bed of broken glass.

Jimmy ripped the leg off of a table. He stood over Kantke. He raised the club.

The ticking grew louder and louder as the piano fought it.

Angel seized Jimmy's arm. Jean screamed.

Peacoats arrived and pulled Jimmy away from Kantke.

Red Steadman was behind them, dressed as an admiral. With him were Boney M and Little Evil, but it was Steadman himself who seized Jimmy by the neck, lifted him off his feet.

"*Not here!*" he yelled into Jimmy's face.

But then the ornate clock chimed.

The ship's bells began to sound.

Steadman released Jimmy.

Kantke got to his feet.

Jean stepped back.

The men and women on the floor lifted their hands.

Angel took Drew's hand in his and lifted it.

"What?" Drew said.

The piano player stood, lifted his hands.

Was it praise or surrender?

Jimmy looked at Jean. She was terrified.

He closed his eyes and raised his hands.

Steadman raised his hands.

The ship's bells ceased.

There was stunning silence, the silence at the end of the world.

Someone started crying.

The blue pulsed so brightly it hurt the eyes.

And then, as one, as if there was no time in the world, as if there was no *Now,* only *Always,* all in the room *spoke a line,* as one . . .

> *"Come The Flood, we will say goodbye*
> *to flesh and blood . . ."*

Jimmy's voice could be heard.

Angel's voice, loud and prayerful.

Steadman, rough, impatient, chafing at obedience.

Drew, repeating the line a half beat late.

The room hummed with expectation.

There was a long, hollow moment . . .

The Last Minute of Eternity

And then a man collapsed where he stood.

And then another.

And then the man who had brought the pregnant woman, falling dead away.

All in, twenty or more of them.

Drew watched them fall.

And then there were no more. "Whoa," he said.

Jimmy opened his eyes.

It was over.

He scanned the room. There was Angel, still on his feet, tears in his eyes. Scott. Krisha. Connor.

Steadman.

Behind him, Jean knelt over her father's body. *He was gone.*

Jimmy went to her, leaned over and put a hand on her back. She looked up at him.

She shook her head. Sometimes what you have to do is walk away. She got up. He didn't try to stop her as she pushed through the others, left them all behind.

The piano man began again, a tune that started out sad, and those who remained began to tend to the bodies around them, crumpled forms in the clothes they last wore living.

CHAPTER 28

AS FIRST LIGHT CAME, A FISHING BOAT WITH NO name rode the swells of the gray water off Long Beach, well out from the shipping lanes. Jimmy and Angel and Drew were at the rails, steadying themselves as the boat climbed and fell. The engines idled and the captain tried to keep it headed into the wind but the ride was rough.

Steadman was forward, directing several peacoats bearing the first of the bodies, strapped with weights, wrapped for sea burial in unbleached cloth. As the bearers carried a body by, every man on deck reached out a hand to touch it. Drew did as the others did. He was back in his blue cap. Then the body was lowered over the side, sucked down feet first with hardly a sound.

As the peacoats went forward for the next, Angel and Drew went with them to help. There was a truce now, for this.

Steadman came to Jimmy.

"You know you won't stop me," he said. "Even with everything you know, you still don't understand, do you?"

Jimmy didn't answer him.

"We'll win," Steadman said. "We will win."

"You probably already have," Jimmy said.

Angel and Drew and the peacoats came back with another wrapped body. Jimmy reached out to touch it.

Steadman blessed it, too, but left his eyes on the breathing man before him.

CHAPTER 29

JIMMY WAS ON THE ROOFTOP PATIO OF JEAN'S apartment. It was clear with one of those once- or twice- or three-times-a-year views, all the way to Catalina. The traffic below on Sunset was heavy but the sound was reassuring, people in motion, full of purpose, everything shiny and bright and clean.

Jean came out with a bottle of water. Jimmy cracked the seal and took a drink.

"Do you believe in heaven?" she said.

He took another drink.

"No," he said, "but I believe in a whole bunch of places they've never given a name to."

She smiled and walked to the railing.

"It really is over with your father," Jimmy said behind her.

She nodded.

She turned to face him.

"When you said that you can't know everything, I guess this was what you meant."

He looked at her. "At the time I think just meant . . . *generally.*"

She wasn't close to him

"So you just wait . . . for the next blue moon?"

Their story was over. At least for now. They both knew it.

"Nah, we were just kidding about all that," he said and tried a smile.

"I'm moving," she said. "To San Francisco."

He nodded.

"Maybe, after awhile . . ." She trailed off. He didn't help her finish the sentence.

"I have something for you," she said.

She went into the apartment and came back with something closed in her hand. She stood in front of him. She opened her hand.

It was a glass bottle, perfume in a functional but elegant glass bottle. He took it. It was a beautiful color.

"It's what your mother wore," Jean said. "They don't make it anymore. I had it synthesized. The scent was still on her dress in the case."

He took her hand.

"Maybe this will help you remember her," she said.

CHAPTER 30

JIMMY WHIPPED AWAY THE COVER—LIKE A MAGI-
cian!—on the last car in the garage. It was a snow
white 1969 Chrysler 400 convertible with white
leather interior, with three-foot fins and what the
lowriders called monster whitewalls, though his
mother certainly never called them that.

It was her last car and Jimmy rode with the top
down and good music on the radio over to Hollywood
and then down to the 10 past Parker Center and Union
Station, the sky still full on blue, and holding, in daylight, the diminishing moon.

Some days people are happy. There wasn't any ex-
plaining it but today people were happy. They waved
at the sight of the huge white car, big as a boat. Jimmy

wore a light green jacket that looked like '69, like a college man in '69, and they were happy with him, too.

He waved back.

The traffic broke open, as it always did, just past San Bernardino, the long hill up to the wide-place-in-the-road town called Beaumont. Jimmy stopped for a Coke at a drive-in. He always stopped at the same place. It was usually only twice a month but the high school girl there knew him and the Mexican boys who did the cooking knew the car.

He sat on the red-enameled picnic bench out front. It was over a hundred and yet there was snow on the mountains behind them.

California.

The desert road, Highway 62, curved away from the Interstate just past Palm Springs, four-lane but wide open, the exit curving and canted so perfectly that at high speed it was like banking in a plane. Ahead, a pass through the mountains, into the high desert, through valleys named for Indians and spiked trees, past copper-colored hills and the Marine base.

Teresa Miles sat in the sun in a wooden chair being read to by a nurse who looked up and smiled as Jimmy walked across the grass toward them. The rest home—now they called it *Extended Care*—was very private and very pretty, three low adobe-style buildings the same color as the desert mountains around them. There was an oasis in the center of it, a few palms around a pond. It was restful. It was constant.

It was the kind of place that could keep a secret.

The nurse bent over and told Teresa Miles her son was there. She had her eyes closed. Her expression didn't change.

It would be polite to say that the movie star still had the same magic in her skin, in the bones of her famous face, but it was gone, or almost gone. She was very white and her skin seemed much too thin, almost like the shell of an insect when the shell is left behind.

Like a woman who when her only son dies, steps off the roof of a hotel above Sunset, and she is left behind.

The nurse walked away.

Jimmy bent over and kissed his mother.

"I saw a coyote with two pups," he said.

She opened her eyes but her expression didn't change.

Jimmy sat on the grass next to her chair. A hawk turned circles in the sky over the oasis and then, just as he was noticing the grace of it, dropped onto something unseen in the brush.

He took the perfume bottle from his pocket.

"I brought you something," he said.

Her hands were in her lap. He put the bottle in her hand. Her fingers tightened around it. Jimmy uncapped it. He touched the glass stopper to her cheek and, under the expanse of our sky, a little more life came back to her eyes.

The debut novel that's a
masterpiece of modern suspense—

THE STRAW MEN
by
MICHAEL MARSHALL

Three seemingly unrelated events are the
first signs of an unimaginable network of fear
that will lead one unlikely hero to a chilling
confrontation with The Straw Men.
No one knows what they want—or why they
kill. But they must be stopped.

YOU KNOW WHO THEY ARE...
IF YOU'VE EVER KNOWN FEAR.

0-515-13427-9

J006